TWILIGHT CROOK

FLIRTING WITH MONSTERS
EVA CHASE

BOOK
2

Twilight Crook

Book 2 in the Flirting with Monsters series

First Digital Edition, 2020

Copyright © 2020 Eva Chase

Cover design: Yocla Book Cover Design

Ebook ISBN: 978-1-989096-76-5

Paperback ISBN: 978-1-989096-77-2

1

Sorsha

I hadn't always wanted to end the world, even after it'd started to seem that a significant portion of the world wanted to end *me*.

The specific people who'd been after me most recently might still be lurking on the other side of the plywood wall I was now eyeballing from the sidewalk across the street. I couldn't see much other than the skeleton of steel girders rising up above it.

Construction workers perched in their neon vests at various points across that skeleton. That was new. Before, it'd looked like the construction site that hid my enemies' secret facility was just a front. Surprise, surprise: apparently all those beams and boards were actually going to construct a building.

"Okay," I murmured. "I'm going in."

If you were watching, it'd have looked as if I crossed the road alone. I was counting on my monstrous companions—four of them now, up from a trio to a quartet—slinking after me through the shadows. More properly called "shadowkind," beings like them had gotten the name both because of the darkness of their natural realm and their ability to sink into and travel through the darkness in ours. Which also conveniently meant they could leap out of that darkness and tackle anyone who tried to tackle me.

We were pretty sure the crew of monster hunters and torture-happy scientists we'd faced off against wouldn't attack me in broad daylight with multiple witnesses, but I wasn't tossing all caution to the wind. Three cheers for supernatural bodyguards!

The buzz of a saw carried from deeper within the construction site. As I walked over to the half-open gate where the workers had driven a couple of trucks in, the tang of fresh-cut pine wood in the warm summer air tickled my nose.

I'd kind of hoped that simply strolling in would get me where I wanted to go. A lot of the time, looking like you knew you were allowed to be someplace would convince everyone around you of it too. No such luck today.

A guy with a gray helmet, an orange vest, and a moustache so bushy a squirrel could have borrowed it as a substitute tail stepped into my path and held up his hand. "Where do you think you're going, Miss?"

For those of you taking notes: you can get good mileage out of a well-placed giggle too. "Oh," I said with a little laugh. "I'm sorry. Something of mine blew over the fence—I just wanted to grab it."

A couple of the other workers sauntered over. Mr. Moustache glanced around. "Do you see it here? I didn't notice anything."

I tapped my lips, pretending to scan our surroundings. "No, maybe it drifted farther in. Couldn't I just take a quick look around? It doesn't look like you're doing anything at the moment that'd make me fear for my life." I raised my eyes to the girders above.

One of the younger guys chuckled, but the moustache dude shook his head. "Sorry, Miss, but we could get in a lot of trouble if we let pedestrians wander around. What is it you lost? You can give us your contact information, and we'll keep an eye out for it."

It needed to be something that could have easily slipped from my hand and been caught in the wind. The words tumbled out before I'd given them much thought. "It was a napkin. A paper napkin with a phone number on it."

Did they look skeptical? I folded my arms over my chest and put on my most convincing tone. "It was from a really hot guy, okay? I don't want him to think I couldn't be bothered to shoot him a text."

The guy who'd chuckled now waggled his eyebrows. "We could give you a few phone numbers to make up for the loss."

Very funny. In reality, I was getting more than enough action these days. Sure, it was from men these dudes wouldn't believe existed, but that was part of what I liked about my new lovers.

Before I could answer, Mr. Moustache handled the come-on for me. "We haven't got time for this messing around. After all the delays on continuing construction, they'll hand us our asses if we don't get on with it." He bobbed his head to me. "If you give me *your* phone number, I promise I'll only call if one of us turns up your napkin."

I sighed dramatically. "Oh, well, if it's drifted off that far maybe it's just not meant to be. Can't fight destiny! Thanks for your help, though." I sauntered out without waiting for their response.

Since it wouldn't exactly do for the regular mortals to witness my monstrous companions emerging from the shadows as if appearing out of thin air, I couldn't confer with them until I reached the dim alley a few blocks down the street. A trash bin farther down the narrow space was baking in the summer heat, giving off a lovely bouquet of broiled kitchen scraps. I wrinkled my nose and glanced around to make sure no one human had followed me between the looming concrete walls.

A moment later, four figures solidified around me like smoke condensing into physical form.

"A hot guy's phone number on a napkin—really?" Ruse teased, his hazel eyes twinkling beneath the fall of his rumpled chocolate-brown hair. "Or have you already gotten bored with the pickings here?" The incubus gave me his typical smirk, which cracked a dimple in his roguishly gorgeous face. I'd "picked" him a couple of times already, and I was happy to report that getting it on with a sex demon was everything you'd expect from the package and more.

Next to Ruse, Snap's forehead had furrowed, barely putting a dent in the divine beauty that made him look like a youthful sun god. "The napkin was made up," he protested in his bright voice, and turned his moss-green gaze on me. "It *was* made up, wasn't it?"

I patted his slim arm. "A total fabrication. I have no phone numbers whatsoever, nor do I want any."

The devourer made a pleased humming sound and stepped closer—not to touch me, but as if he simply wanted to soak up my presence. I'd *also* gotten it on with Snap not that long ago, in a tamer if no less satisfying fashion while he eased into the whole concept of physical desire. What could I say? I'd been busy lately... although with a whole lot more than *getting busy*, I promise.

Waking up Snap's carnal awareness had also stirred up a possessive instinct I hadn't counted on but couldn't help finding kind of sweet. He might stand a full head taller than me, but he was about as frightening as a gamboling fawn. Of course, at this point I knew more about the feel of his body than why the others called him a devourer, which was still a mystery to me. Whatever his greatest power was, just the idea of it made *him* shudder in terror, so he hadn't exactly been eager to chat about it.

As usual, the third member of my original trio was all business. "It didn't appear as though you got close enough to make out anything of the inner facility, m'lady," Thorn said somberly. The ruggedly handsome hulk of a man, a smidge taller even than Snap and filled out with muscles galore, had never met a subject he couldn't approach with grave severity.

He could be plenty intimidating without even trying, although right now his imposing air was impaired by the little dragon squirming from one broad shoulder to the other, displacing Thorn's long white-blond hair with little snuffles of discontentment. Pickle hadn't spent much time around anyone other than me since I'd rescued him from a collector ages ago. It'd taken a lot of coaxing—and quite a bit of bacon—to warm the lesser shadowkind creature up to Thorn enough for him to let the warrior carry him into the shadows, out of mortal sight.

"I couldn't see anything," I agreed. "But it seems like a bad sign that construction has started up again. I can't imagine the sword-star group would let the workers wander around the site if there was anything incriminating left to see." The covert group of hunters, scientists, and who the hell knew what else we'd spent the past week battling marked some of their equipment with a symbol like a star with sword blades for two of its points, which was the only way we'd found to identify them so far.

The fourth shadowkind in our group—the one I'd only met last night after we'd broken him out of the facility that'd been hidden in the construction site—shifted on his feet. His voice held a ring of authority as cool as his icy blue stare. "I think you should hold off on making sweeping assumptions until we've had an actual look inside the place."

I wasn't totally sure what to make of Omen, the guy my trio referred to as their "boss." He shouldn't have stood out in the bunch—not as tall or as muscle-bound as Thorn, not as languidly sensual as Ruse or as breathtakingly dazzling as Snap. Other than those piercing eyes, he was attractive enough with his tawny, short-cropped hair and sharp features, but hardly otherworldly. I hadn't determined what monstrous feature he'd been unable to shed in his mostly human form, either. No shadowkind could pass for fully human on close inspection, as Thorn's crystalline knuckles, Snap's forked tongue, and the curved horns that poked from Ruse's hair could attest to.

All the same, Omen radiated power and menace with every movement of his body, every word that fell from those Cupid's bow lips. When we'd opened his cell last night, he'd lunged out more beast than man—he'd slaughtered two of the guards in a blink. That capacity for violence lurked somewhere beneath the controlled façade he was presenting now. At least with Thorn, who could be monstrously brutal too, the warrior frame and the scars lining his face served as plenty of warning.

Thorn adjusted that frame now, giving Pickle a careful nudge to keep the tiny dragon from tumbling right off him. "We could slip through the shadows right now to survey it. Two of us go and two stay to watch over Sorsha." He'd already smashed through an apartment building and torn heads from men's bodies to keep me safe—he took his self-assigned job as my protector even more seriously than he took most other things.

Omen had held up his hand before the warrior had even finished speaking. "No. Whatever we find, we'll want our devourer testing it to see what he can glean, and he can't do that while there are human witnesses around." He glanced at the sky. "It'll be a little longer before their work day is finished. Since we'll want a vehicle of our own to rely on as we proceed, we may as well take the opportunity to pick up my car and then return."

He definitely lived up to the title of boss—as in, bossy. Since we *had* just met, and I wasn't confident he didn't have some supernatural power that would eviscerate me if I pissed him off too much, I meant to keep my mouth shut and go along with his plan. The trouble was, the next words out of his mouth were to me, with a slight sneering edge: "Since you can't travel through the shadows, I'll give you the address. You can meet us there."

I blinked at him. "You're telling me to head across town on my own?" The other three had refused to let me out of their sight for more than a few minutes since they'd shown up at my apartment, even when I'd *wanted* them to let me handle one thing or another alone.

Omen gave me a narrow look. "I would have thought

a woman of your many supposed talents could manage a simple cab ride."

"Well, yeah." But the sword-star crew had a bad habit of showing up unannounced, weapons blazing. I was only alive thanks to the efforts of my trio—my shoulder throbbed dully where I'd taken a bullet yesterday before Thorn had yanked me out of the way of one that would have blasted straight through my heart. It was still daytime, though, and I sure as hell wasn't going to let Bossypants make me look like a weakling.

"Here's a thought," Ruse said, smooth as ever. "A cab can whisk any of us across town much faster than we can flit through the shadows. Why don't I charm a driver into zipping us to our destination as one happy family?" He slung a playful arm over my shoulders and grinned at Omen.

Omen frowned, but even he didn't have the authority to change the fact that motorized vehicles offered superior speed. "Get on with it then," he said with a flick of his hand toward the street as if it'd been his idea in the first place, and rattled off the address.

He must have made some other gesture of command, because as Ruse strolled past us, Snap and Thorn faded into the patches of darkness that lined the alley. Omen lingered a moment longer, eyeing me with an intentness that set my nerves twitching, and then vanished as well.

The boss had put Ruse on his team for good reason. It took all of a minute before the incubus had a taxi driver eagerly beckoning us into the back seat of his cab as if we were great friends and letting him give us a ride was a huge favor to *him*. Ruse swept his arm toward the open door. "Ladies first."

The other three stayed out of sight, but I assumed they hopped from the shadows along the street into the darker corners of the cab. We couldn't see them, but from what I understood, they'd be able to see us just fine. I doubted Omen would eviscerate me in full view of at least one unknowing mortal, so this seemed like the perfect time to pay him back for his obvious disdain for my presence.

"Nicely done," I said to Ruse as the cabbie hit the gas, and scooted over to grasp the silky fabric of his shirt. The incubus flashed a brilliant smile before meeting me halfway for the kiss I'd planned to claim.

The moment his mouth caught mine, it was definitely him doing the claiming. Holy mother of mistletoe, the guy could kiss. Sure, bodily pleasures were his stock and trade, but still, mark this one A with a thousand pluses.

For a few seconds, I forgot where we were. I forgot the onlooker I'd meant to piss off. I was lucky I remembered my name. My lips parted for Ruse's sly tongue, and my body melted into his, my skin sparking where he trailed his fingers down my side.

Why had we put a hold on our very enjoyable nighttime escapades again? Oh yeah, because he'd broken his promise and used his paranormal voodoo to take a peek inside my head. But he'd told me why with an explanation I could believe, and he'd been on excellent behavior since. I should definitely look into rewarding that behavior soon, shouldn't I, especially since the reward would be gratifying for both of us?

The driver gave a little cough, and that broke me out of the bliss enough to ease back. Heat crept over my cheeks. Ruse shot me another smile, but I'd swear even he looked a tad flushed. I gave myself a mental high five. If Omen was fuming right now, especially since he couldn't actually tell us to knock it off, so much the better.

The cab took us to a derelict storage facility on the outskirts of the city. Most of the garage-style doors were dented and rusted, many of them half-open with only dust and litter scattering the cement floors beyond. But the place must have been at least somewhat operational, because the unit Omen strode straight to had its lock in place and no sign of deterioration. He jerked up the door to reveal...

"You drive a station wagon?" I said, unable to keep the incredulous note out of my voice.

Omen shot me a frigid glance and patted the boxy brown hood. "Betsy here is as reliable as they come, and when evading one's enemies, that matters much more than glitz. She's also got a glamour on her windows that gives a false impression of who's inside, courtesy of a former fae associate of mine. I do *also* have a motorcycle, but that's kept elsewhere."

And it wouldn't really lend itself to carting all five of us around town, at least not when the others were in physical form. But seriously—he'd named his car *Betsy*? I held in a snicker, but the sharpening of his glare suggested he'd noticed the twitch of my lips. I did have to admit that the glamour spell would be awfully useful for keeping the pricks we were up against off our backs.

Thorn peered into the darkness of the storage unit, where wooden crates and metal chests were stacked along the walls around the car. "This space could also serve as a place for Sorsha to sleep—out of the way, and—"

Omen spun to face him, cutting him off with a curt voice. "Don't be ridiculous. Would you have her lead this group right to my stash? We shouldn't linger here any longer than we already have."

Thorn looked so stricken my throat constricted at the sight. It wasn't an expression that belonged on a man of so much strength. "My apologies," he said quickly. "I should have thought the matter through more carefully."

"It seems you haven't been very careful with your thinking in general these past few months, or I wouldn't have spent most of those months acting as a lab rat for a coterie of vicious mortals. Why don't you keep your mouth shut from now on and let me do the thinking?"

I hadn't realized it was possible for the warrior's face to fall even more. Bristling on his behalf, I lost control of my tongue.

"*You're* the one who got yourself trapped by those mortals," I said. "You have no idea how much Thorn has been busting his ass trying to get you back. He's the most dedicated person—being—whatever—I've ever met, often to the point of being incredibly irritating about it. So maybe you should shut up about things you apparently know nothing about."

I could tell Thorn had turned to look at me, but I didn't dare take my eyes off of Omen to check the warrior's reaction. I'd given Thorn a hard time about his single-mindedness in the past, but he'd proven he was holding in plenty of real emotion under that strict exterior—and plenty of passion I'd only gotten a taste of so far. He'd beaten himself up enough for failing to prevent Omen's capture without the very person he'd been obsessively trying to rescue adding to that agony. I wasn't going to stand around while this jackass laid into him for the one thing he couldn't possibly be criticized for.

If I'd thought Omen's gaze was frigid before, now it was cold enough to flay me down to the bones. His carefully slicked-down hair had risen in little tufts as if propelled by a swelling rage. My hands clenched at my sides as I braced myself for an onslaught of anger, but he kept his voice as tartly cool as before.

"If you hadn't insisted on crashing this party, none of us would need to worry about where you spend the night in the first place. Don't make yourself too much of a hassle."

The implied threat sent a shiver down my spine. Why had Omen agreed to keep me around anyway?

It could have been because of the emphatic references I'd gotten from his companions. Snap stepped closer to me, curling his long, slender fingers around my fist in solidarity. "It's because of Sorsha we managed to find and free you at all. She's just as important as any of us."

Pickle let out a chirping sound of what might have been agreement, fluttering his wings anxiously. He lost his hold on Thorn's tunic and ended up clinging to the warrior's hair in his panic to hurl himself back onto his perch. Thorn unfastened him with a long-suffering sigh, but a hint of a smile crossed his lips. I hustled over to take my sort-of pet off his hands.

Omen watched all of this with the same detached disdain and then shook his head. "We'll see," he said darkly. "For now—all of you, in the car. Let's discover what's left of my former prison."

To my relief, he drove with more care than Ruse did, making it back to the neighborhood of the construction site without prompting a single blared horn. By that time, I'd determined that the middle cushion in the back seat popped out to allow access to the trunk and had let Pickle scuttle through. The little dragon was now soothing himself by constructing a nest out of an old plaid blanket that'd been folded there. I decided I wouldn't mention to Omen that his beloved Betsy might end up with her felted trunk lining shredded.

The sun had sunk below the roofs of the nearby high-rises, but the summer evening was still warm and relatively bright. Thorn stole through the shadows around the site before giving us the go-ahead: no sign of the sword-star bunch. Around the back of the site, he hefted a section of the barrier wall aside to let me walk in while the others took the shadow route.

The half-finished framework of steel and cinderblocks wasn't exactly welcoming in the late afternoon light, but it provoked a lot fewer goosebumps than it had in the eerie glow of security lamps through the darkness last night. I suppressed a wince at the creak of the metal beams above in a gust of wind. Then my feet stalled in their tracks as I came into view of the facility we'd stormed last night.

Or rather, *didn't* come into view of it—because where the concrete building with its flood lamps had stood less than twenty-four hours ago, there was nothing but bare, packed earth and a shallow pit of rubble.

As I gaped, my shadowkind companions emerged around me. Ruse let out a low whistle.

A disbelieving laugh sputtered out of me. "These people don't do things by halves, do they?" Just yesterday morning, they'd battered one of their own men beyond identification to cover their tracks. I shouldn't be surprised.

We ventured closer, Thorn striding ahead to patrol the wreckage, but it didn't take long to determine that our enemies had left nothing incriminating or useful behind, only smashed concrete. Snap bent over various spots around the pit, flicking his forked tongue into the air just above the chunks to test for impressions that might still be clinging to them, but more hope seeped out of his face with each attempt.

Omen had lingered near me by the edge of the clearing, letting his companions do the work. No trace of emotion showed on *his* face—not discomfort at returning to the site of his torment, nor satisfaction at seeing the place in pieces, nor frustration at how utterly our enemies had obliterated the evidence of their activities.

There'd been several other shadowkind experimental subjects being held in the facility—beings we hadn't gotten the chance to free. We hadn't managed to figure out what exactly their painful experiments were meant to accomplish either.

"We have to find out where they've taken the other shadowkind," I said. "And then shut down the sword-star crew's operations completely. They can't keep getting away with this."

Omen didn't move. "Obviously."

That was all he had to say about it? I frowned at the barren stretch of ground. "It was hard enough getting just you out with the four of us working together. There are plenty of shadowkind who come mortal-side regularly or even live in this realm these days. Maybe we could ask around and see if any of them would join—"

Bossypants interrupted me with a dismissive snort. "Have you *met* many of our kind that linger in this realm? They're no less self-involved here than they are back in the shadows. All they care about is themselves and perhaps their immediate circle. The greater good of our people means nothing to them if it requires them to lift a finger. Why do you think I was tackling this menace with such a small group to begin with?"

I *had* seen those selfish attitudes in other shadowkind. The group of humans I worked with to protect the creatures that traveled into our realm had reached out to local shadowkind gangs and the like before, but they rarely opted to get involved unless it affected them directly. Still...

"This is a much bigger deal than solo hunters or small collectives snaring lesser shadowkind for profit. All the higher shadowkind are at risk. Don't you think that would matter to the others?"

Omen grimaced. "If it did, this 'sword-star crew' would never have managed to establish themselves as firmly as they have."

He vanished into the shadows, putting a definitive end to that discussion. Such a lively conversationalist.

With a grimace of my own, I picked my way along the fringes of the clearing. Maybe a bit of useful debris had blown this way in the midst of the destruction and been missed during the clean-up. I scanned the piles of boards and the interlocking beams to see if anything caught my eye, squinting into the lengthening shadows of the approaching evening.

I'd made it about halfway around the destroyed facility when a warbling sound from above caught my ears.

My head jerked up. I flinched and stumbled backward just in time to dodge a streak of fire that plummeted down at me.

The blazing thing whooshed past me close enough to singe a few flyaway strands of my hair before it hit the ground. My pulse lurched. The flames flared higher, and I scrambled farther back, my arms flying up defensively. A bolt of pain shot through my bandaged shoulder. The fire flickered in the opposite direction and then slowly dwindled as its fuel ran out.

As I lowered my arms and edged closer to the now only smoldering object, Thorn charged over with Snap and Ruse close at his heels. I clenched my jaw against the ache still burning in my shoulder, and we all stared at the thing that had nearly landed on me like a flaming toupee.

It was a charred... pair of work jeans? Yep, with a sharp chemical scent that indicated how the fire had caught on them so enthusiastically. The fabric must have been dosed in some kind of lighter fluid and then been tossed down from above.

Thorn sprang back into the shadows, presumably to search for my attacker. Snap checked me over carefully. His eyes stark with concern, he fingered the singed strands of my hair, which he'd admiringly compared to the color of a peach when we'd first met.

I took his hand in mine with a reassuring squeeze. "I'm all right. The jeans, not so much."

Ruse cocked his head, still considering them. "Well, that is something, all right."

I peered up at the gridwork and knit my brow. Who would have done that—*why* would anyone have done that? There were a hell of a lot more deadly things here than discarded construction pants.

A nervous quiver ran through my chest, but I wasn't going to be shaken by something this ridiculous, not if I could help it. Mangling the lyrics from my favorite '80s songs always bolstered my spirits. I waved my hand in front of my nose and sang a little tune: "This is what it smells like when gloves fry."

While Ruse snickered, Snap knelt down. His tongue flitted through the smoke. "A man was wearing them this morning—he spilled something sticky and black on them, had to change, left them in a waste bin. I can't sense anything after that." He frowned.

Omen had returned to join us sometime during the chaos. He contemplated the burnt jeans, the structure around us, and then me, his gaze so penetrating I could almost feel it digging through my skull. "Fire seems to like you."

"A lot of the time, I like it too, but only when I'm the one setting things up in flames." I resisted the urge to hug myself. "Someone's messing with us. Trying to keep us on our toes."

"You're lucky you didn't get the slightest bit burned."

What was he implying—that I'd been prepared for fiery legwear to fall on my head? "Three cheers for good reflexes," I said.

Thorn burst out of the shadows so abruptly the air rippled against my skin. "There's no one else on the site right now. Either it was another shadowkind who slipped away quickly or a trick set to go off automatically."

Ruse raised his hand. "Seeing as we weren't getting anything useful out of this ruin anyway, I'd like to vote that we take off before any other 'tricks' come at us."

I expected Omen to argue like he seemed to whenever anyone other than him suggested a course of action. Instead, he nodded. "We aren't getting any farther here."

He stared at me for a moment longer before shifting his attention to the incubus. "Why don't we make use of that computer adept you mentioned? Our enemies will have left a trail somewhere—we just need to pick it up, and quickly."

2

Sorsha

I was starting to notice that Omen's station wagon had a particular smell to it. I inhaled deeply where I was sitting in the back seat, trying to place it. A hint of charcoal, a little salt, something a bit chalky, and a note that was maybe... meaty? Brick-oven pizza, I thought, except it was hard to picture Bossypants chowing down on a slice in his beloved Betsy. Anyway, the scent was too dry, no tomato-y juiciness.

While I contemplated the lingering odor, Ruse, who'd kept his physical form, gabbed away at his boss about the hacker he'd worked his charms on.

"Managed it over the phone," he said, leaning back in his seat with his arms crossed behind his head. "It only took a few minutes before we were such close friends she'd happily delve into an obviously stolen computer. A little internet tracing shouldn't be any problem at all. The original effect won't have worn off much yet, so it'll hardly be any work."

"Wonderful," Omen replied in a voice so devoid of emotion I couldn't tell whether he was truly pleased or being sarcastic, but Ruse's commentary had reminded me of another responsibility. I owed my one actual close friend a call.

I settled deeper into the worn leather cushioning of the back seat, which I had to admit was pretty comfy, and pulled out my phone. Vivi had inadvertently gotten herself tangled up in our conflict with the sword-star crew despite my efforts to keep her out of the line of fire. Okay, maybe even because of those efforts. My caginess had gotten her so worried about me that she'd tracked me down while we were following the bad guys and blown our cover. Since the baddies would have seen the car she was driving, which belonged to her grandmother, I'd ordered them both to go into hiding.

Vivi picked up on the first ring. "Sorsha?"

Hearing her vibrant voice sent a wash of relief through me. "The one and only. I take it you're still hanging in there out at that cottage?"

"Yeah, just bored." A matching relief sparkled through her laugh. "I'm so glad you're okay. I've been spinning out crazier than a cuckoo bird in a blender wondering what's going on."

Vivi had a way with metaphors. I cracked a grin. "Well, we solved one bit of the problem, but we've got a much bigger part to tackle next. The assholes who murdered Meriden are still on the loose, so you'd better hang tight."

"Actually..." I could practically see her twirling one of her tight ringlets around her index finger. "All this time cooped up gave me a chance to think about return strategies. I might have figured out a way I could come back—and give you a real hand—without doom raining down on me."

My chest tightened a little at the idea of my best friend back here in the line of fire, but I'd promised her I wouldn't keep shutting her out like I had before. And to be fair, staying clammed up hadn't protected either of us in the end. Vivi had grown up with parents who knew about and wanted to protect the shadowkind. Not the same as being outright raised by a fae woman like I'd been, but while she wasn't quite as comfortable with supernatural beings as I was, she did have a pretty clear idea of what she was signing up for.

"All right," I said. "Lay it on me."

"Well, I figure the main way these people have of identifying me or Gran is through her car. What if I go to the police and report that it was stolen a few days ago? I'll park it somewhere sketchy but obvious, maybe even call in an anonymous tip too so they'll find it fast, and then Gran has her car back but it sounds like we weren't involved in anything it was used for lately. Smooth as butter on a porcelain vase."

"Hmm." I kind of wanted to pick that plan apart so I had an excuse to keep Vivi where she was safe, but the truth was it sounded pretty solid. "Are you sure the baddies couldn't have seen it parked at your Gran's house in between your scouting missions? Besides the car, what about the questions you were asking Meriden's neighbors?"

"Nah, I parked it in a paid lot overnight just in case. And when I talked to the few people I spoke to in person, I had my hair covered by my hood and big sunglasses on —I don't think they could give a very accurate description of me. I can be a *little* stealthy."

I hesitated, wavering between the guilt over shutting my best friend out before and the guilt I knew I'd feel if I led her into more danger.

"Come on, Sorsh," Vivi wheedled. "Let me pitch in. You let me know what you need, and I'll be there, no other messing around."

She might be safer here in the city with a cover story for the car than she was staying in hiding with the sword-star bunch believing she was involved. "Okay. Handle the car thing like you said, and then don't do *anything* you wouldn't normally do until we have a chance to talk more in depth."

"You've got it." She made an air-kiss sound. "Ditto."

"Ditto," I replied, my smile coming back. Our shared love of corny movies included *Ghost*, which had inspired our trademark farewell.

As I hung up, Omen was just pulling up to the corner on a residential street. He glanced back at me, his gaze as intense as ever. "It never occurred to you that I'd expect you to keep quiet about our activities."

My shoulders tensed automatically. "That was my

best friend—the one who already knows all about the shadowkind and that I'm onto something big?" He'd gotten most of the story in roundtable fashion from the four of us last night. "She's been advocating for beings like you her whole life through the Shadowkind Defense Fund. There may be ways she can help. After what she saw yesterday, she knows how serious the situation is."

"Having one mortal in the mix is bad enough."

"Well, she's involved now, so you're shit out of luck."

I kept my tone flippant, but Omen's eyes narrowed anyway. "If she compromises our mission, I'll ensure she can't interfere anymore."

My whole back stiffened. "You don't have to worry about that." *And if you lay one hand on my bestie, you'd better believe the next place you'll find that hand is rammed up your ass.*

Ruse cleared his throat and pointed to a house on the far corner of the block. "That's the place. Basement apartment, separate entrance. We want to encourage our hacker friend to dig up anything she can about the sword-star group's activities, right?"

"Particularly anything that could tell us where they're operating from," Omen said. "Any regular hunting groups or meet-up spots for their business dealings. But you don't need to remember all that. I'm coming with you. After everything that's happened, I think each of you could use plenty of supervision."

"Sure. Absolutely. The more the merrier." Ruse chuckled, but he'd tensed at the implied criticism.

"Thorn. Snap." Omen peered into the shadows next

to me. Before he'd opened his mouth again, the other two shadowkind had emerged, so abruptly I found myself squeezed against the door to make room. Thorn could have used a whole back seat to himself.

Snap gave me an apologetic peck on the temple before turning to his boss with an eager gleam in his eyes. "How can I help?"

"I want the two of you patrolling the streets, making sure no one has followed us or takes too much interest in Betsy here. And since I'd like to keep this 'merry'— Sorsha, you're coming with Ruse and me. It may be useful to have a mortal around in this particular situation."

I rubbed my ears in disbelief, but his impatient gesture and Snap's proud beaming suggested I'd heard him correctly. "You'll see how much she can help," the devourer said. He pressed another kiss to my check before vanishing back into the shadows with Thorn.

"I'm sure I will," Omen said without much enthusiasm, and shoved open his door.

Somehow I suspected Omen's request was more about not trusting me alone in his car—as if *I* might shred the cushions like some kind of wild animal... or, well, like Pickle—than about him developing any respect for my talents. I wasn't going to look a gift horse in the mouth, though. The sooner I proved those talents to him, the sooner he'd put a lid on his condescending comments.

"This mortal is a little... quirky," Ruse said in a low voice as we walked over to the house he'd pointed out as the hacker's. "And I picked up on a certain amount of defensiveness about that. So, let me recommend that you keep any opinions about her clothing choices and décor to yourselves."

He'd called ahead so the woman would be expecting him. As he knocked on the back entrance that was down a flight of stairs from the backyard patio, I braced myself not to react to head-to-toe goth-gear, a raver's rainbow hair and glitter, or possibly a furry costume. It takes all sorts, after all.

I still wasn't prepared.

"Into the Cavern! Quickly!" hissed the figure who opened the door. A figure in full purple latex bodysuit complete with a yellow blaze of lightning on the chest, a glinting black utility belt, matching black vinyl platform boots, and a black cape she whirled with a dramatic *swish*.

Our hacker apparently saw herself as Superhero of the Cybernet, with all the trappings. I managed to keep my expression blasé as we stepped into her apartment, but it was a near thing.

She'd modeled the "Cavern" after the Bat Cave: a huge array of computer screens at one end, glass cases holding a couple of costume changes and assorted comic-book-esque weaponry next to it, slate-gray paint from concrete floor to ceiling, and light streaming in hazy beams from a circle of pot lights mounted overhead. A moped decked out with metallic black plating leaned against the wall by the entrance. Hoo, boy.

I brushed against the moped as we squeezed into the small space between all her equipment, and something flicked against my arm with a scaly swipe. I clamped my mouth shut before I could yelp in surprise, but Ms. Super Hacker here must have noticed.

"Don't mind Freddie," she said briskly, and plopped into a massive leather chair with an arched back that looked more suited to a super villain than a hero. I squinted at the moped and made out a hunched form with scales that blended into the black seat and the gray walls.

She had a pet chameleon. Named Freddie. Right. I should have brought Pickle along for a playdate.

The hacker chugged from an energy drink sitting on the workspace in front of her and waggled her fingers over one of her three keyboards. This one had a green glow around the elevated keys. She glanced up at Ruse with a grin. "What can I do for you tonight?"

The incubus obviously didn't need to do any more charming. He propped himself in front of the farthest screen and gave her a languidly warm smile in return. "It might be a little tricky, but I'm sure you're up to the task. We can't have anyone noticing what you were digging into, though. Our lives could be at stake."

The woman's expression turned more solemn. She nodded briskly. "You can count on me. I'd give my own life before I let those I fight for come to harm."

"Let's hope it doesn't come to that," Ruse said wryly. "We have reason to believe there are people in this city looking to purchase supernatural beings of particular power, as well as hiring mercenaries of some sort for security details. We'd also like to check for any mentions of activity around a construction site last night."

He gave her the address and a few other details that might help narrow down her search, and she dove into the world wide web as enthusiastically as if it were the Fortress of Solitude. The glow of the screens turned her pale face almost luminescent.

There didn't appear to be anything for me to do here. Of course, it wasn't as if Omen was contributing in some brilliant way either. He drifted over to the display shelves, running his finger over what looked like a ray-gun and then lifting a katana to study the arc of its blade.

"Hmm," Ms. Super Hacker said, more to herself than to us. "This could be—oops, no, I didn't need to see that many boobs all on one lady... What about—oh, that's a shipment of counterfeit plushies. Hmm... Yikes. 'Seeing you waiting at the bus stop, I couldn't help succumbing to the radiation of your smile'—nope, definitely not, lots of luck with that missed connection, weirdo. Hey, this is an interesting thread."

She leaned even closer to the screen, as if she might climb right into it in another minute or two. I ambled a little closer, but she was opening and swiping away windows too fast for me to make out much of what she'd unearthed.

Omen was still exploring her display cases with a rustle here and a clink there. I glanced around the rest of the room, searching for an opportunity to show I was more than dead weight. A stack of ramen packages sat on a little shelving unit in front of the moped. Maybe I could offer to cook her up a snack?

Wait, was I reading that right? She had... barbeque octopus balls flavor. And let's not forget the evergreen classic, mocha cheddar corn. Where the hell had she picked up those? More importantly—I averted my face so she wouldn't see me wrinkle my nose—*why*?

She tapped away at the keyboard some more with a rattle like machine-gun fire. I turned to examine the arsenal Omen had found so fascinating—just as he swiveled away from the cases with a metallic flash.

The curved dagger he'd picked up sliced across my bare forearm. A stinging pain sprung up along the line he'd carved. I did yelp then, yanking my arm back toward me so fast a fresh pang echoed through my other shoulder with its bandaged wound. Blood welled along the cut.

Omen swiveled the weapon in his hand with a practiced grace and set it back on the shelf. "I didn't see you there," he said, in the least apologetic-sounding apology ever, and grabbed my hand to yank my injured arm into one of the streams of light. "Let's see the damage."

Ruse had straightened up, eyeing Omen warily and me with a warmer concern. "We can't have you carving up our mortal. Are you all right, Miss Blaze?"

"It isn't much more than a scratch," I had to admit, but the pain was still nibbling across my skin with a similar sensation to the prick of Pickle's claws. Omen was studying the wound as if he thought he'd find the meaning of life in the slow seeping of my blood. An uneasy quiver raced down my spine.

Had that really been an accident, or had it been some kind of test to see my reaction? If it was a test, what in Waldo's name was he looking for?

And had I passed?

Our superhero had glanced up. Seeing my arm, she turned slightly green. She jerked her gaze away, her balance wobbling in her seat.

Fainting at the sight of a tiny bit of blood—not a great quality in a caped avenger.

"There's a first aid kit in the bathroom," she said in a tight voice, waving toward a door in the far corner. Ruse hustled over there while Omen raised my arm to catch the light better. He was frowning as if I'd managed to disappoint him somehow. Had he expected me to produce skin of steel?

Whatever he'd intended, he definitely didn't look remotely worried about my well-being. As Ruse returned, brandishing an adhesive bandage, my stomach knotted. Omen dropped my hand and stepped away, all trace of emotion vanishing.

I couldn't trust him, clearly—couldn't rely on him to care whether he chopped my arm in two. And as long as Bossypants held me in such contempt, I couldn't totally count on my trio either. As much as they'd supported me, they still followed his orders. They'd never leave me in danger on purpose, but all it would take was one risky situation where they couldn't get to me fast enough because he'd occupied them elsewhere, and my ass would be kaput.

As long as the shadowkind quartet were the only people at my back, at least. Vivi was coming home—and maybe I should start thinking about what other allies I could round up who'd follow my lead more than Omen's.

Ms. Super Hacker must have recovered from her blood-induced queasiness. She let out a cry of victory and drummed her hands on the console in front of her.

"I've got something. Someone's set up an exchange to happen in just a couple of days—potent creature of unusual inclinations. Isn't that exactly what you were looking for?"

A hint of a smile curled Omen's lips, but I couldn't say I found it reassuring. "I believe it is. Let's hear the full story."

3

Sorsha

I was stumbling through the dark hallway of a house. Our house, the one Luna had rented the first floor of —and Luna was there by the door, so tense her skin had broken out in its supernatural sparkle. I could almost see the flutter of her fae wings behind her back.

"My shoes," I said, clutching the duffel bag I'd kept packed for emergencies, my head full of a sleepy haze. I had no idea what this emergency was, only that my guardian had shaken me awake with an urgent hiss of my name. "I can't find them—"

"Never mind that. Someone's coming, Sorsha. I can feel it. Wear these, and we'll go." She grabbed her sparkly sneakers off the shoe rack and shoved them at me. As I tugged them on, they pinched my toes. Her feet were at least a size smaller than mine.

"Are you sure we're actually in danger?" I whispered

as she eased the door open. The only real concern my self-centered sixteen-year-old brain could process was: where the hell were we going to go *now*? "We've moved how many times already, and no one's ever—"

She tugged me with her outside, ignoring my protests. As Luna crossed the lawn, I stopped to try to wriggle my feet more solidly into the shoes. When I looked up, she'd reached the sidewalk—and several figures sprang at her from the night.

Whips that seemed formed of light slashed through the air; a blade flashed; someone hurled a glinting net. Luna whirled around with a shocked squeal. The bindings squeezed tight around her skinny form before I could so much as cry out. Her body shuddered—and then burst into a firework of sparks.

I jolted awake with my shriek still locked in my throat. The air around me was glittering, but it was the gleam of sunlight through crystal, not the sparkly shattering of my guardian's death. Sunlight through several crystals, actually—there were about a dozen of them dangling from silver chains in front of the window in the little cabin we'd found not too far outside of town.

The clang of horror faded from my nerves. I rubbed my forehead and sat up, but my stomach stayed clenched.

The fae woman I'd called Auntie Luna—the woman who'd saved me from the hunters who'd murdered my parents, who'd given me the best mortal childhood a shadowkind could, who'd never made me feel anything less than unreservedly loved—had died more than eleven years ago. I hadn't dreamed about that night in ages. It brought the same old questions back to nibble at me: if I'd just moved a little faster, left my own freaking shoes somewhere I could easily put my feet into like she'd reminded me a million times...

But all those what ifs didn't change the fact that she'd died at the hands of attackers with the same weapons the sword-star crew used, at least one of those weapons marked with that sword-star symbol. I might have screwed up, but *they* were the ones who'd killed her. While I couldn't change anything I'd done back then, there was plenty I could do to make them regret *their* life choices now.

They weren't going to get away with what they'd done to her or any of the other shadowkind. Including Omen, as big of an asshole as he could be. On the balance of things, I'd take him over the men with whips and nets any day.

Rolling my shoulders carefully to test the injured one, I got up. It appeared the property we'd ended up on had once been used for New Age-y retreats. Along with the crystals, three bunk beds were crammed into the single open-concept room between posters with nature photos and encouraging phrases like, "Believe in the sunshine of your spirit!" We'd found a heap of rolled yoga mats in the shed outside. But based on the dust that had coated nearly every surface and the weeds choking the driveway, no one had made use of the place in months, if not years.

I stepped out into the yard where Omen had parked the Oldsmobile under the shelter of an oak tree hung with fraying dreamcatchers. They swayed in the warm morning breeze. In that first second, it appeared I was alone on the property. Then my four shadowkind friends shimmered from the shadows into the daylight.

They didn't look all that friendly. Omen's mouth was set in a tight smile, his gaze holding its usual chill as it came to rest on me. The other three were watching him. Thorn stood with muscles tensed, his frown even deeper than usual, and Ruse's expression looked uncharacteristically serious. Snap's eyes had widened with worry.

"There's no need for all this fuss," Omen said, clearly picking up the thread of a conversation they'd been having out of my hearing. "If she's half as competent as you've spent so much time trying to convince me she is, she'll handle this without any trouble at all."

"But we shouldn't be trying to make things harder for Sorsha," Snap protested.

I walked over, raising my eyebrows. "What exactly am I supposed to be handling that's so very hard?"

Ruse's lips twitched as the incubus no doubt thought up a few suggestive remarks he could make in response, but he settled for a subdued smirk. Omen lifted his chin with the authoritarian air that was getting on my nerves more each day.

"We're attempting to turn the tables on our enemies at the hand-off tomorrow evening," he said. "Enemies who've already proven themselves very skilled at overwhelming us. If you're going to play any part in the ambush, I want to be sure your mortal clumsiness won't ruin our chances."

If I was so clumsy, he was lucky I didn't trip right now and accidentally ram my knee into his junk. But sure, he hadn't seen me in action—maybe it was understandable for him to be skeptical. I'd just bash that skepticism into the stratosphere, and if he was still being a jerk after that, then we'd see where my knee ended up.

I shrugged. "Fine. Hit me with your best shot."

Omen swept his arm toward the other men. "You see. She doesn't require your protection."

"She does occasionally take on more than even a shadowkind would think is wise," Thorn muttered. To be fair, it was true that he might not have needed to save me from any bullets if I hadn't insisted on handling that job alone.

"I'm sure Omen doesn't have anything *too* horrifying in mind," I said, and smiled sweetly at the other guy. "Do you?"

Omen gave me an expression even more openly disdainful than usual. "We'll start with this: my colleagues and I will take Betsy into the city. *You* will make your own way there, by whatever means you can come up with. I expect to see you at the Finger no later than noon."

It was a trip of nearly a hundred miles, and it was already past nine. Ruse tsked with teasing disapproval. "I did hear you like to play hardball with the mortals, Luce."

"Luce?" I repeated.

"Short for Lucifer." Ruse cocked his head toward

Omen. "Not that the actual prince of Hell actually exists —or Hell itself the way humans conceive of it, for that matter—but from what I understand, our boss here used to make a game out of convincing mortals he held the title."

Omen cut his icy eyes toward the incubus. "That was a long time ago and is hardly relevant. I'd rather you did away with the nickname."

"But it suits you so well. You even have the tai—"

"Enough!" Omen barked. "You're wasting her time." His tawny hair rippled, a few tufts rising. So, there were a few topics that could get Bossypants emotional. Interesting.

And what had Ruse been going to say he had? The memory rose up of the tail with the devilish tip I'd caught a glimpse of when Omen had sprung from his prison cell in beastly form. Maybe *that* was the shadowkind feature he kept even in human form—the slacks he was wearing were loose enough to conceal it.

I yanked my gaze from Omen's behind to his face before it became too noticeable that I was checking out his ass, as fine an ass as it was. Such a pity it was attached to a massive jerk.

My time to complete his challenge was ticking away. How in holy heathens was I going to make it downtown in less than three hours without a vehicle? Even if taxis came out this far into the middle of nowhere, my phone had no reception here.

Back out now, and I'd never live it down. I waved

toward the car. "Go on, then. I'll see you at the Finger by noon."

Omen strode toward the station wagon. The others followed more hesitantly, Snap lingering on the lawn until I shot him a smile more confident than I actually felt. He immediately smiled back, beaming back at me with so much certainty in my abilities that I had a spring in my step when I ducked into the cabin to grab my backpack full of my cat-burglar gear.

As I re-emerged, Betsy roared away down the dirt driveway. I slung the straps over my shoulders, careful of the bandaged wound, and set off at a jog. No time for dillydallying, as my Luna would have said.

It was hard to imagine what she'd make of the woman I'd grown into. Would she have been proud of everything I'd done to rescue the mistreated shadowkind in this world so far or horrified by how much I'd stuck my neck out? True to Omen's comments about shadowkind attitudes, during the time I'd been with her she'd never shown concern for anyone other than the two of us. I could easily imagine her racing past a hundred caged creatures to spare me from a splinter.

She definitely wouldn't have approved of the all-black outfit I wore for my thievery—I knew that much. Stealth and sparkles really didn't mix.

I headed down the New-Age retreat's overgrown driveway to a quiet road bordered by fallow fields, stretches of woodland, and the occasional farm house. As I loped alongside the ditch, I scanned all of those for anything worth putting those thieving skills to use on.

The sun crept up across the sky, and the heat intensified with it. Sweat trickled down my back.

I must have covered at least a couple of miles before I spotted my salvation: a mud-splattered bicycle leaning against a fence post, ratty tassels drooping from the ends of its handlebars. Not my typical plunder—I was more a gems and rare coins kind of gal—but right now I'd take that bike over the Hope Diamond.

No, let's be real: I'd take the Hope Diamond, but then I'd steal the bicycle too.

It was obviously a kid's bike, but a big kid's, at least. I couldn't have pedaled it while perched on the seat without hitting my chin with my knees. So, I gripped the gritty plastic handlebars and took off with my ass up in the air like I was about to race in the Tour de France.

As methods of transportation go, you'd be better off not following my lead. I bounced along the potholed country roads for the better part of an hour, until my thighs and back ached almost as badly as my wounded shoulder, and my eyes were stinging with sweat. Thankfully, my vision wasn't so blurry that I missed the delivery truck at the pumps of a gas station up ahead.

The delivery truck with its back door ajar.

There weren't many places around here that a truck that size would be taking its cargo to. I dropped the bike at the edge of the station and slunk over. The driver had his elbow leaned out the window as he chatted with the attendant who was running his credit card.

"Not my favorite type of load, but you've got to take

whatever you can get these days. At least it's a short drive to the city."

Jackpot. I eased the rear door farther up and squeezed under it.

I found myself in a dim, hot space that smelled like straw and shit. Rustles filled the air all around me, punctuated by an occasional... cluck?

I was surrounded by chickens. A hen in the cage closest to me attempted to peck me through the bars.

"Mind your beak," I whispered at her, thinking various curses very intently in Omen's general direction, and hugged my legs to my chest as I prepared for a long ride.

By the time I made out city buildings through the gap under the door, I probably smelled like a chicken coop myself, but I'd made it to my destination with a half an hour to spare. I rolled out when the truck stopped at a red light, summoned an Uber while picking bits of straw off my clothes, and told the driver who showed up to take me to the Finger.

The Finger wasn't the official name of the gigantic statue that loomed in the middle of one of the largest downtown squares, but good luck finding anyone who could tell you what else it might be called. Erected a few decades ago by some avant-garde artiste, the tower of chunks of varnished wood held together by steel struts looked like nothing so much as a massive hand giving the buildings around it the middle finger. Naturally, it was the city's most popular landmark.

When I hopped out at the edge of the cobblestone

courtyard at ten minutes to noon, several tourists were clustered around the Finger taking selfies. There was no sign of any shadowkind, but I wouldn't have expected to find them basking in the sunlight. As I strolled over to the structure, the four of them appeared as if they'd simply stepped from around its other side rather than straight out of the shadows.

"You see," Snap said happily if carefully, to make sure no one around us noticed his forked tongue. "Of course she made it."

With his baseball cap on to cover his horns in mortals' view, Ruse sauntered over to pluck something out of my hair. He tapped my cheek with a chicken feather. "I won't ask."

Funnily enough, Omen didn't look remotely pleased. "You cut it close," he said, as if even making it at the last second wouldn't have been an incredible feat, and immediately turned away. He jabbed a finger toward a police officer who'd paused to buy a hot dog from a stand at the other end of the square. "I hear you consider yourself some kind of master thief. Steal that cop's cap for me."

Oh, he wanted to up the ante now, did he?

Thorn tugged at the fingerless leather gloves that disguised his crystalline knuckles but always seemed to irritate him. "Omen," he started.

I shook my head to hold off the warrior's protest. "Not a problem. I'll just need a moment to prepare."

Omen crossed his arms, giving me a disbelieving scowl. I ignored him as I took the lay of the land. He was going to find out soon enough that I wouldn't give up—not until the bastards we were both after met a fate at least as horrible as they'd given to their shadowkind victims.

I could use a strategy I'd seen Auntie Luna turn to more than once when her fae glamours and other spells wouldn't do the trick. Collide and divert. I wasn't quite as petite and bubbly as she'd been, but I could pull it off nearly as well.

While the cop chowed down on his street meat, I jogged around the nearby streets until I found a performer with an open case strumming her guitar at an intersection. I held out a twenty and patted my wallet when she grabbed it.

"I'll give you four more of those if you scream as loud as you can, five minutes from now," I said, pointing at her watch, and added at her quizzical look, "Set it to music if you want. No scream, no cash."

There wasn't going to be any cash anyway, but hey, just the twenty was a lot of money when I'd lost nearly all my earthly possessions last week.

I hoofed it back to the square, watching the minutes tick by on my phone. When there was only one left, I took off across the cobblestones at a breakneck run.

The cop had just finished his hot dog. He dabbed at his mouth rather daintily with a paper napkin—and I slammed right into him, looking back over my shoulder as if I were paying more attention to something behind me than to where I was going. Still, I managed to swing my heel against his ankle to knock him right off his feet.

We both tumbled over, my arm flying up and smacking his cap to ensure it detached from his head. Since I wasn't a total fiend, I jerked my elbow to the side before it would have rammed him in the throat. We hit the ground with a shared grunt.

"Oh my God, I'm so sorry, so so sorry," I babbled, scrambling up. "It's just—There was—" I gestured wildly toward the direction I'd come from, widening my eyes as far as they would go.

The cop had barely righted himself when the street musician let out the scream I wouldn't be paying her for, high and shrill—and maybe with a riff on her guitar, but I didn't think the cop noticed that. He bolted up faster than anything, too alarmed to bother with his cap, and dashed off to see what devious crime was being committed two blocks away.

I swiped the cap off the cobblestones and ambled back to where Omen and the others were waiting. With a bow, I presented the prick with his prize. "Ta da. Please, don't hold your applause."

Ruse chuckled and clapped. Omen glared at me. "If you think this will—"

"I think," I said, already backing away, "that you've got nothing to complain about in my performance, and I deserve a little break as my reward. I'll meet you all back here at five—or I'll hitchhike my way back to the cabin, if you'd prefer."

I gave Bossypants a cheeky salute, and then I spun on my heel and hailed a passing cab.

Between his knife trick last night and this round of

testing, Omen couldn't have made it clearer how he felt about my presence. I'd just have to show him what humans were capable of when they had allies of their own kind at their back. I needed a shower and a moment to breathe, and then I was going to steal myself a little mortal support.

Only after I'd already picked the lock to the apartment and snuck inside did it occur to me just how bad my approach to a surprise visit might come across to someone who wasn't in the habit of breaking and entering on a regular basis.

Ellen and Huyen, the married leaders of the Shadowkind Defense Fund, were film fanatics. They owned a second-run theater just down the street from the apartment, where they usually held the Fund's meetings to discuss how we could protect the shadowkind creatures in our realm from the humans who preyed on them. So it wasn't surprising to find their walls adorned with framed vintage movie posters and mounted memorabilia like a Godfather fedora and a license plate from North by Northwest. They even had a literal gun on their mantelpiece.

Based on the movies they'd chosen to display, it looked like suspense flicks and film noir were their favorite genres. Which meant they'd probably watched at least a dozen scenes where a character walked into their darkened home only to find an unexpected intruder waiting, sitting casually in an armchair, perhaps with a dramatic clicking on of a lamp.

I wanted to ask the Fund's leaders for their help, not give them a heart attack. At least it wasn't all that dark at three in the afternoon, when I knew they always popped back home for a late lunch break after the first round of matinees. Taking the sneaky route was the only way I could talk to them without any chance someone from the sword-star crew would see me with them and decide to make the two women their next targets.

I might have risked relocking the door and waiting for them in the hall, but before I'd quite decided, their key clicked in the lock. Oh well, I guessed I was stuck doing this the creepy way.

The couple walked in, Ellen in mid-sentence exclaiming about her ideas for new popcorn flavors to inflict on Fund members at upcoming meetings. Seeing me in the living room doorway, they both halted in their tracks. I raised my hand in an apologetic wave of greeting. "Hi?"

Ellen glanced between me and the door and back again, strands of her frizzy, graying hair flying around her face where they'd escaped from her loose bun. "Sorsha, what on earth—How did you—"

I held up both my hands before she could finish that question. "Let's not worry about that right now. I'm *really* sorry to surprise you like this. I just didn't think it'd be safe to talk anywhere else. There's something big going on—something that's hurting a whole lot of shadowkind."

I'd known that fact would override every other aspect

4

Thorn

"You went *where?*" Omen said. His voice had become even flatter and colder than it'd been for most of the past two days, but I'd known him long enough to recognize the crackling undercurrent of heat that ran through it. To say that he and our mortal lady were not getting along would be putting it very mildly.

Sorsha set her hands on her hips. She was always rather striking to behold, now that I'd allowed myself to acknowledge it, but I enjoyed watching her most when circumstances brought out the ferocity in her temperament. Unfortunately, recently those "circumstances" had mostly been our commander.

"They're the leaders of the local branch of the Shadowkind Defense Fund," she said. "If anyone can give us a hand with our investigations, it's them. We *are* dealing with mortal enemies, after all. Who better than mortals to figure out what they're up to?"

Omen rolled his eyes skyward. It wasn't the most awe-inspiring view, standing where we'd gathered in a laneway between a glossy office building and the slightly taller residential tower beside it. A rich but bitter scent wafted from the coffee shop on the office building's ground floor. The clientele exited through the front, though, and the tower had no balconies below the tenth floor, leaving the laneway quiet.

Which meant Omen didn't need to raise his voice even slightly for it to cut crisply through the silence. "It's bad enough having any mortals entangled in our affairs. I'm not interested in shepherding a whole flock of them."

"You don't have to see them or talk to them," Sorsha said. "I'm the go-between; I'll handle everything. You never asked me *not* to try to bring them on board."

His eyes narrowed. "I assumed you were sharp enough to realize that without my saying it. Apparently not."

"We got some useful tips from Sorsha's Fund friends before," Ruse put in. "They led us to the hacker. Why not see what they come up with?"

"Yes," Omen said with a sarcastic edge, "why not find out how quickly they can turn our efforts into a total clusterfuck?" He turned back to Sorsha. "You want to do things your way? I'm still not convinced even you can keep up with us. Do you think you're up to another challenge, or will you run away again?"

"I didn't *run away*." Sorsha sighed. "Lay it on me,

Luce. What death-defying stunt have you got for me now?"

Omen's eyes narrowed at the nickname, and I restrained a wince. Of course the incubus with all his teasing would have brought that up—but our lady couldn't know just how charged that reference to our commander's long-ago exploits was for him. Omen had been quite a trickster himself when I'd first known him, but everything about his demeanor since he'd recruited me to his current cause showed how utterly he'd erased that past from his being. If he could have erased it from all memory as well, I expected he would have.

As he cast his gaze upward again, I braced myself. It seemed he had gotten something out of the view after all, because a moment later, he pointed toward the top of the residential tower. "There's a flower pot with an orange blossom on the highest balcony, by the far corner. Do you see it?"

Sorsha peered upward. "Yep. What about it?"

"I'd like to see you steal *that*... without taking advantage of the building's elevator or stairs. Without going into the building at all."

My defensive instincts sprang to the forefront with an inner clang of alarm. Sorsha might be able to scale the outside of the building—once she reached the lower balconies, it wouldn't require too much of a jump between them—but with each floor she climbed, she'd be tempting a fall. And by the time she made it to the twentieth or so floor, that fall would almost certainly be fatal.

Omen was smiling. It didn't matter to him whether she lived or died. I was starting to think he'd prefer her dead.

It'd become clear that arguing with him about Sorsha's worthiness wouldn't convince him. From the determined clenching of Sorsha's jaw, I knew she wouldn't refuse the trial. I was hardly going to stand here and watch her throw caution—and perhaps herself—to the wind without a care, though.

The thought of what I was about to offer sent a constricting sensation through my chest, but I could handle it discreetly. I stepped forward. "I'd like to confer with the mortal one for a minute."

Omen frowned at me, but I caught a flicker of curiosity in his eyes too. He knew I didn't bestow my loyalty liberally.

"Talk her out of the attempt for her own good," he said.

I ushered Sorsha farther down the laneway to where the others wouldn't hear what I had to say.

"You're not going to talk me out of it," she said before I could begin my appeal.

I let out a dismissive grunt. "Do you think after everything I've seen of you, I'd be witless enough to even try to? You'll retrieve that flower pot for Omen, m'lady. *I'll* see that you do. You only have to send Ruse and Snap off on some errand first."

Her brow furrowed. "Why? What are you talking about?"

"Omen wanted you to find a way to get to that

balcony without entering the building. He didn't put any other limitations on the task. I can be your way. It would only require a matter of seconds—I'll fly quickly enough that no mortals catch more than a glimpse they'll believe they imagined."

Sorsha stared at me. "You're offering to show your true shadowkind form and fly me up to the top of the building, just to get a flower pot?"

I *had* impressed on her rather emphatically that I didn't want her revealing what she'd discovered about my nature to the others. The wingéd—what mortals tended to call "angels"—had a long-tarnished history, one I had no wish to open up to the incubus's teasing jokes or the devourer's unbridled curiosity. But I'd allowed my wings to come forth once before in the service of saving our lady's life. This was no different.

"It's more than retrieving a flower pot," I said. "It's proving to Omen that you belong with us. You've fought too hard by our sides for him to dismiss you now. If I can make the process easier—and less of a threat to your survival—then I won't hesitate."

The thought of the valor she'd shown throughout our time together outshone the irritation I'd once felt at her often flippant attitude. After everything we'd faced together, looking at her stirred a much deeper and more poignant emotion, one so unfamiliar I couldn't put a name to it. I only knew it would be a near thing not attempting to sever Omen's head from his body if she died because of his distrust.

That emotion gripped me even harder when Sorsha

offered me her softest smile. A matching tenderness shone in her eyes. "I appreciate that, Thorn. I know you wouldn't make an offer like that to most people. But I really can handle this myself—and it'll prove much more to Omen if I do. Are you doubting my strength?"

She flexed her biceps and didn't quite conceal a wince. I couldn't hold back my protest. "You're *wounded.*"

"But feeling better with every passing hour." She patted her shoulder and then reached up to pat mine as well. Her touch brought back the quiver of sensation that had passed through me when she'd caressed my wings the other night, stirring a much more heated emotion I recognized perfectly well even if it hadn't come to me often. Ah, yes, that was desire.

I allowed myself just a fragment of remembering what her lithe body had felt like against mine when I'd captured her mouth so briefly, of imagining what it might feel like if I claimed her completely—and then I yanked myself back to the present.

"I was listening closely to Omen's requirements too," Sorsha continued. "I've got this. And on the off-chance I'm wrong, I trust that you'll catch me."

She bobbed up to give me a quick peck on the lips that sent an unreasonably hot flush through the rest of my body and sauntered back to rejoin the others.

"Just to be clear," she said to Omen, adjusting the straps of her backpack, "the only rule is that I *can't* go inside this building, right?"

He gave her a narrow look. "And you bring me the

pot and flower unbroken. Those are the terms."

"Perfect. I accept. Now excuse me. I won't go in *this* building, but I am going into *that* one."

A delighted laugh escaped Snap as our lady sashayed over to the office building next door. Omen's expression turned murderous for an instant before he steadied himself with that nearly impenetrable cool calm he'd held in front of him like a shield since we'd first spoken to him after his escape.

"It still won't be easy for her," he said.

Ruse leaned back against the wall and tilted his head up to watch the balconies. "Oh, I wouldn't be so sure about that."

"This wasn't my idea," I told our commander. "I didn't know that's what she'd planned. She rejected my suggestion entirely." He didn't need to know exactly what that suggestion had been.

Omen eyed me, but he knew I wouldn't outright lie to him. He let out a huff. "Let's see what she thinks she can get away with like this, then."

Snap headed down the laneway where he could get a slightly closer look at the flower pot in question, and Ruse trailed after him. I glanced at Omen and judged it safe enough to say, keeping my voice low, "I can tell you that she's as honorable as she is determined. She—It came about that she witnessed my full form. I asked her not to speak of it with the other two, and she's kept her word."

Omen betrayed a hint of surprise at that. He gestured up and down toward my body. "She's seen you—wings and smoldering eyes and all?"

"Yes," I said. And she'd appeared to like what she saw, where most mortals might have screamed. A flicker of the heat she'd provoked raced through me again.

"Hmm." Omen went back to watching the upper reaches of the buildings, but I thought with a little less rancor.

It didn't take terribly long for Sorsha to emerge. She appeared at the edge of the opposite rooftop, a gleam of sunlight in the red hair she'd pulled into a tight ponytail. After giving us a jaunty wave, she swung a grappling hook she must have been carrying in that pack of hers across the distance.

It caught on the requested balcony with a clatter. She paused, but no one emerged from the residence. Grasping the rope, she leapt off the roof.

My breath started to hitch, but before I even had to recover it, she'd already planted her feet on the railing of the balcony below. She climbed the rope in a swift scramble, pausing just briefly with a suppressed wince only my battle-trained eyes might have picked up on, tucked the flower pot under her arm, and tossed the hook back toward the roof she'd descended from.

Less than five minutes later, Sorsha pranced out of the office building and held out the flower to Omen. "As you ordered. Now are we done with these stupid games or what?"

Omen glared at her. "For the time being," he said, as if he wasn't quite finished with her, and I knew it was too early to be truly relieved. When Omen put his mind to something, he was as unshakeable as—well, as a hound.

5

Sorsha

"Wait," Vivi said, lowering her half-eaten butterscotch chocolate-chip cookie. "So, this badass shadowkind boss named his station wagon *Betsy*?" A snicker escaped her. Then she half-choked on the bite she'd just taken and sputtered several coughs, still managing to sound amused.

I grinned back at her. "That's right." Basking in the hot late-afternoon sun across the glass-topped café table from my bestie, I found it easier to let go of the uneasiness Omen had stirred up in me and simply laugh about him. Sweet cinnamon sparkles, had I missed having Vivi here to shoot the breeze with.

The only thing that might have elevated our reunion more was if we'd felt confident enough to drop in on our favorite dessert place near her parents' house, which we'd visited nearly every week when I'd stayed with her family in the first year after Luna's death. But this new spot, where we'd nabbed a table on the sunny back patio, had already more than met my best friend's approval. After one nibble, she'd declared her cookie was "the cream of the icing on the cake."

"And how does Omen feel about you hanging out with me, if he's so down on mortals in general?" she asked now.

My spirits sank a little, but I kept my smile. "I convinced him you'd cause way less carnage if I gave you the low-down than if you were running around the city without the full story. He still attempted to burn a hole through my head with his glare."

Vivi made a show of checking my face over. "Didn't work. Not so powerful after all, I guess." She paused, her own grin fading. "*Is* that the full story now?"

"All the important parts. If I went into every detail, we'd be here for a couple of weeks." And I wasn't sure I wanted to fill her in on every detail when those details included things like Thorn tearing the heads off of guards to avenge my shoulder wound. It was hard to see moments like that in a positive light if you hadn't been there.

I wanted Vivi to keep a positive outlook on my new companions specifically because I'd predicted her next question. She leaned her elbows on the table and gazed at me coyly through her eyelashes. "And when am I going to meet your incredibly hot new boyfriends?"

I'd skipped most of the details there too, but maybe I shouldn't have mentioned just how friendly I'd gotten with my trio at all. I popped one last bite of my blueberry pie into my mouth and waggled my fork at Vivi. "They're not exactly my boyfriends. It's not as if a mortal could really *date* a shadowkind guy, let alone three of them."

She waved my protest away. "Okay, your new cuddle-buddies. Whatever you want to call them, the question stands. I promise not to try to steal them away from you, but you've got to at least share the eye-candy."

"We'll see. I'm not sure I want Omen knowing any more about *you* than he already does." And I also wasn't sure she wouldn't think I was bonkers once she took in the full reality of the trio. I'd gotten to know them—in ways both literal and biblical—enough that their oddities didn't faze me, but Vivi had never been all that close with any shadowkind before. I didn't think she could even totally understand the bond I'd had with Luna.

For all the polite language they used and all the work they put into protecting shadowkind creatures, most of the Fund members never stopped thinking of those beings as monsters.

"Fine." Vivi wrinkled her nose at me and recovered her grin. "You are at least going to let me help out now, right? I need to get in at least one grand adventure before I hit thirty, or what the hell am I doing with my life? I can be very useful, I'll have you know. Look at me, all professional poise."

She gestured to her outfit, which as always was white

from neck to toe: an ivory blouse and wide-leg dress pants over strappy sandals with a reserved twinkle of gold at the buckles. Even with the explosion of dark curls that burst at the back of her head from the tight braids along the rest of her scalp, she did exude a certain elegance that I doubted I'd ever pull off. Being raised by a shadowkind left a person a little feral in ways it was difficult to shake.

"I'll give you that," I said. "Let's see what comes out of the, um, meeting tonight, and I'll let you know where we need you."

She gave me a questioning look at that statement, but I held up my hands in a gesture for mercy. I wasn't shutting Vivi out this time around, but I sure as sugar wasn't dragging her off to a direct ambush of the murderous and potentially psychotic sword-star crew. Especially when she still saw this as an adventure, even if she realized it was a dangerous one now.

I had to get going to prepare for that ambush. As we left the café, I gave Vivi a tight hug, as if I could absorb her cheer into me to bolster me through the battle ahead. We said our "Ditto"s, and I headed for the spot where the quartet was meant to pick me up, singing a little song to inspire myself. "We'll touch and surround, I'm on the hunt this af-ter-noon."

Omen eyed me as I got into the back seat of the station wagon as if checking me over for mortal cootie contamination. I was mature enough at that particular moment not to stick my tongue out at him in return. The other three were sticking to the shadows as they often did in the car, but I took a little comfort in knowing I wasn't actually alone with the dude.

"Vivi's going to be chill," I told him. "She won't stick her nose in unless I ask her to—and I'll only ask her with something really specific that none of us can do."

Bossypants let out a grunt that seemed to say he couldn't imagine there being any task fitting that criteria and switched the car into drive. I drew in another sniff of that odd smell that clung to the vehicle's interior. Dry, smoky, a little savory, with that trace of minerals... Maybe he crisped chicken wings on a tray of scorching crystals in his spare time? It could be some weird shadowkind hobby no one had bothered to tell me about.

Ruse's charmed hacker had dug up the details of the hand-off we were heading to. It was supposedly taking place an hour after sunset in the parking lot of a mini-golf course. Not your typical spot for illicit exchanges of creatures the average mortal didn't even believe existed, but when we slunk over after leaving Betsy a short distance away, I could see why they'd picked it.

The course with its candy-bright painted fixtures—a windmill here, a castle there—surrounded the parking lot on two sides and was big enough that no one farther afield would have been able to see what was happening in the lot. A dingy warehouse offered a windowless brick wall on the third side, so no witnesses there. At the road, someone had conveniently left a dumpster full of construction rubble where it blocked most of the view of the span of asphalt, and the nearest streetlamps had burnt out. By a total coincidence, no doubt.

We'd arrived just as the sun was setting. The shadows of the miniature structures stretched twice as long as the actual fixtures across the patches of green. Ruse slipped through the shadows to unlock the gate so I could follow them in.

"Your only job is to hang back until we have our prize," Omen ordered me. He pointed to the roof of the hut that held the ticket sales booth and equipment. "Thorn will boost you up there. Stay out of view and watch the transaction. I only want to hear or see you if you spot something from up there that the rest of us need to know. Once we've trapped one of their number, then you can jump in to remove protective wards as necessary."

"And to open the cage to let their shadowkind prisoner out," Snap piped up.

"Yes, that too," Omen muttered as if annoyed at the reminder that I would be useful in more than one way. He fixed his stare on me. "Got it?"

"Aye, aye, captain," I said dryly. I suspected he'd have tried to lock me in the car instead of letting me tag along at all if he'd thought there was any chance that car could hold me for more than a minute. But even he couldn't deny the value of my immunity to the materials that deflected shadowkind powers.

Just in case I found a good use for it, I picked up one of the mini-golf clubs and swung it experimentally through the air. A little light, but it had decent heft to it. For good measure, I stuffed several of the small but incredibly dense golf balls into the pouches on my belt.

I'd decked myself out in full cat-burglar gear for this operation. If I didn't move or speak, I'd be nothing but a shadow on the rooftop, even my red hair hidden under the black knit cap. Thank flaming eels the evening was already starting to cool off, or I'd have been a puddle of sweat in a matter of seconds.

Thorn gave me a boost to the edge of the roof, and I scrambled across it to duck down behind one of the fake gables. Peeking over the protruding section, I could make out the edge of the golf course and all of the parking lot.

The shadowkind quartet had discussed their plans in more depth while I'd been chatting with Vivi. As I settled into my position, they vanished into the shadows. From what I'd gathered, they were going to station themselves in a rough circle around the parking lot. The idea was to watch the hand-off long enough to determine the sword-star crew's usual procedures, and then—unless the squad appeared too well-equipped—charge in, free the shadowkind the collector was selling to them, and snatch one of the sword-star employees for later questioning.

I shifted my position on the clay tiles a few times, my back getting stiff and my shoulder achy from my hunched posture. Every time a car rumbled by through the deepening evening dark, I froze. Finally, a black van that looked like the sort of vehicle used to transport large livestock pulled into the lot. It parked in the far corner where the golf course rubbed up against the warehouse.

Only one figure stepped out—the collector, I assumed. At first glance, he could have passed for an evil-genius supervillain from the type of comic books I was guessing our hacker had read too many of. The dome of his bald, bulbous head shone in the faint light from the far-off streetlamps, and he wore a gray suit with its square collar buttoned right up to his chin. I half expected him to produce a monocle from his chest pocket.

Then I noticed the sheen of perspiration that caught even more of the light than the pale skin of his scalp. The dude might have supervillain fashion aspirations, but super-confident he was not.

It took another ten minutes before a second vehicle growled into the lot: a white delivery truck with a bakery logo painted on the side. A fake business, or another front like the discount toy store the sword-star crew had run some of their operations out of? I made a mental note of the name in case it was the latter.

Five figures emerged from the truck. They wore the silver-and-iron helmets and plated vests that we'd seen before. All shadowkind found one if not both of those metals repellent, but they couldn't block Thorn's physical strength or whatever concrete tricks Omen had dreamed up.

One of the figures appeared to have a whip, probably one of those glowing laser-y ones, at his hip, but they weren't holding any weapons. It looked like they didn't anticipate dealing with any hostile parties in this transaction.

Exactly as we'd hoped.

The sweaty collector opened the back door to his van. Searing light spilled out—he'd have bright lamps set up all around the cage that must be holding the powerful creature to prevent it from slipping away into the shadows. The sword-star bunch wheeled a container like an oversized gym locker out of the back of their truck and set it facing the van. It looked like they meant to transfer the cage from the van into that box, which must have lights of its own.

Before they got that far, four shadowy forms hurtled into the lot. I couldn't make out much of their faces through the blur of darkness still clinging to them, but the massive shape bashing two of the sword-star crew off their feet was obviously Thorn.

The other three shadowkind didn't dare get quite as close to our enemies and their noxious armor. Ruse lashed some sort of rope at the collector's legs and yanked it so he tumbled onto the ground, his knees locked together. As the not-at-all-super villain started sniveling like a kindergartener, Omen and Snap tossed thick sheets over the two attackers Thorn had felled. Whatever those were made of, the material was heavy enough to hold the men in place.

Thorn was still dealing with the rest of the sword-star crew. He snatched the man with the whip by the wrists and hurled him over the fence to crash into the mini-golf castle. The dude slumped, one of the turrets wobbling and then plummeting to smack him in the head for good measure. Another asshole got a punch in the throat with the warrior's crystalline knuckles. A gurgle escaped the gaping wound as he collapsed in a bloody mess.

The last of our enemies had taken advantage of Thorn's distraction. The guy thrust a metal rod at the warrior's back, and sparks spurted against Thorn's tunic. The huge shadowkind shuddered, a spasm gripping his limbs for a second as he wrenched himself around. Meanwhile, the prick who'd broken the poor castle was managing to pick himself up, whip in hand.

Oh no, he didn't. "Thorn!" I called out in warning, springing to my feet. My hand had already shot to one of my pouches. My fingers curled around a golf ball, and I flung it at the guy with the rod.

It nailed him in the back of the helmet with a dull clang—I'd call that a hole in one. With a victory whoop, I pitched another few his way, pelting him for long enough that he wasn't prepared for Thorn's punch. The warrior's rigid knuckles smashed right into his face. I averted my gaze from the spurt of blood.

Good thing, because the castle dude was dashing back toward the chain-link fence, whip ready. I leapt from the hut's roof onto a plaster drawbridge and from there to the ground. As the guy moved to heave himself over the fence, I thwacked him across the ear with the golf club, just below the base of his helmet. His head swayed, and I aimed the putter at the top of the helmet this time. With one solid swing, I smacked the protection right off him.

Omen was there as if he'd been waiting for just that chance. The second the helmet careened off, our leader slammed the sword-star guy's forehead into the bar along the top of the fence hard enough to shatter his skull.

Okay, then. He might not have Thorn's bulk, but he

6

Sorsha

Interrogation was much less painful when you had an incubus in play, both for those of us on the interrogator's side and, I had to assume, for the victims. No need for water torture or trolleys laid with knives and pliers when a little charmed conversation would get them spilling their secrets much more effectively.

Ruse had chatted up our two captives while they'd still been pinned against the ground. As soon as they'd been thoroughly under his thrall, we'd let them up and marched them into the back of their own truck. Now, we were parked in an isolated part of town, standing in a semi-circle facing the two star-sword dudes, who sat against the wall of the compartment.

The incubus might have softened up these two, but naturally Omen was determined to handle most of the actual questioning. His eyes gleamed, even narrower than usual under the stark glow of the one lamp we'd turned on—one that'd been meant to hold other shadowkind as prisoners under much harsher circumstances.

The specifics of those circumstances was clearly the largest question on his mind. He crossed his arms over his chest, appearing to just barely hold himself back from shooting the two guys a death glare. Ruse's illusion that we were all fantastic friends would only hold if Bossypants didn't push them too far in the opposite direction.

"What were you planning on doing with the shadowkind being you were buying from that collector?" he asked.

One of the men stirred, a hopeful expression coming over his face as if he wanted nothing more than to please his kidnappers with his answer. "We'd meet with the other truck and hand it off."

This was at least a two-stage manoeuvre, then. Not surprising, considering the lengths we'd seen these people go to for caution's sake before.

Omen frowned. "And where would the other truck have taken it?"

"We don't know," the other guy said. "The people who give us our instructions, they like to keep all the pieces separate. They say it's more secure that way. It's a good thing—what if someone who wasn't looking out for us had grabbed us instead of you?"

My lips twitched, but I managed to swallow a laugh. Had Ruse wiped the memory of what Thorn and Omen had done to their colleagues from their minds, or had he simply convinced them that those guys had been asking to have their skulls bashed in?

It would have been nice if we could have tracked down the second set of Company lackeys, but they'd have realized the hand-off had gone wrong by now. Wherever they'd been meant to meet these dudes, they and anything they could have told us would be long gone. So much for finding the new base of operations.

Omen didn't look remotely satisfied with the answer he'd gotten either. "Do your 'people' tell you anything about what they do with the shadowkind they're gathering once they have them?"

The first guy brightened. "Yes. A little. They're looking for ways to end the beasts' evil influence on our world. The Company of Light will eradicate all the monsters that prey on us. But they're slippery demons— just killing some here and there isn't good enough. They're looking for a better way."

I wasn't even one of those slippery demons myself, and I automatically bristled on behalf of my companions. Snap tucked his arm around my waist in a gesture of comfort, but his divinely sweet face was drawn. I squeezed his hand in return. He'd spent little time mortal-side before now—he might never have heard a human talk about how much they detested beings like him before. This supposed "monster" was more compassionate than most human beings I knew.

A hint of otherworldly smolder flickered in Thorn's eyes. The huge warrior took a deliberate step closer, looming almost to the roof of the compartment with an aura of menace, but Omen held up his hand. His mouth had formed a rigid smile.

He didn't like what the guy had said, but it was exactly the attitude he'd expected.

"The Company of Light," he repeated. "Is that what your organization calls itself?"

The man nodded. "We have to keep our cause secret, because backlash from the monsters could end us all, but with the work we're doing, our light will burn away all the shadows."

"But you don't know what exactly your Company's experiments are supposed to achieve."

"Experiments?" The man's brow furrowed. "That's not my area. I just know whatever they're doing, they're working toward destroying every fiend that dares set foot here—and maybe all the ones back where they come from too."

Lovely. A chill collected in my gut. He was discussing literal genocide as if it were the most glorious purpose he could imagine. Had any of these sword-star— excuse me, *Company of Light*—assholes ever even talked with a higher shadowkind?

I'd be the first to admit that beings like the four around me didn't subscribe to the exact same sense of morality humans did. And sure, some of their kind did prey on mortal beings. But plenty of mortals preyed on each other too. The answer was to fight back against the ones committing the actual crimes, not to mass murder everybody. I didn't think this Company would like it if the shadowkind turned their logic back on humankind.

"That does sound like an honorable goal," Omen said, his voice so edged with sarcasm I half expected it to slice right into our captives' flesh. He paced from one end of the compartment to the other as he considered his next line of inquiry. "Are these hand-offs with the collectors the only way you contribute?"

"They call on me once every few weeks for a job like this," the first man said. "Otherwise, I keep quiet and keep out of the rest of their business."

The shadowkind's gaze slid to the other guy. "And you?"

"I don't do anything else with the beasts, but I've done a little other driving—bringing equipment for the events and that sort of thing."

"Ah. What sort of events would those be?"

The guy shrugged. "I'm not sure. They have some parties with a bunch of rich folks now and then. With all the equipment they must need and the cash for buying off the collectors—I guess they've got to raise funds somehow or other."

Another laugh tickled my chest, this one sharper with irony. Of course the Company of Light would need to hold fundraisers just like Ellen and Huyen's group of defenders did. While we gathered money to protect the shadowkind, they gathered money to hunt and torture them. From the scale of our enemies' operations, they had to be a lot better at it than we were. Maybe we could pick up some pointers along the way.

Omen grilled the two more—about how they got their equipment, where they were trained in handling shadowkind, and anything else he could come up with relating to the structure of the Company of Light. Unfortunately, our enemies had been awfully sly all around. The training sessions happened at random locations that changed every time, the equipment showed up on the guys' doorsteps along with the orders for their next assignment, and they didn't know much else.

We stepped out of the truck to confer where they couldn't overhear us.

"It's not a total loss," I said. "We freed the shadowkind they were going to buy—we put the fear in that collector and hopefully a bunch more in his network. We know what their hand-offs look like now, and maybe we can get at them through these fundraising events somehow."

"It's still less than I'd like." Omen eyed the truck broodingly. "Maybe I can come up with another angle that'll be more productive."

A new chill tickled down my back. "What are you going to do with them when you've run out of questions?" I'd avoided prying into that subject until now, but that hesitance was starting to feel cowardly. The guys in there were prejudiced dicks, but they'd talked with us peacefully. I didn't like the idea of watching my companions slaughter them in their defenseless state.

Omen looked as though he'd like it just fine, but then his mouth twisted as if he'd bitten something sour. "It would be better if their 'Company' doesn't realize we held this interrogation. Ruse, you can charm them into keeping quiet about our chat, can't you? Convince them that they have to claim they drove from the scene of the attack unhindered?"

The incubus saluted him. "Give me a little more time, and I can manage it."

I glanced around at the darkened street. The shadowkind quartet didn't really need me here anymore —and there was something else I'd wanted to accomplish while Omen was distracted with this business. My stomach grumbled, giving me the perfect excuse. I hadn't eaten since that slice of pie with Vivi.

"Unlike the rest of you," I said, "I need dinner or I'll keel over. Meet you back where we left Betsy in a couple of hours?"

The thought of me fulfilling my mortal needs brought out Omen's disdain. He waved me off and yanked open the truck's back door again.

I trotted several blocks from the interrogation scene, weaving right and left at the intersections, and then called an Uber. I *was* planning on getting something to eat—but not anywhere Omen would have approved of.

As I settled into the car's back seat, something jabbed my leg in the bottom of my backpack. I felt inside, and my fingers closed around the cool, smooth surface of a little box. My throat tightened.

I drew out the box, the city lights outside the window catching on its pearly sides. My fingers moved automatically to pop open the lid.

This keepsake was the only thing I had of my parents'. There hadn't exactly been time to stop and pack when hunters had stormed into my parents' house while

Auntie Luna and I had been playing in the backyard. At my mother's scream to her, Luna had grabbed three-year-old me and fled—but she'd had this box with the folded notepaper inside to offer me when I was old enough to read it.

The note didn't say much other than that my parents had loved me and wished things hadn't turned out this way but that Luna would protect me. They'd obviously realized there was a chance the assholes they'd stood up to would lash out at them.

I didn't know whether those assholes had been connected to the Company of Light just as Luna's attackers had been or whether they'd been just a random bunch of vengeful hunters, but either way, it only proved what psychotic monsters *humans* could be. And how much some of those humans needed to have their evil plans upended.

So I'd damn well use every tool I had, whether Omen approved or not.

I clicked the box shut again and tucked it into my purse this time, wanting to keep it even closer to me. The car slowed, just reaching the bar I'd given the driver the address to.

As I stepped through the doorway to Jade's Fountain, I scanned the room for anyone who didn't fit, but it looked like the usual crowd of quirky mortals and the occasional shadowkind partier who could blend in here. There was a mortal girl wearing a cat-ear headband, and two tables away a dude whose lizard-like eyes I suspected weren't contacts. Exactly as it should be. The burble of the water that cascaded down the far wall and the mineral scent in the air settled my nerves for the first time in days.

As usual, Jade was working solo behind the polished quartz bar counter, the dark green hair that would have marked her as a shadowkind to anyone who realized it wasn't dyed tumbling down her slim back. I headed to the seat at the far corner reserved for those of us already in the know.

The shadowkind woman ambled over a moment later. I thought her eyes were more wary than usual. Either she'd picked up word on the street about the hijinks I'd been caught up in, or those hijinks had made *me* more paranoid than usual.

"What'll it be tonight, Sorsha?" she asked.

"A Jack and Coke and one of those turkey paninis." I motioned to the little fridge where she kept prewrapped meals ready to pop into the toaster oven.

"Late dinner tonight?"

"It's been a busy one."

She hummed in response as she prepared the sandwich and poured my drink. When she set both in front of me with a clink of the glass, she lingered there, leaning one elbow onto the counter. "What's up?"

I paused to take a large bite of my panini and licked melted cheese grease off my fingers. Yum. "I know you don't like to get too involved in the Fund business and that sort of thing, so I'm not going to ask you to. I'm just going to say: if something major were going down— something that put *all* the shadowkind who've come mortal-side and maybe even the shadow-side ones in danger—do you know any higher kind who *would* want to stand up against the mortals involved?"

Her expression turned even more guarded than before. "Are you suggesting that something like that is happening *now*?"

I held her gaze steadily. "How much do you really want to know?"

She hesitated, and then her lips pressed flat. "Point taken. Maybe it's not worth the risk of even asking around, then."

"I guess you've got to weigh the odds. Would it be worse to do nothing at all and one day soon this bar gets stormed, or to just put out some very careful feelers that you can divert toward me?" I took another bite and chewed while she thought that over. Then I added, "I've never seen anything like this before, Jade. You know I wouldn't be making an ask like this if it wasn't important."

A couple of college-age kids with facial studs that might have been disguising an actual horn or two had come over to the counter farther down. Jade sighed. "I'll think about it—even if I check, I'm not sure I've got anyone for you. But if I do... I'll reach out to your private number?"

"You've got it. Thanks, Jade. I appreciate whatever you can do."

It was late enough that a few of the patrons were starting to sway with the music beside the tiled pond people used as both wishing well and, when drunk enough, wading pool. I hadn't planned to dance, hadn't planned to stick around longer than it took me to gulp down the rest of my meal, but as I tossed back the last sweet-and-sharp swallow of Jack and Coke, warm hands gripped me by the waist. The now-familiar bittersweet scent of cacao laced with caramel wrapped around me.

"I've finally got you alone," Ruse said in his equally chocolatey voice, tipping his head so his lips brushed the shell of my ear. Just that small contact, not even a kiss, sent an eager shiver through me.

I swiveled on the stool and looked up into his languid eyes. My heart might have skipped a beat at the heat in his gaze. Even with that silly baseball cap on his head to hide *his* very real horns, there wasn't anyone sexier I'd ever seen.

He couldn't have worked any of his seductive voodoo on me while I had my protective badge pinned to my undershirt in its usual place over my heart—just in case I happened on any shadowkind whose motives I *couldn't* trust—but he had plenty of totally non-supernatural charm to go around too. Taking the allure out of the incubus would have been as impossible as taking the purr out of a cat.

"We're hardly alone," I had to point out, motioning to the crowded room. "Did you follow me here? I thought you were taking care of your new best friends?"

Ruse grinned. "Oh, they're well taken care of. Sometimes I impress even myself. I just had a suspicion I'd find you here. I know who you turn to for information and reinforcements."

"I'm not sure I've gotten either." I gave his solidly muscled chest a nudge, more playful than designed to push him off me. "You've found me—what are you going to do with me now?"

His grin stretched wide. "Why don't we start with a dance? That seemed to work well for us last time."

The last time we'd danced together—in my old apartment after he'd put on an '80s dance mix to cheer me up—I'd pulled him into bed with me later that night. I still wasn't totally convinced that diving under the sheets with him again was a great idea. All the heights of bliss he could take me to were offset by that whole emotional manipulation side of his powers. He'd promised never to poke around inside my head again, but he'd promised that before the first time he'd done it too.

As he led me onto the dance floor, my uncertainty wavered. I'd forgotten just how good his hands felt against my body—trailing now from my waist over my hips and down my thighs. He stayed close as we shifted and swiveled with the music's haunting rhythm.

When I stopped for a moment as one song faded out, Ruse pressed a kiss to the bare skin at the side of my neck. I couldn't stop my breath from hitching at the jolt of pleasure.

"Hmm," he murmured against my hair. "The devourer has joined us in the shadows. I'm getting the impression he'd like to have you this close always. You know, my offer to show him the ropes between the sheets —perhaps literally, if you'd enjoy being tied to the bedposts—still stands. Imagine all the fun we—"

Before he could finish that torturously tempting offer, another of our companions pushed through the dancers toward us. Omen's eyes blazed so furiously in their icy way that even Ruse went still.

His boss came to a stop right in front of me and jabbed his finger at my chest. "What the hell do you think you're doing here?" he demanded, low but cutting.

"Dancing?" I said with an innocent smile.

"I know who runs this place. I know she talks with your *Fund*." He said the last word with a sneer. "I told you, we can't count on the other shadowkind for this. We're handling it ourselves."

"I never agreed to that. And anyway, I barely told her anything. I'm not an idiot."

"As far as I'm concerned, the jury's still out on that one." He jerked his hand toward the doorway. "Let's go. You've interfered enough for one night."

My body balked at the idea of following his orders, but his arrival had reminded me that it probably wasn't the safest for me to stick around here anyway. I was pretty sure the Company's people had looked for me here once before. From Ruse's reaction, he wasn't up for more dancing anyway.

"Interfering, huh?" I said, jabbing my finger right back at Omen. "That must be some brand-new way of saying, 'Provided an essential component to my masterplan.' You're welcome, by the way. Lucky for you, *Luce*, I'm ready to call it a night."

"You," Omen growled, but a second later he reined in the temper I'd known that nickname would provoke—

even if I wasn't totally sure why—with a flick of his gaze toward the crowd.

He couldn't keep his cool forever. One of these days, I'd get under his skin enough to break the beast right open.

Maybe I'd better hope Jade had sent a few buddies my way before that explosion.

7

Sorsha

The New-Age cabin didn't have electric lights, but I'd scrounged up a huge candle in a glass jar. The label said *Lawn Mower*, and the scent fit: like fresh-cut grass with a hint of diesel. I could tell why that one had been abandoned in the closet. It was better than the stale, dusty smell that had filled the cabin before, though.

As I blew out the flame for the night, Pickle let out a sleepy, squeaky murmur from the amethyst incense bowl now filled with shredded gauzy scarf. I'd set it in the shower stall in the tiny bathroom to give him the sense of a cavern. He'd have preferred a whole tub to trundle around in, but we were both making do with what we had.

I tucked myself in under the sheets on the cramped lower bunk, lay my head on the thin pillow—and all at once the warm weight of another body solidified against mine, making the space twice as cramped as before. I flinched with a lurch of my pulse. Then I registered Snap's breathtaking face gazing down at me in the dim moonlight that seeped through the cabin's window, his sweet but dark scent, like clover and moss, filling my nose.

He was already pulling back at my initial panicked response. Balancing precariously on the edge of the mattress rather than leaning against me like before, he stroked the side of my face in apology. "I'm sorry. I forgot that you can't tell I'm here until I come out of the shadows. It's started to feel so much like you're one of us that I find myself thinking you have the same awareness."

"That's all right." I didn't mind his company in my bed now that I knew it was him. I gave him a gentle tug toward me before his tall but slim frame tumbled right onto the floor. His body settled against mine again—chest to chest, one toned leg tucked over my thigh, those golden curls nearly brushing my cheek—and a hungrier heat formed low in my belly. I couldn't resist tracing my fingers along his smooth jaw in return. "Was there any particular reason you decided to drop in on me in bed?"

His smile looked a little sheepish, but his eyes gleamed with a hint of their monstrous neon green, unable to disguise his eagerness. "I was thinking—after seeing you and Ruse at the bar—I wanted to be that close to you again. We don't have to do anything other than this. I'd be happy to just lie next to you while you sleep."

Oh, my darling man—if I could even call him a man. I'd never have thought a being who was apparently capable of inflicting horrifying magic could be so enticingly adorable, but Snap somehow managed to be both in one.

I let my fingers trail down to where the collar of his Henley shirt splayed open over the lean muscles of his chest. "So you came here just to cuddle, huh? No interest in anything more?"

Another flash of neon flared in his eyes. "I didn't say *that*." His head dipped, his lips grazing my temple with his next words. "I would like very much to taste you again, Peach. Maybe in ways I didn't get a chance to last time?"

"Hmm. The truth comes out," I teased.

Snap drew back an inch to meet my eyes again. "Not just for me. That night, what we did together—it felt better than anything I've ever experienced in this realm or the one of shadow. But mainly because of how we connected so completely, sharing in the sensations. I want to do it again and again, but only if you're with me, wanting it too."

He spoke so earnestly it made my chest ache, both because of the adoration in his tone and because I knew how much of his affection was probably due to the novelty of the experience.

Sexual pleasure wasn't something shadowkind instinctively sought out in their own realm—it appeared to be the domain of mortals like me and mortal bodies like the ones he and his kind wore here. Many higher shadowkind sought out that bliss once they discovered it, and some like the cubi kind needed it to sustain themselves, but Snap hadn't spent enough time mortal-side to have stumbled on those desires until now.

"That attitude is a good one to have," I said. "But it won't only be me you can experience this with, you know. You'll find you can feel just as good with other women—maybe even men too—when you broaden your horizons."

He let out a soft huff. "No. There wouldn't be anyone else quite like you. I've never seen—the courage you show, so willing to fight for us even though we're not like you—your patience as we adapt to this world. You don't shy away even from the parts of us that make others call us monsters. You stand up with us against our enemies even without the same sorts of powers, no matter what you've lost... I only hope *I* can be strong enough to match you."

My throat constricted with a pang that shot straight through my heart. Okay, he might have made a pretty solid case there, even if I had trouble seeing myself as half as valiant as he did. Not being willing to stand by while living, feeling beings were caged and slaughtered was a pretty low bar to label someone a hero.

I caressed his jaw again, running my fingers up it and into his soft curls. "Well, I think you're pretty amazing too. This world can be a shitty place, but you manage to find every bit of beauty in the simplest things. You want to understand everything just for the sake of understanding it—most people only care about what's going to help them get ahead. I've never met anyone who wanted so badly to help and create joy in every way they can. I have no idea how I'm going to let you go."

I felt the ache of that uncertainty even more when he beamed down at me. He kissed my temple where his lips had teased me before, and then my cheek and the crook of my jaw. "Then don't."

For a moment, I tried to imagine what it would be like if the devourer didn't leave my life once this mission of ours was over. Could he really be a boyfriend, despite what I'd said to Vivi? Sharing an apartment with him, introducing him to all the other mortal pleasures like my favorite movies and music and—of course—food. Going out on the town with him, sharing in his wonder. Meeting up with friends...

How would I explain our relationship to anyone from the Fund? I wasn't sure even Vivi could manage not to be weird about it.

Would I get tired of his awe once I'd been around him for a while? Would he end up irritated by my many flaws as the initial glow of attraction faded? I'd had enough trouble making any kind of ongoing relationship work with actual human dudes. My track record suggested this would be the longest of longshots.

There was no point in saying that to Snap, though. It'd only ruin what we had right now. When we didn't know if we'd even survive to the end of the mission, it hardly mattered anyway. If we both got to have a future, one where maniacal organizations weren't attempting to eradicate his entire species, then we could worry about the practicalities—if we hadn't already determined that we were headed nowhere fast.

Right now, I wanted him as badly as he clearly wanted me. That was the only answer I needed.

Instead of talking, I drew his mouth to mine. He leaned into the kiss with all the eager passion I adored in him. As he deepened it, his tongue slipped between my lips, twining around mine with that skillful forked tip.

Mmm, yes, I definitely wasn't in any hurry to give this up.

The first time, days ago, we'd taken things slow while Snap explored his desire, and had gotten each other off with only our hands. The devourer had gathered confidence since then. As he kissed me again, ardently enough to coax a whimper from my throat, he was already tugging my undershirt up, placing his hands to avoid the silver-and-iron badge I left pinned to it out of habit.

The moment I eased back to pull it the rest of the way off, he palmed my breasts. In a matter of seconds, his long, lithe fingers had tweaked both my nipples into hardened nubs. Quivers of bliss flooded my chest, drowning out the twinge of my injured shoulder as I tossed the undershirt aside.

I yanked Snap into another kiss, but he didn't linger in it long before making good on his wish to taste me. He slicked his tongue over the peak of one breast and then the other, the forked end teasing my nipples even stiffer with the most incredible sensation.

I groped at his shirt, wanting to feel his naked chest against mine. Snap reached for the hem and then paused with a neon glitter passing through his eyes. He grinned with an unusual slyness, blinked—and the shirt simply disappeared.

Scratch that—*all* of his clothes had disappeared. I gazed down his sinewy frame to the erection jutting from between his thighs, and a fresh flush of desire washed through me. I'd known the shadowkind constructed the clothes they wore separately from their bodies when they emerged into the physical space, but I'd never seen that fact put to use to quite such enjoyable effect. Two thumbs up for instantaneous nudity.

"Very smooth," I said, and Snap looked even more pleased with himself for the second it took before he was kissing me again. He continued fondling one of my breasts to blissful effect while his other hand trailed heat down my side all the way to my hip. I arched to meet him automatically, and his knee slipped between my legs. His thigh pressed against my sex with the most delectable friction. I shivered in delight, unable to stop myself from rocking into that contact.

Snap smiled against my mouth and shifted his leg, his erection rubbing against my hip, moving with me until I moaned. Pleasure surged from my core. My fingers clenched where I was grasping his shoulder and his hair, my desire taking on an urgent edge.

The same urgency appeared to have gripped Snap. His breath stuttered over my lips. He kissed me again, hard, and then said in a voice so strained with need it rocketed my own hunger even higher, "Maybe more tasting can wait. I want to be inside you—that's how it's supposed to be, isn't it? That's what feels right."

My own breath was coming shaky. "Yes," I managed to say, never so grateful that shadowkind didn't reproduce the same way mortals did, because I sure as hell hadn't gotten a chance to stock up on condoms. "I mean, there are all kinds of ways that are totally right, but that's the one—that's what most people like best."

The devourer made a wordless sound of acknowledgement and yanked at my panties, which I couldn't conveniently will out of existence with a blink, more's the pity. I squirmed out of them and splayed my legs, reaching down to help guide him. As my fingers stroked the hot, silky length of his cock, Snap groaned, but his instincts led him well. Without any further direction, he teased the head of his erection over my slit and in, in, in with a deliberate care that had me burning for more.

When he'd pushed all the way to the hilt, pleasure radiated from where we were joined all through the rest of my body. He went perfectly still, his eyes locked on mine through the darkness, wide with a delighted sort of wonder. A short, breathless laugh escaped him. His rapturous expression choked me up all over again. I resisted the urge to buck against him and propel this union toward its climax faster than he seemed to intend.

"This," he murmured. "*This* is the best. With you."

"Snap..." I didn't know whether I was going to return that tender sentiment or beg him to drive me on to further satisfaction, but then it didn't matter, because, thank all that was taut and tingly, he started to move. Pulling back and pressing forward, gently and then with more forceful thrusts, watching my face with avid attention.

With each whimper that fell from my lips and each rush of bliss that sent my eyes rolling back, he adjusted his rhythm, his angle, his speed, until every plunge of his cock inside me set off rising waves of ecstasy. The bunk bed squeaked as our hips smacked together, and a giggle just as breathless as his laugh tumbled out of me. The realms really ought to thank me for waking up this potential in him, because he was fucking *brilliant* at fucking.

"If you get there before me, it's okay," I said around another gasp, but he shook his head. His features had tensed against his release even as he held the same rapt attention on my reactions.

He ran his fingers over my hair and across my thigh, fitting us even more tightly together. One thrust, and another, and another, each searing a headier pleasure through me.

With a little cry, I careened over the edge in a burst of bliss. Snap's groan and the clutch of my hair told me he'd followed.

His body slackened, but he held his muscles tensed enough to stop his full weight from squashing me into the mattress. He lowered his head to claim one more kiss. I reveled in it, my limbs gone boneless with release.

"There isn't much room," he said after, and I understood the question he was asking. He was a cuddler, as much as he enjoyed other activities too. Tonight, I could embrace that part of his nature. Maybe a small part of *me* could even believe I deserved this devotion.

"You can stay." I scooted over so my back leaned against the wall. Snap settled onto the mattress beside me, pulling the sheet back up to cover both of us. It was a tight squeeze, but our bodies interlocked as if they'd been meant to fit together. I nestled my head beneath the devourer's chin and brushed my lips to his chest. Snap's arm tucked around me, holding me there, secure.

Our breaths evened out in harmony. Shadowkind didn't need to sleep, but in physical form, they could. After a few minutes, Snap had relaxed completely against me. When I traced my fingertips over his bare torso, he didn't stir. My own eyelids drifted down. The ache swelling around my heart was nothing but contented now.

"It's quite the feat," I sang under my breath, snuggling closer. "In your eyes, I am so sweet." And maybe, come what may, that would be enough.

8

Snap

When I woke up, only a faint haze of dawn light showed through the window. Sorsha lay peaceful in my embrace, her red hair providing a bright frame to her pale face. Her fiery sweet scent lingered in my nose and on my lips.

I wanted to hold her like this forever. I wanted to slide back inside her and return to that wonderful, slick melding that had brought such pleasure to both of us. But the first option was impossible while we still had Omen's jailors to bring to justice, and the second would have meant breaking her much-needed sleep.

Instead, I settled for slipping away into the shadows and reforming outside, meaning to check the car for any food she might have bought and left there that I could offer her as a breakfast when she woke. That's what I would have done, except Omen was leaning against the car, his arms folded over his chest and his gaze piercing as it fixed on me. I might not have been an expert at reading emotions like Ruse was, but I could tell he wasn't happy.

"What exactly is this mortal's draw that all three of you are slavering over her?" he said in a cool, flat tone. "Even *you*. Are her nether regions laced with heroin?"

I blinked at him. I didn't like how hard and cold he'd been since we'd freed him. The Omen who'd asked me to help with his quest, the one who'd guided me through our first few ventures into the mortal world, hadn't exactly been cheerful, but he'd smiled with warmth. Made jokes now and then. Laughed at *Ruse's* jokes at least as often as he'd glared. He was angry because of what the other mortals had put him through, this Company of Light, and that made sense, but still, I didn't like it.

And also... "I don't know what that means."

He sighed and pushed himself off the car to straighten up. "Of course you don't. Never mind. The point is, you're awfully attached to this woman, aren't you?"

Did he simply know what we'd been doing last night, or had he managed to overhear some of the things I'd said to her as well? I wouldn't take any of them back.

"Why shouldn't I be?" I asked. "You haven't given her a chance—you weren't there to see how much she did for us, how incredible she's proven herself to be. Weren't your tests enough? Or how she helped us in the ambush last night?"

"That's not the point. She could deliver us the elixir

of life and she'd still be a mortal. No good has ever come of a shadowkind getting hung up on one of them. We're not the same sort of being—we don't mix well. It's a losing game."

My hackles rose. "It isn't a game. I care about her."

He waved a finger at me. "That's exactly the problem. Caring tangles your fate up with hers. You haven't been on this side enough to know—mortals are fragile, Snap. Damned fragile. Why do you think they're always coming up with new ways to try to screw us over?"

"Because they think we're monsters?" I ventured.

"That's just the name they invented to justify how they feel. And how they feel is fucking terrified of us." He scoffed. "They're afraid of so much, and they want to destroy whatever scares them."

I paused, remembering a different sort of terror I'd sensed before we'd gotten Omen back. One he might have experienced as much as the creatures who'd left those impressions had. Was that what had changed him?

"I know what they did," I said quietly. "The Company, in their experiments—not every aspect of it or any hint of why, but we investigated one of their labs. I tasted... over and over again, so much agony to so many shadowkind. It was horrible."

"You don't need to tell me that," Omen growled.

"But I do need to tell you—Sorsha isn't like that, not at all. She hates the people who did that as much as we do."

"It doesn't matter. Even the ones who aren't outright

hostile end up making more trouble than it's ever worth. The only thing it's worth doing with mortals is killing the ones out to harm us and giving all the others a wide berth. I guarantee you, she'll make you regret doing anything else."

"You don't know her. *She* isn't fragile." I couldn't imagine that word ever properly describing Sorsha. The power she wielded wasn't anything like Thorn's or Omen's—or any other shadowkind—but it was still power. I could recognize the determination and resilience in her as surely as I could glean impressions of the past from any objects in my grasp.

Omen had tried to hurt her or to put her into situations where she'd be hurt, but she'd overcome his challenges. Why couldn't he see?

"She is fragile," he insisted. "You just don't understand yet. It always comes out at the worst time. We've got too much at stake to risk it."

"We'd risk a lot more if we stopped her from helping us. And I might not be very familiar with the mortal realm yet, but I know enough to recognize that."

"Fine. She's helping us. I haven't sent her away, have I? Just have a little self-respect and stay out of her *bed* if you know what's good for you." He grimaced and stalked away.

A jittery sensation ran through my body in the wake of his words. The thought of Sorsha becoming fragile, of her breaking in some way, set all my nerves on edge.

I made myself investigate the car as I'd planned to. After a minute, I came up with a gas station store bag still holding some sort of chocolate cake-like confection that I expected would serve well enough, but I couldn't rouse much sense of victory. I flitted back into the cabin and set the food down on the little table under the window.

Sorsha had dozed on. There *was* a sort of delicateness to her features when they were relaxed with sleep, a vulnerability in the softness of her skin. When we shadowkind took physical bodies in this realm, we could be gouged and shattered too, but unlike her, we could escape into the shadows to avoid a blow.

I'd already had to dig one bullet out of her. That had been painful—for me as well as her. Perhaps that was what Omen meant about her supposed fragility causing trouble.

The answer was simple, though. It rang through me clear as anything as I gazed at her lovely form.

I wouldn't *let* the few who were vicious enough to wound this woman get close enough to do so. No mortal or shadowkind would uncover any frailty in her. She'd saved me from a cage that would have burned me and the searing of the lights in a collector's home—and I would save her when she needed me to. Over and over, if it came to that. When a battle turned bloody, it wasn't as if Omen needed my abilities in that moment to serve his purposes anyway.

Whatever other shadowkind he'd known who'd mingled with mortals, they must not have cared the same way I did. She was mine, and she'd called me hers, and nothing had felt more right in my entire existence. He didn't need to worry about how much she mattered to me precisely *because* of how much she mattered to me.

Satisfied with that conviction, I eased down on the bed next to her to soak up a little more of her warmth. If I was particularly lucky, she'd share a morsel of that chocolate delicacy with me when she woke up.

9

Sorsha

When I returned after placing the police cap I'd stolen a couple of days ago on the head of a ten-foot-tall horse-and-rider statue in the park, Omen barely gave it a glance, even though he'd given me the challenge. "All right," he said. "Now let's see you collect, oh, we'll say ten wallets. You never know when some mortal cash might come in handy."

I stopped myself just shy of glowering at him. It was a hazy afternoon, the sunlight filtering through a thin layer of grayish clouds overhead, but warm enough that plenty of people were roaming through the park around us. Nabbing ten wallets wouldn't be tough. But we really *didn't* need cash when Ruse could charm anything we needed out of just about anyone—and at this point I was pretty sure that Omen's tests weren't meant so much to confirm my abilities as to arrange my arrest or some disabling injury. Maybe he'd have liked both.

I'd thought he was done with the Sorsha Trials after yesterday's ambush, but apparently not. Ellen's phone call this morning appeared to have set him off. I'd only spoken to her for a few minutes to get the plans for a Fund meeting in an undercover location this evening, but Bossypants had been fuming behind his controlled exterior ever since.

My own patience was wearing so thin you could have severed it with the blunt end of a spork. I also didn't love the idea of screwing over ten random innocent bystanders who'd just wanted to enjoy the last few days of summer.

I set my hands on my hips and smiled thinly at Omen. "How about I do you one better? I'll steal the wallets, lift the cash, and return them without the marks ever knowing what they lost."

"A thief with a heart of gold," Omen said with a hint of snark. "I'll be watching to make sure you collect the full ten."

"I'm counting on it."

I slipped through the park, focusing on purses left by picnic blankets and on larger gatherings where I could blend in with the crowd long enough to score. I only took a bill or two out of each wallet rather than all the cash, because Omen wouldn't know how much I'd left behind. When I'd replaced the tenth and walked back to the edge of the park where he'd parked Betsy, I had a hundred and fifty bucks and no intention of playing this game any longer.

"Here you go," I said when he emerged from the shadows between the trees, and handed him the money. "Buy yourself a better attitude. Somehow I'm guessing you didn't put the shadowkind guys through half this much work to prove they belonged on the team."

"I *picked* them, knowing they already belonged." Omen grimaced at the bills as if he found them distasteful and stuffed them into his pocket. "You don't get to decide when we're done. I'm feeling like a snack. Get me a pie from that shop." He pointed to a bakery across the street.

Was he kidding me? I opened my mouth to tell him where he could shove his pie... and then realized there was an even better option. Instead, I gave him another smile. "Does it have to be stolen, or can I buy it? And any particular flavor you'd like, boss?"

Really, calling him "boss" should have tipped him off. I could almost hear Ruse's snicker from the patches of darkness nearby. But Omen either wasn't paying enough attention or assumed he'd actually persuaded me of his ultimate authority. He waved dismissively at me. "An expert thief shouldn't need to spend any money, right? And I'll take apple or cherry."

So generous of him, giving me two options. I gave him a mock curtsey and strode across the street.

A beautiful cherry pie was sitting on the top shelf of the glass display cabinet beside the cash register. I asked for one of the tarts next to the pie, and once the clerk had opened the cabinet door, "accidentally" knocked her tip jar onto the floor. As she scrambled to grab a broom to sweep up the broken glass and scattered coins, I thought a silent apology at her and liberated the pie. If she'd understood what good use I was going to put it to, surely she wouldn't have minded.

When I returned, Omen was leaning against his car, looking way too smug. I had the perfect cure for that.

I gave him a broad grin as I crossed the street. "Here's your pie. Enjoy!" Then I lifted his just dessert and planted it smack-dab on his face.

I moved quickly enough that the unsuspecting shadowkind didn't have a chance to dodge. He jerked away an instant too late, sputtering as chunks of golden pastry and syrupy globs of cherry filling dribbled down his face and onto the front of his shirt. A couple of passersby snickered at the sight. He couldn't blink away into the shadows to remove the mess in front of witnesses.

His eyes flashed with the fiery glow I'd seen in the Company's facility. "*You.*" With a wordless growl, he snatched my wrist and spun us around to slam me into the car.

The impact radiated all through my back, making my healing shoulder throb, but it was worth it—to see his sneering face covered in fruity gore, to watch his rigid control snap and let out the heated rage underneath. To prove *he* wasn't the perfect model of cool authority he liked to pretend he was. As he raised a fist, I stared right back at him, daring him to use it.

My trio ruined the fun. All three of them dashed

from the shadows in the same moment. "Omen," Thorn said in protest, and Snap leapt to my side.

Ruse cocked his head, studying my masterpiece. "You did want her to show she can stand up for herself, didn't you? You've pushed her pretty far. Looks like sweet payback to me."

Omen's shoulders had already come down. His teeth flashed as he bared them, and then, with Thorn's massive form hiding him from view, he slipped into the shadows and back again so swiftly his body only seemed to stutter before my eyes. Just like that, the mashed pie was gone other than the bits that had fallen to the sidewalk. The lingering scent smelled pretty damn good. Almost a waste of a tasty dessert—almost.

Snap eyed the splatters on the ground as if he was thinking the same thing, but he stayed next to me, his arm coming around my waist. Omen glanced around at his supernatural companions, his expression back in its chilly mask but his stance tensed and the ice in his eyes searing.

"*I* decide when she's done," he said, and shifted his gaze to me. "Was that prank supposed to convince me of your self-discipline?"

"No," I said. "I was just getting the pie to your mouth in as speedy a fashion as possible. But it probably does show my self-discipline too, considering I'd been *wanting* to do something like that for ages. I've met all your challenges. Either I'm in or I'm out, Luce. Or are you not very disciplined at making up your mind?"

A renewed spark of anger danced in his eyes, but he held it in check. His chin rose to a haughty angle. "I was confirming how much shit you were willing to take. Always important to know the limits of those you're working with. That can be enough for now."

He didn't want to find out what he'd get in the face if he started up his tests again. I eased myself off the car and brushed my hands together. "Excellent. I'm glad we got that sorted out. You all can even enjoy a little bro time hitting up that hacker for more dirt while I'm meeting with the Fund tonight. Wins all around."

As hard as I'd been working to stay part of the shadowkind quartet's investigations, I had to admit I was looking forward to getting in some human socialization. Of course, I wouldn't have chosen to be climbing up walls while I did it.

I eyed the rock-climbing gym Ellen had told me to meet the group at skeptically before stepping inside. The vast room smelled like rubber and sweat. Carabiners clinked and voices echoed off the high walls. A pang ran through my still-healing shoulder. Well, I'd grinned and borne it through worse in the past few days.

Vivi was waiting by the check-in desk, decked out in a tee and velour sweatpants—both white, naturally. She bounded over at the sight of me.

"Interesting change in scenery, isn't it? Come on, sign the waiver and get your gear. Ellen and Huyen booked a private alcove, but we've still got to look as if we're using it to actually climb while we're talking."

I laughed. "A workout and a debate in one. This should be fun."

Vivi hefted a climbing harness over her slim shoulder. "Do you really think they're going to argue that much about getting involved? These Company of Light people are obviously into some seriously shady shit."

"Yeah, but I can't tell them about most of that without giving away how much I was hiding from them before. And you know how a lot of the members are—they don't want to extend any more effort than showing up to chat at the meetings and writing up a few outraged emails."

It didn't appear that all that many members had even made the effort to show up at this new location. In our reserved alcove, Huyen had already scaled nearly to the top of the wall. A few other regulars were poised at various points lower down, their feet braced against the handholds that looked like something out of an abstract art exhibit. Ellen and one of the younger guys were standing near the edge of the wall, the guy pitching an idea to her in a low, urgent voice.

"We'd raise so much more money that way. It's not *really* lying. Okay, so we wouldn't actually be trying to save the abused dogs in the photos, but we are rescuing some kind of creatures—and some of them are furry!"

Ellen didn't look convinced. Since most of the mortal population would never have believed the shadowkind existed—and the ones who lived mortal-side weren't in any hurry to draw attention to that fact—we couldn't be completely truthful about our goals when we campaigned for donations. Slapping photos of a cause that wasn't ours to gain sympathy points rubbed up against our leaders' conscience.

"Sounds like a great idea to me," I said as I passed them, clapping the guy on the shoulder and shooting Ellen an encouraging smile. Maybe that was how the Company of Light could afford a gazillion people on staff and fancy equipment out the wazoo: pictures of cute fuzzy animals in distress.

"Huyen and I will talk it over," Ellen said to the guy as Vivi and I picked our spots along the wall. "You know we try to avoid outright falsehoods—it could come back to bite us if anyone follows up."

Okay, so there were practical reasons to avoid blatant lies too. Knowing the Company as well as I did now, they just offed anyone who poked their nose too far into their business.

As I hooked up my equipment, another sort of hook-up slunk into the space with all the shine of a storm cloud. Leland dropped his harness at his feet and stared up at the wall gloomily.

After spending so much time around my supernaturally stunning quartet, it was hard to remember what I'd found particularly attractive in that boyish face and top-heavy physique. Especially since these days my ex-friend-with-benefits turned even more sour whenever he glanced my way.

He was all the evidence I needed that I had no idea how to make an even semi-romantic relationship work with a fellow human being, let alone a shadowkind. *All* we'd been doing was hooking up, and somehow I'd failed to handle that well enough to end things on good terms. I wasn't even sure what exactly Leland had wanted that I hadn't been delivering, since he'd never outright asked for us to become more—or acted interested in anything about me other than what I could offer between the sheets.

Men. Maybe I should stick to one-night-stands from here on out. How big a catastrophe could I create when I spent less than twenty-four hours with a guy?

Huyen had bounded down the wall with impressive springiness, and the other members who'd been partway up descended as well. Ellen beckoned us together into a circle.

"Why are we meeting *here*?" one of the other women asked. "Is something wrong with the theater?"

Both of the Fund's leaders glanced at me. "Sorsha came to us with a somewhat... unusual situation," Ellen said. She tapped her fingers against her lips, and I wondered what popcorn flavors she'd been experimenting with to stain the tips that shade of purple: lavender? Eggplant? "For the sake of caution, we decided it was best to discuss it in a setting we've never used before. Sorsha, why don't you explain the rest?"

I dragged in a breath and laid out the scenario to the other members the same way I'd explained it to Ellen and Huyen, as succinctly as I could. I was just finishing up when one of the gym employees ambled our way.

"Hey," she said. "Everything all right over here?"

It must be getting noticeable that we weren't using the equipment. "Just doing a little catching up before we climb some more," Huyen said cheerfully, and shot us all a look that said, *Get moving*.

Time for the fun part. I checked my rope and gripped it tightly before wedging my foot against one of the lower holds. Leveraging my weight with my good arm, I hefted myself up. Maybe I'd just hang out right here.

"We need to look into these people," I said over my shoulder to the others, who were gathering along the wall around me. "Find out where they're operating out of, how they're raising their money, and anything else we can about them. But we've got to be careful to make sure they don't catch on that we're interested. Whatever we find out, we can pass on to the higher shadowkind and they'll decide how to handle it."

Those higher shadowkind would just happen to be the ones I was currently shacking up with.

"I don't know about this," said a middle-aged guy named Everett as he edged his way from one handhold to another. "It sounds like this organization is very... intense. If they *do* find out we've been meddling with their business, how are they going to crack down on us?"

"Hey," Vivi said, bouncing a little against the wall. "We've managed not to clue any outsiders in to what we're actually working on for however long the Fund has existed, haven't we?"

I shot her a grateful look. "And we won't be *meddling*," I added. "I don't want us to stick our necks out that far—I agree that it's not safe. Better to let the shadowkind"—*and me*—"handle any actual response. We'll just be information-gathering."

"If this is your pet project, I don't see why you can't gather information on your own," Leland muttered.

To my frustration, a couple of the others murmured noises of agreement. What the hell had they joined up for if they were going to turn chicken the second the shadowkind *really* needed us?

I bit my tongue against asking that out loud. Thankfully, I'd said as much in politer terms to our leaders the other day, and they hadn't forgotten. Ellen hefted herself a little higher and peered down at the rest of us. "This is the whole reason the Fund was created. We shouldn't claim we're out to support the shadowkind however we can if we won't get involved when they're in the most danger they've ever faced."

"We didn't realize we'd be up against some big, secret army or whatever when we joined," Everett protested.

"Yeah," said the woman who'd asked about the change in location. "Let the shadowkind deal with the info-gathering and everything else if it's so important to them. Half the time they don't even help *us* helping their own kind."

That was sadly true, as Omen well knew. "This is different," I started.

Leland cut me off with a scowl. "Only because you decided it is. These people have been operating for who knows how long already. If the shadowkind haven't figured it out yet, that's on them."

Did he really care about the beings from our sister realm that little, or was he taking his animosity toward me out on them? Ugh, why had I ever thought this dude was worth letting anywhere near me, let alone *into* me?

Vivi spoke up before I had to. "Look, you just explained why it's important that we pitch in. It's clearer than a crystal under a cloudless sky. The shadowkind *haven't* been able to figure the problem out on their own. They're not used to mortal-realm resources and strategies. We are, so obviously we could find out some things they haven't been able to."

"Exactly." I wished I wasn't dangling from a rope partway up a wall so I could have given my best friend a hug. Put a dunce cap on me for ever thinking Vivi wasn't up to facing off against this conspiracy. I'd gotten so caught up in trying to protect her, I'd forgotten how strong and smart she was.

Another round of murmurs carried along the wall, but this one sounded less decisive. Huyen, up at the top again, cleared her throat as she headed back down.

"As always, participation in our activities is optional. I think Sorsha and Vivian have made a reasonable case. We'll proceed with caution, of course, but we can at least put out a few feelers. Especially—how are these people raising their money? Coming at them from that angle could reveal all sorts of things the shadowkind aren't aware of, since it'll be all between the organization and other mortals."

Leland descended from his perch with a huff, but to my relief, at least a couple of the other members nodded, if hesitantly. Vivi's brilliant grin bolstered my spirits.

"I'm going to talk to my contacts tonight," I said. I

wouldn't mention how much more intimate I'd gotten with most of them beyond talking. "I'll see if they know anything about the fundraising side that could point us in the right direction. You all could look through public records to check for any big events with a purpose that sounds suspiciously vague."

"And we should all know what that looks like from our own efforts." Huyen chuckled and soared through the air the rest of the way to the ground. "You heard her, people. That's this week's assignment. Let's not let ourselves down."

10

Ruse

"Well," I said, peering out of Omen's car at the farm we'd driven up to, "this place is gloom personified, isn't it? I have to say I preferred mini-golf."

By all appearances, the property was abandoned. The barn door hung open at an odd angle, and only weeds grew in the fields in uneven tufts, their yellowing leaves turned eerie by the moonlight. When I slipped out of the station wagon, the smells of dry dirt and old wood met my nose. A lopsided weathervane creaked as the night breeze briefly spun it.

Sorsha made a face where she'd gotten out beside me. "I see your gloomy and raise you ten creepies. But I guess the Company of Light needs the cover of darkness to do their dirty work."

We'd been directed here by the hacker girl who now saw me as the bestest friend she'd ever had. It'd been a particularly productive session on the computer, uncovering not just this hand-off with a collector who clearly hadn't gotten the message from the last one but also a fundraising gala happening in a few days. This Company had gotten away with an awful lot, but mostly because they hadn't faced off against an opponent who could really challenge them. The four of us with Sorsha in the mix were basically a dream team, if I did say so myself.

The location of our current ambush looked more like a nightmare. Thorn and Omen uprooted a couple of wilting shrubs to conceal the car more thoroughly where our boss had parked it behind a shed. The meetup was supposed to happen on the far side of the barn and not for another hour, but I wasn't going to argue against their caution. I had no desire to spend another second behind silver-and-iron bars.

Snap had ventured into one of the fields. He bent to sniff—and taste the impressions around—one of the taller weeds.

"Nothing has touched this except the wind and the rain," he said, and glanced toward the brick house in the distance. There might have been a FOR SALE sign outside it once, but it appeared to have fallen off the wooden post it'd hung from. "Isn't this a place for growing food?"

I came over, giving him a teasing tap with my elbow. "You're not going to find anything to eat here, my friend. I'd bet this place hasn't grown crops in years."

The devourer made a vaguely disappointed sound

and headed toward the barn. We'd agreed that he would
test the area for any sign of past transactions. There were
only so many secluded spots in and around the city—the
Company had to reuse some of them, especially if they'd
been operating since the time when Sorsha's fairy
guardian had been attacked.

We all stole across the field after Snap, Sorsha
rubbing her arms even though there was only a slight chill
to the summer night. Her gaze twitched at another creak
of the weathervane.

"Doesn't it seem a little strange that they'd arrange
another hand-off so soon after the last one?" she said. "If
they were bringing in new shadowkind every week,
they'd have needed a much bigger facility than the one
where they were holding Omen."

"Many of them might be lesser shadowkind—smaller
ones with some unusual or extreme powers," Thorn said.

Omen nodded. "Or they could have other facilities.
They certainly moved their operations from that
construction site quickly enough. It took the woman quite
a while to dig up the details of this one, which I wouldn't
expect if they'd wanted us to find it. But that is possible—
which is exactly why we're going to proceed with just as
much care as always. Let's see where we can place our
mortal so she won't create any catastrophes."

Sorsha shot him a withering look, but I thought he'd
said it with a little less animosity than usual. As much as
her trick with the pie had infuriated him in the moment, I
suspected he'd gained a little more respect for her at the
same time.

We'd just passed into the thicker darkness of the barn's shadow when Thorn, who'd taken the lead, barked a warning and lashed out with one of those rock-hard fists of his. I stiffened, expecting the meaty *whack* of that fist meeting flesh... but instead there was a soft *whoomph* and a woody cracking.

We hustled closer and found the lunk standing over his toppled foe: a tatty scarecrow with straw now burst from the split canvas of its head. I couldn't resist clapping Thorn on the back. The great hero of our time. "Excellent work. Now it won't hurt anyone else ever again."

The warrior glowered at me. Omen nudged at the straw with the toe of his boot. "Better overly fast reflexes than not fast enough. Let's see what our devourer has turned up."

Snap was still edging along the side of the barn. He moved from there to the sagging wooden fence, his normally cheerful face gone solemn with concentration. Finally, he straightened up and came to join us.

"I caught a trace of a person passing by in a few spots," he said. "Also, at one time there were younger humans who'd been drinking something with alcohol and were dizzy with it—they were gathering in the barn. I don't think they had any connection to the Company."

"Drunken teens? This would be the perfect place to party." Sorsha glanced around. "They cleaned up after themselves pretty well."

"We haven't looked *in* the barn yet," I pointed out.

"And it might have been years ago," Snap added. "I

can't judge the timing all that narrowly. I didn't pick up anything to do with shadowkind, but if there've been other hand-offs here before, the people involved wouldn't necessarily have touched anything to leave impressions."

He drooped a little as if he felt he'd failed us by not discovering more. I'd have cracked a joke to perk him up, but Sorsha was already grasping his arm with the warm little smile she seemed to have invented just for him.

"You didn't pick up any sign of a threat," she said. "That's good to know."

He beamed back at her, his discomfort eased, and while I'd meant it when I'd told her that I was happy to see her take her pleasures wherever she could find them, the sight of them gazing at each other like that started an uncomfortable sensation nibbling at my gut. I wouldn't call it *jealousy*—what kind of incubus would I be then?— but it was something. Something I didn't want to look any more closely at. We had bigger fish to fry here.

Omen was in full admiral mode. He motioned to each of us in turn. "Thorn, watch the road and alert us if you see *any* vehicles heading this way. Snap, bring the rest of the equipment from the car. I don't smell any humans around the barn now, so it should be safe. Ruse, you figure out Sorsha's best vantage point with her. I'm going to check over the grounds farther afield."

My assignment suited me just fine. I offered Sorsha my elbow with a playful dip of my head. "Miss Blaze, if you would accompany me?"

Her lips twitched with amusement. Even as she rolled her eyes, she accepted my arm. "I think I can figure out my own vantage points, but I won't say no to having company. Maybe you can turn on that glow of yours so we can see in there."

She was joking, but Omen cut his gaze toward us anyway. "No special effects, please. We're trying to keep a *low* profile."

"Don't worry," I said. "I can manage to resist the urge to shine up the place." Besides, it would have felt strange shifting into my full shadowkind form anywhere other than in bed. We shadowkind revealed our true selves so seldom in the mortal realm that our more human guises were what came naturally after a while.

The inside of the barn *was* dark, though. Once we'd stepped much past the doorway, I could only make out the outlines of the shapes around us—some sort of large metal milk tank here, a row of stalls there. The odor of musty hay wafted around us. Not the most delightful perfume. Sorsha brought her hand to her nose as if stifling a sneeze.

I spotted a couple of squashed beer cans when I wandered close to one wall, but otherwise our mortal was right—the partying teens hadn't left much trace of their adventures here. Or else someone had come by since the partying and done a quick cleaning job.

A hay loft loomed high above our heads in the larger room, but if there'd been a ladder to access it, it was long gone. Sorsha frowned at it. "I think there's a window up there—that might be a good place for my stake-out. I just need a way up."

"We could have Thorn toss you," I suggested.

She swatted my arm and headed down the aisle beside the stalls. As I followed her, her pace sped up. "Oh, wait. Maybe that's—"

Whatever she was aiming for, she didn't make it there. One of the stall doors burst open as something large and heavy slammed into it with a metallic groan.

My supernatural skills might not be in the realm of combat, but I was still plenty quick on my feet. Sexual prowess required a certain nimbleness. The knobby monster of machinery careened toward Sorsha, and I dashed forward. I yanked her out of the way into a nearby stall on the opposite side—almost fast enough.

The mass of steel clipped her wrist, just shy of smashing her hand into the post beside her, and a bone snapped. We careened into the stall together, hitting the wall next to the door.

Sorsha gasped, the sound tight with pain. As she bit her lip, her eyes squeezed shut for a moment. Her left hand hung limp from her injured wrist, which was already swelling.

My pulse lurched. I held her motionless against the wall as another mechanical groan carried along the aisle with a heavy thump. If Omen had been wrong—if there were Company soldiers lurking in here—Thorn would be all the way down at the road by now, and the boss who knew where. I wasn't equipped for a fight.

Sorsha blinked, her lips parting with a shaky breath, and I caught her gaze. "We have to stay quiet," I murmured, and then, because it was the only way I could help her stay that way, I brought my mouth to hers.

I couldn't have imposed any of my supernatural intoxication on her to heighten the sensations while she wore that noxious brooch—and I wouldn't have regardless, having promised her as much—but I was plenty skilled as a lover without that enhancement. And I knew this woman now in ways I doubted even Snap did.

I swallowed any sounds she might have made and coaxed her tongue to twine with mine, leaning my body close enough to meld against hers, careful of her wrist and her still-bandaged shoulder. Her left arm stayed rigid at her side, but the rest of her melted into my embrace. I hadn't lost my golden touch yet.

As she kissed me back, her other hand came up to grip the back of my neck. She was throwing herself headlong into my attempt at distracting her from the pain —and damn if her response wasn't distracting me too. Why had I started this again?

No further noise reached my ears from the rest of the barn. Had the apparent assault really just been a precarious piece of farm machinery tipping over and not some kind of trap?

I didn't really want to stop this to find out. Sorsha's body adjusted against mine so pliantly, heat coursing between us. Shadows above and below, I'd never longed for anything more than to throw myself headlong into this burning, even though the tremors of energy that passed from her into me were barely more than a trickle thanks to her brooch.

No, I wanted to incite the passion in her just for the carnal satisfaction of it. To be inside her again—to feel her eager slickness around me—to know *she* wanted to be that close to *me* despite everything else...

A chill cut through the flames of my desire. That last longing, to be embraced fully by her not just in body but mind and heart as well—I had no business thinking that way. That kind of desire had nearly wrecked me before.

I'd learned my lesson. I damn well better have.

I pulled back, leaving Sorsha flushed and breathless against the wall. A faint glint caught in her eyes in the darkness—a shimmer of tears that had formed before I'd taken her mind off her injury.

"No one's coming," I said. "I think it was just an accident, not an attack. We should do something for that wrist. I mean, something more permanent than my immediate efforts."

I winked, and she managed to grin at me, her mouth twisting as the pain must have caught up with her again.

"I can still do my part in the ambush," she insisted in a strained voice as we crept out of the stall. "I'm not letting any of you tell me otherwise."

How was my heart supposed to be still when she talked like that, all ardent defiance? But I hadn't spent centuries dealing in desire to fail at curtailing my own, even if it wasn't quite the desire I was used to. I made a flourish with my hand for her to leave the barn ahead of me, as if this had all been a bit of fun.

When Omen returned, he didn't even try to argue with Sorsha. He knew battle wounds well enough to fashion a rough splint for her wrist, glaring at the limb the whole time even though I'd made it clear she hadn't been remotely careless. But it turned out none of us had any parts to play. The hour of the supposed hand-off arrived and passed, and another hour after that, until each passing minute left my stomach balled tighter.

"They're not coming, are they?" Snap said finally.

Omen scanned the farmyard, his expression grim. "No, it appears they aren't. Let's hope that means they got scared off by our last ambush and not that they have something worse planned. Time to move out—and make sure that as far as they can tell, no shadowkind were ever here."

11

Sorsha

My nerves stayed jittery the whole way back to the cabin. I didn't like that the Company had apparently changed their plans, not at all. They'd never been the fickle type before.

Omen took the windingest of winding routes, and every honk or laugh that carried from the street around us had me jerking around with a hitch of my pulse. Which wasn't great, because every sudden movement took my probably-broken wrist from the deep but dull ache it'd settled into back to sharp, stabbing throbs for the next few minutes. I couldn't even bring myself to ponder the mystery of the car's smoky-savory-minerally car smell.

But even though the eerie stillness of the farm had been supremely suspicious, we made it back to the New-Age retreat unobstructed. I wouldn't have minded popping into a hospital on the way, but Omen seemed determined not to make any more stops tonight, and I wasn't going to tell him I couldn't take the pain.

"First thing in the morning, we'll find a quiet little clinic where I can 'encourage' a doctor into giving you a proper cast," Ruse assured me when we got out by the cabin.

"I might have a better solution than that," Omen said curtly, and didn't follow up that proclamation with any further detail. Just Bossypants being super helpful as always.

I yawned and considered both the makeshift splint and my exhaustion. "Well, I think I'm tired enough to sleep as long as I don't put any pressure on it." I paused, eyeing both the incubus and Snap. "So, I'll need the whole bed to myself, no company. Just FYI."

Ruse let out a chuckle that sounded oddly emphatic. "Have no worries on that score, Miss Blaze."

"Do you need anything else?" Snap asked, as if he could have produced whatever I asked for out of the woodlands around us.

"No, rest and a doctor in the morning sounds perfect. But thank you." I gave him a quick peck for good measure. When I glanced at Ruse, meaning to offer him the same gesture, he averted his gaze and turned as if to inspect the trees. All righty then. I could recognize a brush-off when I saw one, even if I had no idea what bee had gotten into the incubus's bonnet.

Picturing Ruse swapping his baseball cap disguise for an actual bonnet and taking way too much amusement from the image, I headed into the cabin. By the bunk bed

I'd been using, I stopped to fumble with my cat burglar outfit's belt. Maybe I should have asked one of my lovers to join me for just a little platonic action. Undressing one-handed was pretty tricky.

I settled for only removing the belt with its dangling tools and stuffed all that into my backpack with a sharp tug of the zipper. At the sound, Pickle came scampering out of the bathroom. I'd barely had time to give him a scratch under his chin when the world went to hell around me.

A crash split the air, then a thump and a volley of shouts, most of them voices I didn't recognize. My heart stopped. No time for that rest right now after all, unless I wanted to be doing it six feet under.

I snatched up my backpack and my purse—and, shit, Pickle. Scooping up the little dragon one-handed, I tossed him into the purse with so little grace he squealed in protest. As I wheeled around, pawing at the backpack for the tools I'd just put away, a figure in silver-and-iron armor crashed through the cabin window.

Shards of glass pelted the arm I raised to protect my face. Thankfully, my fighting instincts kicked in, honed by the self defense classes Luna had made me take—I sent up a silent apology to her spirit for ever complaining about those. The guy lunged at me, and I knocked his feet out from under him with a swipe of my leg. As he caught himself on the post of one of the bunk beds, I groped with my good hand for any hard object I could turn into a weapon.

My fingers collided with a big, jagged hunk of rose

quartz on the tiny dresser. Time for it to do something other than look pretty and emanate loving vibes.

The guy swung at me again, but *his* weapon—one of those blazing whips—wasn't much use in the tight space. Before he could fling it at me, I walloped him in the head with the pointy end of the crystal. He swayed but managed to throw a punch that clocked me in the jaw.

I reeled backward, my head spinning, and he smacked the crystal out of my hand. I grasped hold of the next nearest object, which turned out to be my lovely lawnmower candle. Thank goodness for thick glass jars. I mashed that right into his nose, hard enough that blood spurted from his nostrils.

As he swore at me, I fled out the cabin door. Pickle squeaked in distress at the bumping of my purse against my ribs, but I didn't have a chance to steady him, especially when my one functional hand held my only means of defense.

Outside was even more of a shit-show. The moonlight glinted off protective helmets and vests all across the clearing. Thorn let out a bellow as he thwacked a few of our attackers off him, but their weapons had slashed across his bulging arms deeply enough that even in the darkness I could make out hazy mist trickling out of the wounds.

Shadowkind didn't bleed like we did, not that red liquid mess. Sever what should have been a vein or an artery, and their essence wisped out as black smoke.

Another form careened through the night, chomping and gouging unshielded calves and bellies left and right.

I'd barely seen more of Omen than a blur when he'd first barged out of his jail cell, and then he'd been flickering somewhere between his shifted form and his more human appearance, but I knew this had to be him—and now he was all beast.

The enormous, hound-like demon-dog could have stood shoulder-to-shoulder with me, and I was no shorty. In place of the icy blue eyes I was used to, its gaze blazed a fiery orange. The same searing glow coursed amid its dark gray fur like rivulets of molten magma across a volcanic plane. Fangs as long as my index finger gleamed with each snap of its jaws. The devilishly pointed tail I remembered lashed through the air, wrenching a knife from one attacker's hand.

I'd never seen a shadowkind like that before, but Luna had told me stories of some of the more frightening creatures you could encounter, mostly to dissuade me from begging her to find a way to take me into the shadow realm so I could experience it for myself. I was looking at what most mortals would have called a hellhound.

In the midst of the chaos, I was struck by a fleeting eureka moment. So *that* was the source of Betsy's smell. Instead of your typical doggy odor, Omen's presence had marked it with sulfur and hellfire.

The Company's people clearly hadn't caught him by as much surprise as during their first ambush, but despite his ferocity and strength alongside Thorn's, our attackers were closing in on us. They hadn't skimped on manpower.

One guy sprang at me, and I beat him off with the

candle jar, just as another came charging toward me from the other direction with one of the Company's nets. Did he figure *I* was a shadowkind, or did they just want to take all of us alive for questioning? My breath hitching in my throat, I lobbed the jar at his face.

He must have been holding a lighter or something that I hadn't seen. The candle's entire wick flared to life as the jar's mouth smacked into him, and hot wax splashed into his eyes. He dropped the net with a howl.

Thorn barreled toward me just as another attacker swerved my way. The warrior pummeled him three feet in the air with one of his mighty fists and spun to shield me. "Take cover—the car!"

Abandoning him to keep fighting on my behalf sent a jab of guilt through my gut, but *he* wouldn't leave until I had a safe route out of here. And the station wagon was my only hope of a quick escape.

A figure already sat in the driver's seat—a blond surfer-looking dude. Confusion washed over me for a second before I realized it was the disguising spell on the windows. The guy inside had to be Ruse, having slipped inside through the shadows now ready to make a getaway.

I was just a few steps from the door when the Company people must have noticed my mad dash. A louder shout rang out, and something shrieked through the air over my head. I had just enough sense left in my spinning head to duck, my good arm coming up over my head.

Whatever explosive our attackers had hurled, it hit

the hood of the station wagon—and blasted a burst of flame all across poor Betsy. I hit the ground, my skin stinging from the heat. A lance of pain shot through my injured wrist, a duller throbbing waking up in my bandaged shoulder. I hissed, nicking my lip with my teeth.

Someone grabbed my good arm—Ruse, his cacao smell turned smoky from the wafts of heat streaming off the station wagon. "This way!" He hauled me onto my feet and toward the drive.

I glanced back toward Thorn and Omen. "But—"

"We're not leaving them behind. I'm a firm believer in back-up plans."

Snap wavered out of the night up ahead and beckoned us onward. "I found it! There's only one man there—I think he has the keys—" He gazed past us to the crackling mess that had been our previous method of transportation. "And we need them, don't we?"

"Lead the way," Ruse said. "And make it snappy, Snap."

The devourer had enough sense of humor left to give a flicker of a smile as he whipped back toward the road. "Down the road this way," he said, pointing.

The gray shape of a large van came into view beyond the trees. Ruse smiled. "Perfect. We'll go through the shadows and only emerge when we're as close as we can get. Between the two of us, we should be able to knock him over. Sorsha, you can get his gear off?"

I gripped the strap of my purse, crisscrossed with the backpack I'd never gotten the chance to take off, thank

Merlin's magic. My jaw was aching from clenching against the pain in my wrist. "I'll do my best."

Ruse nodded and turned to Snap again. "Then I can convince him we're all just having a friendly party. As soon as he's subdued, you bring Omen and Thorn."

Without another word, they both vanished into the darkness again. I pelted onward, sweat beading on my brow. "Just another manic run-day," I sang to myself under my breath, but even The Bangles' bouncy tune couldn't lift my spirits right now.

The guy guarding the van looked up at my footsteps when I was still a short sprint away, but my shadowy companions had gotten there first. His hand jerked up, a pistol clasped in his grip, and Ruse and Snap appeared right behind him, slamming his legs so he toppled over.

I dropped to my knees to wrench off his helmet. Ruse grasped the man's head and Snap sat on his legs while I fumbled with the snaps on the vest.

"A lot easier with two hands," I muttered, but after what felt like a million years, I was yanking that off too.

The incubus immediately started speaking in his smooth, cajoling tone. A magical thrum resonated through his voice. "We're all just having a little fun: a night-time game of tag. You and your partners had the wrong idea coming in here. No one wants to hurt anyone else. Happy times all around."

I raised my eyebrows at him, but the guard was already falling into a subdued daze. "Yes," he said. "I'm sorry. No one passed on the message."

Snap flitted off into the darkness. As Ruse kept

charming the guard, I checked the guy's pockets for the keys to the van. "Don't mind me. Just a little friendly groping."

He didn't look offended. I fished the keys out and opened up the driver's side door. *I* obviously wasn't driving in my current state, but I'd shit silver dollars before I let myself be crammed in the windowless cargo area.

I settled my purse and the deeply disturbed Pickle on the floor by the front passenger seat, tucked my backpack beside them—and ducked as a gunshot rang out from someplace much closer than I'd ever have preferred.

Ruse's voice rose. "If you could do me a quick favor, pal? Run on over there and tell your colleagues that there are more shadowkind coming from the north. If they hurry, they can tag 'em all."

"Yes, right, of course," the guard said, and trundled off toward the figures I could see just emerging from the driveway.

"Buckle your seatbelt," Ruse said breathlessly, diving in behind the steering wheel. He obviously didn't trust that his gambit would delay our pursuers long enough for us to laze around.

I shoved the keys into his hand, he gunned the engine, and to my vast relief, three figures popped into the space behind us with a whiff of Snap's mossy scent, the sulphuric odor I now knew belonged to our hellhound shifter, and far too much of Thorn's smoky blood.

Ruse hit the gas and hauled at the steering wheel.

The van screeched around in as tight a U-turn as he could manage, engine sputtering, and roared off down the country road with bits of gravel rattling like machine-gun fire against the undercarriage.

Two more shots rang out behind us. One clipped the side mirror beside my door, and I flinched. But then we skidded around a bend and left our enemies far behind.

"Well," I said, with as much optimism as I could summon, "we all got out alive. And in one piece... I hope?"

Omen's cold voice carried darkly from behind me. "All of us except Betsy. Any thoughts on how you're going to repay that debt, mortal?"

12

Sorsha

"Just keep quiet and let me handle everything," Omen said as we walked down the street, the others trailing through the shadows around us.

I grimaced at him. "I know, I know. You've been telling me how much I should shut up ever since you brought up these friends of yours."

"They're not my *friends*. They owe me a favor. A few favors, really. Which is a good thing for you, considering I'm down one heavily enchanted car."

"Hey, I'm not the one who must have led them to our hide-out."

He stopped in his tracks to glare at me. The late morning sun searing off his blue eyes turned them almost as fiery as when they'd been the color of flames last night. My skin itched with the suspicion that if I pushed that line of thought harder, he might transform into his hellhound self so he could literally bite off my head.

"It was your human hacker contact who pointed us in the wrong direction," he said. "And we wouldn't have needed a hideout in the first place if your mortal body didn't require sleep. I don't think it's in your best interests if we start tallying up the full score."

I didn't see how it was *my* fault his car had gotten blown up. How the hell had I been supposed to get to it without running toward it? But to be honest, while the shadowkind boss had grumbled plenty about the loss since we'd ditched the Company's van in the wee hours of the morning, he hadn't been quite as caustic with me as I'd have expected.

Another suspicion itched at me: something was up. Maybe he was being slightly less awful to me for the time being because he was about to offer me up to his past associates as dinner?

He set off again, walking fast enough that I had to hustle to keep pace. Then I saw the building he was leading us toward, and all other questions fell to the wayside.

"*That's* where they run their business?"

The parking lot he'd moved to cut across sprawled outside of a sleek, dusky block of a building with a sign that would have been lit up in neon if it'd been opening hours yet. A sign with a buxom lady in a bikini holding a martini glass, next to the words, *Paradise Bar & Dancers*. If you looked up "strip club" in an encyclopedia, it'd probably have a picture of this place.

"*Quiet*," Omen said in a harsh undertone, and added, equally low. "It's not for the male members of the gang. They've got a succubus in the mix—this allows her easy feeding."

Right, and I was sure the shadowkind men who ran their criminal syndicate operations out of the place didn't get so much as a smidgeon of enjoyment out of the boobs and butts on display.

Maybe Ruse would perk up in the presence of another cubi type. He'd seemed a little down this morning, his smirks pale around the edges. Unnerved by the fact that the Company had tracked us down yet again despite all our precautions? Or was whatever had turned him standoffish last night still eating at him?

I did manage to keep my mouth shut as Omen rapped on the glass door. A woman in a dress designed to draw your eyes to exactly the few body parts it covered opened it and waved us in with a bored expression. Omen had called ahead so his friends—excuse me, owers of favors—would be expecting us.

The woman who'd let us in didn't appear to be the succubus he'd mentioned. She went over to one of the little tables by a platform ringed with soft purple lights. A few other ladies with big hair and bigger cleavage were sitting there, nibbling at a plate of nachos. The tangy scent of the salsa hung in the air alongside sour notes of alcohol. They didn't go for the bah-dah-boom music during off-hours, though—in weird contrast to the setting, a classical flute piece was lilting from the speakers.

Pickle squirmed in my purse, and I set my hand on it

to hide his movement. I didn't see anything supernatural about the gathered dancers. Omen strode straight past them and the stage to a door at the back of the main room.

Just before he reached it, a man opened it. Or maybe I should say a goliath. The dude filled the entire doorframe, taller even than Thorn's six-foot-and-quite-a-few-inches and equally muscle-bound.

Not one of the wingéd, though. His skin had a faintly blue-ish cast that I knew from experience meant *troll*. How he explained that to the mortals he dealt with in his gang's activities, I didn't know—but maybe when you were that big and scary, people tended not to hassle you about the exact hue of your skin.

"Omen," he said in a thick baritone, his narrow gaze jerking from the hellhound shifter to me. "And friends." He must be referring to the others he could sense in the shadows.

"Good to see you, Laz," Omen said in his usual cool, even voice. "I appreciate you all making the time at such short notice."

A sharper male voice with a hint of humor carried from the room behind Laz. "Aw, come off it, Omen. We know as well as you do that there'd be hell to pay if we forgot what we owe you, possibly literally. Get yourselves in here, already. Let's have a look at this troop you've assembled."

The troll stepped back, and we walked into a back room that disproved Omen's spiel about the strip club front being all for the woman in the bunch. Pin-up posters hung on the plaster walls, a few of them of hunky dudes showing off the full kit and caboodle, but mostly sprawled women with come-hither eyes.

To avoid having my own eyeballs assaulted by too many pairs of perky nipples, I trained my gaze on the group lounging on the leather sofas that created an L along the far walls.

My nose told me before anything else did that there was a werewolf in the bunch. I'd had dealings with a couple of them before through the Fund's work, and anyplace they spent much time always took on a distinctive smell, like musk and pine and a hint of wet dog. Soon appearing as a new candle scent, no doubt.

From the look of the three figures on the sofas, Mr. Wolf was the guy with the scruffy brown hair and scruffier beard whose eyes glinted an eerie yellow. At his left sat a slim man with skin so pale it was nearly translucent. I wouldn't be surprised if he was fae or some related being.

Reclining on the other sofa was the succubus Omen had mentioned, a voluptuous woman in a lacy baby-doll dress who hadn't bothered to pause in painting her toenails at our entrance. The fall of her wavy honey-blond hair didn't quite disguise gem-like protrusions twinkling like rubies just behind the corners of her jaw. She must pass those off as some kind of piercing.

The trio shimmered into their physical forms around Omen and me. Snap stuck close to my side, his arm tucked next to mine, and when the succubus finally looked up, Ruse tipped his head to her with a knowing glance. Thorn, who was no longer smoking from various body parts thanks to the shadowkind's quick recovery time, flexed his shoulders and appeared to size up the troll. The other dude might have a few inches on him, but I'd bet all my worldly goods—limited as those were at the moment—that the wingéd's fighting skills could overcome that difference no problem.

The werewolf stood up slowly as if he didn't want to look too eager to welcome us. His voice was the one that had called us in—he must be the leader of this pack.

"Quite a collection," he said, and gave Omen a slanted grin. "Even a mortal. Although I see you've managed to break her already."

My jaw clenched at the mention of my bandaged wrist.

Omen shrugged with a casual air. "That's one of the reasons we're here. Birch, you can handle a wrist fracture, can't you?"

The pale man sprang up like a tugged branch swinging into place, and I caught the rustle of the few silvery leaves mixed with his ash-gray hair. Not fae— dryad. The shadowkind with affinities to plants often had healing abilities—something to do with the whole sprouting to life thing.

"I'll need to remove the splint to take a proper look," he said.

Omen nudged me, and I held out my arm. Bossypants was using one of his previous favors to fix up my wrist? Awfully weird when he'd just spent the last few days doing everything he could to set me up for a fall. But while he was offering—

I motioned to my shoulder. "I've got a bullet wound that's still sore while you're at it, if you have the chance."

"That wouldn't take long. Melding flesh is easier than bone." Birch led me to the sofa and sat me in the spot the werewolf had vacated. As he began unwrapping my wrist, I gritted my teeth.

"Broken and shot at," the werewolf said with obvious amusement. "You're usually more careful than that, Omen."

"She's something of a disaster, but useful in other ways," Omen said, lucky I was too busy holding in a pained gasp to chuck something at his head. "And 'careful' wasn't enough to completely protect us last night. There's a particular group of mortals who've taken their vendetta against our kind to another level entirely."

As the dryad gripped my wrist and threads of a warm tingling sensation wound through the pain, Omen gave the gang's inner circle the low-down on the Company of Light. He managed to avoid mentioning the fact that its members had captured and imprisoned him for weeks on end, I noticed.

"We're all under threat," he finished off. "It's clear these mortals won't be happy until they've eradicated every shadowkind in existence."

The werewolf had listened intently to the story, but now he scoffed. "They don't stand a chance."

"You haven't seen the resources they've gathered and the techniques they've worked out for overcoming us, Rex." Omen motioned toward me. "We have to rely on *her* to make it a fair fight. And from what I've heard about the experiments they're running—it's not a simple matter of them looking to kill us all. They've got something more complex they're working toward. Maybe something we can't be prepared for."

"It's horrible," Snap said, a waver running through his bright voice. "The things I've sensed from the places where they worked—they enjoy hurting us and want to hurt us more."

The werewolf—Rex? Well, I guessed that was better than "Fido"—gave the devourer a skeptical look. "I doubt you need to worry your pretty head about it too much, Sunshine." He raised his eyebrows at Omen. "Where'd you dig *that* one up?"

Okay, now they were both lucky the dryad still had a firm grasp on my arm. "I don't think you'll be making jokes about it if they come for the bunch of you and stick you in their silver-and-iron cells," I said.

"I've fought many battles across many centuries," Thorn added in his grim tone. "I can confirm that the strategies this Company of Light is using are particularly —shamefully—effective against our kind, even those of us with strength beyond that of any human."

"Only if they hassle us," Rex said. "It sounds like they've come after you because you've been stirring up shit with them. Why are you sticking your neck out if it's going to get chopped? Any shadowkind stupid enough to get snared can face the consequences for themselves."

"When they run out of the easy pickings," Omen started, but his argument was cut off by a grunt from the troll.

My head jerked around at the squeak that followed. Shit on a soda cracker—while I'd been distracted by Birch's healing efforts, Pickle had squirmed his way out of my purse where I'd set it on the floor. Now he was bounding around by the troll's feet, flapping the wings that couldn't carry him more than a few feet thanks to the collector who'd had them clipped.

"What is *this*?" Laz asked, his lips curling in apparent disgust.

"He's mine," I said quickly, and then, remembering Thorn's initial offense at the idea that I was keeping a shadowkind as a pet, "I mean, because he decided that. I couldn't get rid of him even if I wanted to."

Ruse chuckled. "He appears to like you, Laz."

The troll attempted to ease Pickle away with a push of his foot, but the little dragon just scuttled around it and squeaked at him some more. A smile tugged at my lips. Now that we'd gotten Pickle friendly with Thorn, he probably figured all hulkingly intimidating shadowkind had bacon somewhere on them.

"Pickle," I called with a cluck of my tongue. Proving my point about who called the shots in our relationship, the creature completely ignored me, now nipping at Laz's pant leg.

"Oh, pick it up and give it a few pats," Rex said dryly. "It's clearly not taking no for an answer."

The troll bent rather stiffly and scooped Pickle onto his bulging arm. The dragon immediately scurried up to perch on his shoulder, where he chirped happily. Laz straightened up, his jaw working as if he was holding back a cringe, and watched the creature warily from the corner of his eye.

I stifled a laugh. Not such a tough guy after all, huh?

As the dryad shifted his attention from my now-numbed wrist to my shoulder wound, Omen launched back into his appeal. "I've heard the way these mortals talk. They aren't going to stop until they've wiped us all out—and one of their goals with their experiments is probably to find easier ways to identify us. They won't leave you alone to mind your own business. We have to strike back against them hard and soon, before they become even better at incapacitating us."

Rex clapped the hellhound shifter on the arm. "I know you've been through a lot and seen a lot in your time, Omen, but we've been living on this side for decades. I know mortals inside and out. If they come for us, they'll regret it. This city is ours now—let them try to take it from us or us from it, and we'll paint downtown with their blood." His teeth bared in a fierce grin.

"They already are taking shadowkind captive right within this city," Thorn said.

"The beings who haven't bothered to offer our crew their loyalties can buck up or leave. Most of *them* are a nuisance anyway." Rex turned back to Omen. "I owe you, sure, but not enough to dive into a war of your own making."

"*They're* the ones making it," Omen muttered, but I could see the resignation in his expression. He'd told me from the start that there wasn't any point in turning to other shadowkind for help. But he'd tried to convince this bunch anyway—because seeing them stay alive mattered more to him than it did to them, apparently.

As the faint throbbing in my shoulder fell away with the dryad's magic, a prickling sensation rose up from my gut. The frustration spilled onto my tongue before I could hold back the impulse.

"You know what happens when all you think about is looking after yourself and your friends? You look around one day when everyone who could have used your help has been killed or caged, and guess what, there's no one left to help *you*. But sure, go ahead and ignore the people who've actually dealt with the threat you're dismissing. I'm sure you know *so* much more about what we're up against than we do while you're sitting here in your titty bar playing gangster."

"I'll have you know we've got a lot more than just titties," the succubus said in a wry tone, but Rex whirled on me.

"*You* are just a hanger-on playing at being part of something special and supernatural," he snarled. "I don't need lectures on politics from a mortal."

I stared right back at him. "This mortal hanger-on survived being shot with a silver bullet. Think you could do the same, wolfie?"

Ruse raised his hand to his mouth to cover a snicker.

Omen sighed and shook his head. "Don't mind her. She doesn't know when to shut her mouth. I've still got more favors to call in. We need something to drive and someplace to stay that won't call attention to who or what we are. I assume you can offer that much?"

Rex turned to him without bothering to answer my last question. "Yes, that much I can do for you. In fact, I've got something that'll count for both." He snapped his fingers at Laz. "Quit playing with that little beasty and get me the key to the Ford."

The troll poked tentatively at Pickle, who merely nuzzled his fingers, probably wondering when the bacon was coming. Thorn stepped in to lift the dragon off the troll's shoulder. With visible relief, the big guy hustled away and returned with a key on a leather fob.

Rex motioned for him to hand the key over to Omen. "It's yours, and we're square. You can pick it up in the back left corner of the lot at King and Washington."

Omen palmed the keys and glanced around at the others. "You all relax here while I collect our new ride. You might as well get a breather in after the night we just had. Except you." His gaze settled on me. "You're coming with me before you burn any bridges all the way down."

I didn't have any interest in hanging out with these jackasses anyway. "Thank you," I said only to Birch, because I could be polite *and* an ungrateful bitch. As I tramped after Omen out of the strip club, I reveled at the easy roll of my shoulders. The dryad had some magic, all right. The numbness was already wearing off around my wrist, but that joint moved with only a slight ache now too.

I waited until we'd traveled another block before I said anything in response to Omen's cold silence. "I *mostly* kept quiet. Don't pretend I didn't say exactly what you were thinking anyway."

The corner of his mouth curled upward. Was that a hint of a real smile?

"You did," he said. "If I minded, I'd be reaming you out right now. You saved me having to say it myself. Not that it made any difference—which is why I wouldn't have said it."

All right then. I would have left it there, the silence feeling less tense if not quite companionable, but Omen shot a penetrating look my way. "If you're willing to say all that to a bunch of supernatural gangsters, when are you going to tell me about your fire powers?"

I blinked at him, struck by both confusion and something deeper, something more chilling than his eyes —because I wasn't totally confused. "What are you talking about?"

That slight smile came back, but I didn't like it this time. "You know. I wasn't so caught up in the fight last night that I would miss you lighting that candle with nothing but strength of will. You hide it well—I started to think I'd imagined the wave of heat you sent at the pricks in the Company's facility—but the cat's out of the bag. You're obviously not a shadowkind, or you couldn't handle the metals in their armor. Is it sorcery?"

Wave of heat... I remembered the way the one guard had flinched that night as if burned, but I'd put that out of my mind as just a weird random happening. Like the weird way the fires I set when taking my leave of the collector houses I'd raided sometimes behaved too. Because assuming those incidents were anything other than random, that they had anything to do with *me*, would mean something was very, very wrong.

"For it to be sorcery, I'd have to be a sorcerer, wouldn't I?" I said. "I don't have the faintest idea how to summon shadowkind to do my bidding. I've never even known a sorcerer. So, sorry, I think you're just imagining things. But while we're talking about interesting powers, what's the deal with the whole hellhound thing? Are you going to rain down hellfire on me the next time I piss you off?"

I didn't really believe he would, but changing the subject made for excellent deflection. Usually. Omen *was* rather dogged...

Forgive me the horrible pun. Could you have resisted?

"No," he said. "Although if you try to touch me in that state, I will sear your skin off. But you know one power I do have? I can smell fear. You don't actually think your connection to fire is nothing. You're terrified of the fact that it's *something.*"

I folded my arms over my chest. "For your information, the only things I'm *terrified* of are sharks and being forced to go into witness protection someplace with no decent Thai restaurants."

"Say whatever you like. But if you deny it, you're being nearly as bad as Rex and the rest. You could use that power to help our cause."

"I don't *have* any power," I said, tamping down on the icy jolt his words had provoked in my gut. I couldn't have any sort of supernatural skills. It was impossible by any measure I knew of, and I knew more about the shadowkind and magical goings-on than just about any mortal alive, so it simply... couldn't be true. "And look, here's the parking lot Rex mentioned. Let's get on with more important, *real* concerns like what we're going to be driving."

"You're not going to dodge the subject that— Oh, boils and brimstone."

Omen stopped dead halfway across the lot, which was the point when it'd become obvious what "Ford" Rex had meant and how it was going to serve as both vehicle and home. Parked in the far corner was a vehicle even dorkier than his station wagon had been: the patchy blue shell of a squat camper van.

13

Omen

I could always feel a rift between the mortal realm and our own, even before it came into sight. There was a quiver in the air and a subtle flavor that tasted like salty steam. Here in the docklands, it mingled with the warble of the evening breeze over the river and the marshy scent of algae.

Rex had done me one better than handing over his clunky camper van. He might not want to stick his neck out for the rest of shadowkind, but he always had his people keeping their ears to the ground for potential threats, and he'd gotten a few reports of odd activity near this particular rift that sounded very much like the ambush I'd been caught in. The Company of Light had a few clear patterns, including that they liked to hunt near the rifts, presumably hoping to catch shadowkind who were still disoriented from the transition and so easier to disarm.

We didn't know how often the Company's hunters made the rounds here, but the past reports had all been from Thursdays—and all well before we'd staged our own ambush, so I didn't think the Company had planted that information like they must have for the hand-off at the farm the other night. We'd just have to hope we got lucky. I wanted to hear from someone who could tell us about more of their operations instead of just spouting anti-"monster" bullshit.

My shadowkind associates were surveying the area through the shadows, ready to dart back to me if they spotted suspicious movement. I'd opted to stay in my physical—human-ish—form, staked out on a low rooftop over one of the derelict factory garages, so that I could put the screws to my mortal ally a little more.

Said ally was crouched next to me by the low brick wall that ran along the edge of the rooftop. Sorsha flexed her slender wrist as if she still couldn't quite believe that Birch had mended it.

She knew magic, had been raised by a woman with shadowkind powers, and yet seeing them in practice was still somewhat otherworldly to her. So otherworldly that she seemed determined to deny that she could wield any powers herself.

I knew what I'd seen—not just during the attack by the cabin, but when we'd been escaping the Company's experimental facility and the day afterward, when I'd tested her with that falling fire. The effect *had* been small enough that I could see how she might have explained it away. I'd nearly explained it away after my slicing of her arm had revealed human blood rather than the smoke of a well-disguised shadowkind. None of my other tests had provoked her to using deliberate magic—or relieved me of the problem of deciding what to do with her.

But then the candle. And I'd seen in her reaction when I'd confronted her that she knew there was something more than human about her, as much as she wanted to deny it. I'd just have to prove it to her beyond her ability to deny it.

First I had to figure out what brought out those powers in the first place, since she didn't appear to activate them consciously.

"Shut up," she said before I'd so much as opened my mouth. "I know why you decided to stick with me, so you should know I'd rather tongue-bathe a tiger than talk about *that* anymore."

"Funny that you seem to think you have any choice in what I decide to talk about," I replied. If the universe had seen fit to send me a secret weapon with unpredictable powers, couldn't it have offered up one slightly less mouthy? "We could be facing off against Company people again tonight—people prepared to capture shadowkind. Are you really going to hold up your hands and play the powerless mortal if they get one of their nets or whips around us?"

She shot me with a look as fiery as that red hair of hers. "I've never acted *powerless*. I just don't have any super-special hocus pocus, no matter how much you want to believe it."

"Have you ever really tried to work some 'hocus pocus'? Why don't you see if you can set that stick up in flames?" I nodded to a bit of the debris that was scattered across the asphalt surface around us.

"Why don't I throw it and you go fetch it, dog-breath?"

The worst part about the insult was it did bring out my inner hellhound. My hackles rose, and my lips started to curl with a growl before I caught the searing surge of my temper.

She sparked all sorts of fires. I'd spent ages reining in the wildness that ran through my nature. I was *not* going to let one upstart human blast all that effort to smithereens in the course of a week. It was bad enough that both she and my shadowkind associates had seen me in a bout of unhinged fury when they'd first broken me out of my prison cell. I wasn't going to live that down until I'd shown just how in control of myself and *them* I could be.

I hadn't enjoyed browbeating them back into line, but sometimes harshness was a necessary component of leadership. If they didn't see me as fully in command, they might hesitate to follow an order when far too much depended on it. I hadn't devoted my current existence to this cause to see my efforts fall apart because I placed kindness over authority.

Besides, if I let my temper loose and incinerated the mortal, she wouldn't be any kind of secret weapon at all.

Before I could compose a perfectly calm and controlled yet scathing response, Snap flickered out of the darkness. "Men," he said breathlessly. "With the protections the Company has used before. They're moving toward the dock just east of the rift."

I peered in the direction he'd indicated. Beyond the glow of the nearest streetlamps, a few figures slunk through the darkness and vanished onto the abandoned boats still roped to the docks. Planning to hide out in that shelter while they watched for any beings that emerged, presumably. I frowned.

They'd come in enough numbers to overwhelm me during that first ambush. We had the advantage of surprise this time, but that wasn't a guarantee of victory. They'd shown how formidable a threat they could present at the cabin the other night too. As much as I'd hated it, especially after what they'd done to Betsy, turning tail and running had been our only hope of surviving with our freedom.

We did have the river to work with here, though. Those vests and helmets were pretty heavy—the men wouldn't be eager to swim in them. I cocked my head, considering the possibilities.

"Get Thorn and Ruse, and go through the shadows around the dock to the boats. Cut them loose—push the two far ones toward the middle of the river so they can't reach the dock and the one nearer this way, toward the shore. We'll give them a fine welcome." I jerked my hand toward Sorsha. "Come on."

As Snap vanished, we hurried to the stairs. "Getting a

few flames going on that boat would keep our enemies even more distracted from shooting or slashing us," I pointed out. "Is it really so important to convince yourself you don't have the power that you won't even try to pitch in?"

Sorsha's eyes flashed at me in the darkness, but I thought I heard a hint of hesitation in her voice with her next protest. "I think it's better I focus on the ways I can actually help rather than imaginary super powers."

"Funny, of all the things I could criticize you for, I hadn't taken you for a coward."

Her shoulders tensed. That blow had landed. Now if only it'd push her enough.

Falling into silence out of caution, we slipped out the factory doorway and edged along the side of the crumbling brick building toward the water. As we reached the sprawl of the shipyard that lay between us and the river, shouts rang out from the dock. My boys were getting down to work.

I set off across the yard at a lope, assuming Sorsha would follow, determined as she was to help in one way or another. In the dim light, I made out the motorboat careening across the water toward us. Three figures were scrambling across it, one of them yanking at the chain on the motor, which coughed its last wheeze of gas and died again.

Another brandished a gun. I'd take care of him first.

"You know the plan," I said to Sorsha. "See if you can add to it."

She stared at the boat, but if she was attempting to

stir up a fire, I didn't see so much as a glimmer. Fine. We could do this without any magical help from her. That was *our* area of expertise, after all.

I reached the edge of the concrete yard just as the boat came within leaping distance. One of the men gave a yell at the sight of me, but I was already springing across the gap.

I tackled the prick with the gun, knocking the weapon out of his hand and into the water. Thorn appeared next to me an instant later. He heaved another of the men by his bare arms onto solid ground, a few feet from where Sorsha had come to a halt.

The man landed on his side with a grunt, but he was sprier than we'd given him credit for. Ruse appeared with one of our lead blankets on one side, Sorsha dove to snatch off his helmet from the other—and he swung his leg around so fast he managed to kick the back of her knee. She stumbled, yanking herself out of the way of his next blow, and skidded right over the slick metal lip that jutted over the water.

She fell with a yelp and a splash, the water swallowing her up. Thorn rammed his fist into one of the other men's faces, crushing his skull, and spun to dive for her, but Sorsha had already heaved herself back to the surface. With an angry hiss, she grasped a post to haul her dripping body out of the water.

Ruse had managed to trap the first man under the blanket. The one I'd disarmed threw himself at the shore. He snatched at Sorsha as she swung her legs out of the water, she smacked out at him with her hand—

and just then, a tiny flare glinted along the collar of his shirt.

It was there and then gone. I wasn't sure Sorsha had even noticed it, but I grinned—both at the momentary flame and at the crunch of Thorn's fists pummeling the prick into the pavement a second later.

Sorsha picked herself up. Her drenched shirt clung to her chest and hips, emphasizing every curve of her athletic but undeniably feminine body, and a different sort of heat stirred in me.

Oh, she was something to look at. I wouldn't try to deny *that*. She could light all sorts of sparks, indeed. But those ones, I had no interest in pursuing. She already had enough shadowkind under the spell of desire.

I motioned to the man we'd trapped. "Their friends will be on us any minute now. Get the iron and silver off him and let's go!"

14

Sorsha

We held our second interrogation in the back room of a funhouse. The summer fairgrounds had shut down for the season a few days ago, but they left enough supply trailers and other structures on site year round for the camper van to blend right in.

Omen stalked back and forth in front of the chair where we'd plunked our now perfectly willing captive down. "The docklands, the bridge in the park, and the strawberry-picking place south of the city. Are those really the only rifts your people check regularly? You never go farther afield?"

The Company of Light guy let his head list to one side as he considered with a frown of concentration. Once Ruse had chatted with him long enough, he hadn't even minded having his arms and legs tied to that chair. Bossypants was insisting on extra caution.

"I went out to a town just north of Pittsburgh with the guys once," our captive said, "but I wouldn't call that regularly. Covering those three every week takes up plenty of time as it is. We don't catch many of the monsters, but the Company is happy with what we bring in."

An edge of frustration was creeping into the hellhound shifter's voice. "All right. Let's run through all the Company higher-ups you've dealt with. Names, descriptions."

"It'll make helping them so much easier," Ruse put in with a twinkling of charm, shooting Omen a look of warning not to get too brusque in his questioning.

Pickle, who'd been watching the proceedings with me where I was standing beyond the glow of the single overhead bulb, scrambled from one shoulder to the other with a prickle of his claws and a nervous twitch of his tail. Tension hummed through the small, barren space, most of it wafting off of our leader. After everything we'd risked, this captive wasn't proving much more useful than the first one.

My phone vibrated in my pocket. I stepped out into the evening air with a little relief at the excuse to leave. It wasn't much fun listening to the Company jerks spout off about eradicating "monsters"—and even though they appeared to all be prejudiced and potentially murderous assholes, seeing them in that charmed daze for hours on end unnerved me.

I had my protective badge pinned to my undershirt to ward off supernatural powers, and I trusted Ruse not to use his on me anyway, but still... under certain circumstances, he *could*. He had on at least a few innocent people who had no opinions about the shadowkind whatsoever in the past couple of weeks in the service of our cause.

The phone's screen glowed in the deepening darkness outside. It was Vivi calling. My heart leapt. Kicking at crinkly concession-stand bags, I wandered farther across the desolate concrete yard that had held a Ferris wheel a few days earlier and brought the phone to my ear.

"Hey, Vivi. Did everything go okay?"

"Oh, yeah. They ate up my posh persona like I was caviar with a cherry on top. I told you I could work a crowd."

"You did," I agreed, and I'd known it was true. Vivi's brand of poise seemed to endear her to people almost as well as Ruse's charm. She'd been out this afternoon at a fundraising event. Between the connections the Fund had started tracing and the information we'd gotten from our local hacker, we'd been pretty sure it was a front for the Company of Light. "No one asked any awkward questions?"

"Nah. I've been around this kind of crowd before— just like the folks my uncle would schmooze with when he was running for state office. As long as you look the part, they assume you're some rich professional like them. And they do like to talk. I think I might have picked up a couple of tidbits your little team will find useful."

I perked up, ignoring Pickle nibbling at my ear. "Oh, yeah? What did you get?"

"Well, I made friendly with some of the catering staff and was able to sneak a look at some of their paperwork to check the billing name and address. Not sure how far that'll get you, but it should be worth tracing. And there were some pictures in this slide-show they did—they were claiming they're raising money for a special treatment center for kids with cancer. Maybe Ellen and Huyen should reconsider the whole 'no outright lying' policy for *our* appeals, because man did it work—"

"The pictures?"

"Right, yeah." Vivi laughed at herself. "I wondered if they might have used any from their actual buildings, since they wouldn't want anyone to recognize a place they know isn't really a cancer treatment facility. So I snapped as many pics as I could of *their* pics with my phone. I'll email all that and the billing info stuff to you. I know it's not a ton, but I didn't want to get too pushy my first time out."

"You shouldn't get pushy, period," I reminded her, but a smile had touched my lips despite the desolate atmosphere around me. We were building a real team here. With enough people—mortal and shadowkind—on our side, eventually the Company wouldn't stand a chance.

"I know, I know. Safety first. I did find out they're holding another event like this next month, so I can try to dig up more leads—in non-pushy fashion!—then."

"Perfect." Next month—that felt like forever away.

Of course, it felt like it'd been at least one forever since my shadowkind trio had barged into my life in the first place. I was already down an apartment, most of my belongings, and my sense of certainty about who I was.

That thought led me right back to the insinuations Omen had been making—the last thing I wanted to dwell on. As I shook my uneasiness off, Vivi kept talking.

"I stopped by our favorite bar too—a certain someone there wanted me to pass on a message. I guess whatever she wants to tell you, she didn't feel comfortable talking about it except in person? She wants you to meet her in the FoodMart five blocks east of her place at eleven thirty tonight."

Jade wanted to meet at a grocery store? Well, I'd had dealings in weirder places recently... like right now, looking up at the giant clown face on the front of the funhouse. The shadowkind woman might have come through with something for us. I checked the time on my phone—I wouldn't have to rush to make it there. "I can do that. Thanks for letting me know."

"If there's anything else I can help out with in the meantime..."

"I know, I know. You're eager to get in on the action." But I still wasn't in any hurry to pull my best friend that far into the fray, as hungry as she might be to get a taste of adventure. "I'll keep you in the loop."

I ambled back around the funhouse and slipped through the back door just in time to see Thorn plunging his fist into our captive's smiling face.

Plunge was absolutely the right word. His crystalline

knuckles caved in the guy's forehead and nose with a sickeningly wet crunch and squelched at least a few inches farther into his skull. The man's body slumped—a body that was still tied tightly to the chair. It wasn't as if he could have been any threat.

My stomach lurched. "What the hell!? Since when were we going to kill him?"

Thorn stepped back, blood and gore dripping from his hand to patter on the floor, his mouth tightening as he looked at me. Beside him, Omen—who must have given the order—offered only a casual shrug.

"Since he was a genocidal bastard out to destroy all shadowkind?" he said. "He coughed up everything useful he knew, and some of his colleagues saw us take him— they'd never believe he escaped before we'd raked him over the coals. From the sounds of your past exploits, they'd have killed him for being a loose end. This way he ends up in the same place without spilling anything about us."

He was still spilling—spilling brains all over the concrete floor. I averted my eyes, swallowing down the bile that was rising in my throat.

Omen had a point. The Company had murdered their own people before for compromising the organization through no fault of their own. I'd seen Thorn himself murder several Company employees in the past couple of weeks. They'd just always been actively trying to murder us at the same time, so it'd been easier to keep down my dinner at the thought.

"Well, I'm going to need a ride downtown in about an

hour," I said. "I think I'm going to tour the sights outside until then." I turned on my heel and marched back out before any more of the fleshy stink could reach my nose.

Meandering around the vacant fairgrounds didn't do much to lift my mood, even with the good news I'd gotten from Vivi. I lobbed discarded pop cans at a target game that had been left in place while Pickle rummaged for treats by a snack stall with empty racks. Exerting my muscles distracted me a little, but that gnawing uneasiness lingered in the back of my mind.

I let my voice carry across the concrete yard. "In a messed-end town in a dread-sent world, the beast-blend boys can stress their girls..." Nope, even warping lyrics was taking me in a gloomy direction.

This was my life now: murder and mayhem and never setting my head down anyplace any other human wanted to be. Maybe I wouldn't have anything like a normal life back in a month—maybe I wouldn't next year.

It'd been easier not to think about long-term plans during the hunt for Omen's captors when we'd had no idea who we were up against, and then when it hadn't seemed all that sure I'd even be alive in a few days' time. Easier not to wonder if I was meant for a normal human life at all when I hadn't had an obnoxiously domineering shadowkind insisting I had some kind of supernatural power.

That *was* impossible, wasn't it? The uneasy quiver rose through my chest again, but the memory of Omen calling me a coward hardened my resolve. I glared at a tattered popcorn bag drifting across the concrete and pictured it going up in a burst of flames.

Burn. Burn!

Not so much as a flicker of heat wavered off the paper shell. With a surge of relief that maybe was a tad cowardly, I shook my head.

Of course I couldn't set a piece of trash on fire with will alone. The rest... it had to be a string of coincidences. Heck, when you played with fire as much as I did, was it really surprising that now and then something strange would just happen to happen?

My restless rambling led me back toward the funhouse. As I skirted an ancient-looking transport truck someone had left parked between the building and the now-deserted go-kart track, voices reached my ears. I paused out of view to listen. Hey, long-time thief here— why would you expect me to be above a little eavesdropping?

The first voice was Thorn's, even more somber than usual. "—pick them off a few at a time, and it hardly seems to make any difference."

"We're getting there," Omen replied. "Even I didn't know how complex this mortal conspiracy was going to be. But all that picking away at them will get us closer to shutting them down completely."

"It's not the kind of war I'm used to fighting. *They're* not the kind of opponents I'm used to going up against. To kill one who's been talking to us cheerfully as if we're his comrades..."

"Just because they don't fight the same way as the

armies of times past doesn't make them any less formidable. If anything, they're more so, don't you think? If they came at us in a horde with swords swinging, you'd make mincemeat of them in an instant, and we'd be done with it."

"That's true."

My hackles were starting to rise at the thought of Omen badgering Thorn into acting against his conscience when the shifter's voice softened.

"I do appreciate all you've offered to me and this cause already, old friend. I wouldn't have called you out of your seclusion if I didn't think you could save so many more now than were ever at risk back then. Not that *I* believe you owed anyone more than you gave all those eons ago. You definitely don't owe me anything. While you stick with us, we do things my way—but if *you* need something from me to make the sticking easier, just say the word."

Thorn sighed. "It feels as if time has passed so quickly and yet so little of it has gone by. Someone needs to stand up for our kind, and I'm more equipped than most. I'd just wish for a clearer way if one were available."

"Wouldn't we all?" Omen said with a chuckle, and then paused. "How do you think the others are holding up? You've spent more time in their company than I have by now." To my surprise, he sounded honestly concerned, as if he cared about Ruse's and Snap's well-being beyond how well they could carry out his orders.

Thorn took a moment before answering. "The

incubus is difficult to read, but he's seemed happy enough. Maybe a little *too* merry at times, if anything. The devourer remains steady as long as he's not prodded about his greater power. He has more resilience to him than I might have expected."

"All right. If you get the sense either of them is faltering, let me know. I didn't start this crusade to ruin the only shadowkind willing to stand with me."

Holy hiccupping hellfire, the boss had a heart and a conscience after all. What would he say about *me* when he thought I couldn't hear?

As much as I'd have liked to indulge that curiosity, I had a covert meet-up to get to. I strolled around the truck as if I'd only just arrived back at the funhouse.

Omen's expression immediately sharpened at the sight of me. Thorn drew himself up even straighter as if he felt the need to look extra imposing after the doubts he'd expressed to his boss, but I'd stopped being intimidated by his size days ago. Mostly.

"I've got to get back to the city now," I said. "Important news from a friend—something too delicate to be passed on over the phone. Who's driving?"

I hadn't really figured Omen would volunteer, no matter how much heart he'd hidden behind that authoritarian attitude. "Ruse," he barked. "The mortal needs someone inhuman to drive that human vehicle."

"Hey," I said. "We can't all learn everything. Unlike some of you, I've only been in existence for twenty-seven years, and for all but eleven of those, driving would have gotten me thrown into juvie."

Omen ignored my attempt at defending my honor. As Ruse materialized by the camper van, the hellhound shifter motioned to Thorn. "You go too. Make sure our walking disaster doesn't cause any new catastrophes."

Snap poked his head out from the funhouse doorway. "I can—"

"You," Omen said, "are going to sample that corpse like you did the man that led you to my prison. Maybe he'll be slightly more informative now that he's dead. Let's get to it."

Snap shot me a pained apologetic glance, but he couldn't exactly claim he'd provide more protection than the warrior. I hopped into the passenger side of the van, and Thorn vanished into the shadows in the back. It held two padded benches—one of which was going to serve as my bed tonight—and various cupboards Pickle darted off to continue exploring.

Ruse arched an eyebrow at me. "What are we up to tonight?"

"The thrilling art of grocery shopping," I said.

"Hmm. Maybe this is more Snap's area after all."

Despite his initial joke, he flipped on the radio and drove from the fringes of the city toward the downtown core without attempting any additional conversation. When I made a wry comment here or there about the passing buildings, he offered a smile and a quick response, but nothing to encourage his usual flirty repartee.

The most he spoke was when he had me call up our hacker ally and put her on speakerphone so he could bolster his supernatural influence before I sent her the address and photos Vivi had passed on. "Everything you can find out, as soon as you can find it," he said, his voice dripping with charm. "Your help has been absolutely invaluable."

As I hung up the phone after our next steps were all set, I studied him from the corner of my eye. Maybe this newfound reserve of the past few days meant he was starting to take our current circumstances more seriously than Thorn had given him credit for.

Or maybe, despite all that initial flirting and the heat I'd thought I'd felt between us just a few nights ago in the barn, he was bored of my mortal companionship already. He'd been with who knew how many other women before me, after all, and he didn't usually stick around for much chitchat after the deed was done. I should have felt honored he'd invested as much attention in me as he had.

But to tell you the truth, it only added to the uncomfortable hollow in the pit of my stomach. Call me greedy, but it seemed *I* liked each member of my trio more than was probably wise.

Any worries about Ruse's interest in me or lack thereof vanished when the glowing windows of the FoodMart came into view up ahead. The downtown grocery store took up half a city block, open from the wee hours in the morning until midnight. I guessed even Jade might use it for purposes other than covert meet-ups—shadowkind might not *need* to eat, at least in the traditional mortal way, but many of them enjoyed doing so simply for the pleasure of chowing down. It was just hard to picture the bar owner's sleek, green-haired form amid the aisles of canned veggies and jars of pasta sauce.

There she was, though. I spotted her within seconds of heading inside, Ruse and Thorn following invisibly through the shadows. Her dark hair swallowed up the artificial light, turning the green almost black.

She caught my eye for just a second and then drifted farther down the aisle to contemplate the cereal boxes. Lucky Charms were on sale—now that *was* lucky. I picked up a box and pretended to be fascinated by the nutritional information. What vitamins did they stuff into those marshmallows?

"What's up?" I asked quietly.

Jade turned and inspected a container of peanut butter. "I know this is ridiculous, but we've had a few mortals come into the bar asking rather pointed questions. I think it's best you steer clear of the Fountain until this situation you've gotten yourself into is... cleared up."

My throat tightened. I'd already suspected the Company might have asked around about me at Jade's, but I hadn't meant to bring more trouble to her doorstep. "Understood. I'll be a stranger until it's safe again."

"I do have some—well, possibly—good news too. A couple of occasional patrons stopped by yesterday talking about a conflict with mortals, and I told them you were working on something like that. They seemed interested in joining forces. I'll let you figure out how to reach out to them. Here's Glisten's number."

A shadowkind named Glisten? What sort of shiny being would that turn out to be?

"Thank you," I said with intense gratitude as she surreptitiously passed me a slip of paper.

The corner of Jade's mouth quirked up. "Wait to thank me until after you've met them. They might be of some use. Take care of yourself."

With that, she set the peanut butter back on the shelf and walked away. I gazed longingly at my box of Lucky Charms for several seconds longer, but that was made for people who had things like bowls and spoons and, y'know, fridges in which to keep milk. A.K.A., people other than me at the present moment. Sighing, I put it back and headed for the door.

I came around the corner by the cashiers and stopped in my tracks with a stutter of my pulse.

A lanky man with shaggy black hair was just handing his credit card over to the woman at the counter. A man I'd recognized from his posture in an instant, but he turned his head enough for me to see the profile of his face and remove any doubt.

I'd lived with that man for almost a year, until I... hadn't. It'd been years since I'd last seen Malachi. Our paths hadn't crossed since he'd left—mostly by his design, I suspected.

I'd been as over our relationship as I could have been without any kind of closure, but seeing him out of the blue sent a flush that was half shame and half anger surging through my body. No way in hell did I want to deal with him *now* of all the possible times I could have run into him. A significant part of me would have liked to run him *over*. I spun around and darted for the entrance before he finished paying.

As I clambered into the van, Ruse reformed on the driver's side.

Thorn loomed over my seat with a worried frown. "Are you all right? It looked like—"

"I'm fine," I said quickly. "It has nothing to do with… with anything important. Please, let's just get out of here."

Ruse took one look at me and shifted the van into drive, and I left yet another piece of my old life behind.

Good riddance.

15

Sorsha

Red and purple lights flashed in the old fortune teller booth. The mechanical figure with her cracked plastic cheeks and glittering turban jerked a little to the left, still running on some reserve power source in the fairgrounds.

I popped in a quarter. "Who'll they cast in my role when they make a movie out of this craziness?"

The crone's creaky voice was starting to outright sputter as she ran out of juice. "The answer lies in your hea-a-art."

I nodded sagely. "Okay, so an Eastwick-era Michelle Pfeiffer then." Dye her hair red—it could work. We'd just need to invent time travel first.

I readied another quarter. "Am I even going to survive to see that movie?"

"All things are possible if you find the w-w-will inside yourself-f-f."

The fortune-teller was basically a Magic 8-ball with a face. Since my restless wandering had led me through the night to this part of the fairgrounds, she'd answered my previous questions with cryptic remarks like, "Your chances will rise with your spirits," and "Sadly, my ancient eyes cannot see that far." It was a good thing she only cost a quarter. And also that her owner had left the money collection panel open so I could retrieve my few quarters for repeated rounds.

But maybe I didn't want real answers. Maybe that was why I was interrogating her rather than getting some much-needed sleep. If I lay down with nothing to occupy myself, it'd give my worries a chance to really dig into my brain.

Not that they weren't jabbing plenty of spades into me as it was. As I pushed in one more quarter, my throat tightened just a bit. My next question came out in a rough murmur. "What am I?"

"Seek with an op-p-pen mind, and the truth will become c-c-clear," the fortune teller informed me.

Another voice followed on the tail end of her response, low and sly. "But clearly you're a tall drink of water up way past her bedtime."

My pulse skittered, but only for a second. I knew that voice. I folded my arms over my chest. "Very funny, Ruse."

The incubus sauntered from behind the booth

wearing his typical smirk. "I didn't mean to startle you. You've seemed disconcerted ever since we left the grocery store. I figured I'd make sure you hadn't wandered off too far." He cocked his head, taking me in, and of course at that exact moment a yawn I couldn't hold back stretched my jaw. "And you *should* be in bed, shouldn't you?"

"With you there too, you're suggesting?" I said, not totally against the idea.

The brief tensing of Ruse's features tied a knot in my stomach. *He* was against it, apparently. "I suspect you do need some actual rest at this point," he said.

"*I* suspect I'm not going to be able to get to sleep until I'm at least twice as exhausted as I currently am."

"Let's see if we can't tire you out some more then." He eyed the crone in her plastic box. "This old gal doesn't seem to be doing the trick. Come on."

I was already tired enough that I couldn't be bothered to protest. We wandered across the vacant lots where various carnival rides had once stood until we reached a sort of plaster hill about ten feet high that must have supported some part of a track.

"Mountain-climbing is good, solid work," Ruse said, clambering halfway up the lumpy side and then offering his hand to me to help me. I waved it away and scrambled up to the top on my own.

The peak had enough room for at least three people to sit side-by-side. One of the ride operators must have used it as a lounging spot before we'd discovered it—an open beer can was wedged into a notch at one side. I drew my knees up to my chest and peered out over the desolate fairgrounds in the thin glow of the moonlight.

Ruse settled in next to me, leaving what felt like a careful space between us. Was he shunning all physical contact now? What was up with *him* these days?

Or maybe the problem was me thinking the incubus had to still be into me after our intense but admittedly short entanglement.

I resisted the urge to scoot closer to him, as good as it might have felt to have one of those well-toned arms around me. Which was the right choice, because a moment later, he said, "It has something to do with the man you saw in the store, doesn't it? You knew him, and it wasn't with happy memories."

Since he wasn't touching me, he couldn't feel how much my body tensed up at the question. I gazed determinedly at the city lights in the distance. "There were some happy ones," I said finally. "A lot of them. At least, I thought they were happy at the time."

"Do you want to talk some more about that? Get it off your chest?"

I didn't really want to talk about Malachi any more than I'd wanted to see him, but it could be I didn't have any more choice about the former than I'd had about the latter. As long as I held the thoughts in, they'd keep gnawing at me. It wasn't as if Ruse was going to judge me for my failures in committed relationshipping.

I shrugged, picking at the tab on the beer can. The sour smell of the stale alcohol fit my mood perfectly. "He's the only serious boyfriend I've had. We were together for two and a half years, lived together for almost a year of that... Everything seemed to be going great. I was in love with him, thought I was going to spend the rest of my life with him. I hadn't told him about the Fund stuff or Luna yet, but I figured we'd get there."

Ruse sprawled back on his elbows, watching me with a mild expression. "I sense a rather large 'but' coming this way, and not the sort I enjoy checking out."

I rolled my eyes at him, but my lips twitched at the joke. "Yeah. But." The memory came back to me, so sharply it stole my voice and my breath. I braced myself, summoning all the detachment the years afterward had allowed me to cultivate.

"One day I got home from the job I had back then, manning the cash register in an ice cream shop, and it was like... like he'd erased every trace of his presence from the apartment. All his clothes and books, his shower stuff, the armchair his dad gave us—gone. Oh, except that he'd bought all the dishes and silverware, but he was kind enough to leave me one plate with a knife and fork." I grimaced.

Ruse blinked, looking genuinely taken aback. "Totally out of the blue—no arguments beforehand? Not that up and leaving that way would be normal even under those circumstances, as far as I understand it."

"Nope. As far as I knew, nothing had changed. He left a note..." I swallowed hard. "He said he felt like he was lying when he told me he loved me, that he couldn't seem to fall in love with me because I wasn't quite what he needed. That's the last I ever heard from him. He ghosted me completely. I hadn't even seen him again until tonight."

"This may not be much comfort, but if that's how he deals with his problems, I'd say you're better off without him, Miss Blaze."

"Obviously. I just..." I just had never quite been able to shake the question of what I'd been lacking that had made me unlovable. But maybe I knew now. Maybe there was something not quite right about me that he'd been able to sense even if he couldn't have put it into words.

I didn't want to linger in the chill of that possibility.

"It would have been hard to take when you were so fond of him," Ruse filled in for me.

"Well, yeah." I gave myself a little shake and forced my tone to turn wry. "It doesn't matter. What's so great about a normal life anyway? I'm having way more fun fleeing murderous psychos on a daily basis."

Ruse chuckled. "Your involvement with the shadowkind has brought a certain sort of excitement into your life, hasn't it?"

That was one way of putting it. But I did want him to know— "I don't regret breaking you three out of those cages one bit. I let some of the things that *should* have mattered slide while I was with Malachi, not wanting to risk him getting caught up in any trouble I got into. It was only after he left that I really started going after the collectors, emancipating their zoos and all that. So I suppose you could say I've decided to be married to my work."

"We'd certainly be in a much worse position if it

wasn't for that," Ruse said with amusement, but the intentness of his gaze suggested he hadn't totally bought my nonchalance about the break-up.

For a minute or two, we sat in silence. A plane flew by far overhead, its tiny light flashing. Then the incubus said, "It *might* make you feel better to know that from what I've seen, love doesn't come all that easily to anyone."

I raised an eyebrow at him. "You haven't exactly been pursuing that kind of relationship to speak from experience."

He smiled crookedly. "Not generally, no. But—and I'll thank you not to mention this to any of our companions—there was one woman, a little more than a century ago. She enjoyed our initial interlude so much that I found myself returning to her, and now and then we would talk before or after... or during... and I found I enjoyed much more about *her* than the physical satisfaction."

It was my turn to blink at him. An incubus falling in love? I wouldn't have thought the cubi kind were even capable of that—but maybe that was my own prejudice, as enlightened about the shadowkind as I liked to believe I was.

Ruse didn't meet my gaze, still staring up at the sky. "It was ridiculous, of course. When I attempted to spark something beyond our encounters of the carnal kind, she made it very clear she only wanted me around for getting her off. Put me right in my place. An embarrassing blip in an otherwise illustrious career, but I guess we all have our lessons to learn."

I studied his roguishly handsome face, trying to picture what kind of woman would turn any of Ruse's attentions away. He'd gotten *me* off impressively well between the sheets, sure—I had no complaints there—but my fondest associations with him had nothing to do with the bedroom. There'd been the night he'd gotten us all dancing to one of Luna's old CDs to lift my spirits. All the ways he goofed around to counter Thorn's sternness. The delight he seemed to take in filling Snap in on all the weird and wonderful parts of the mortal realm.

The fact that he'd come after me tonight and made sure I was all right—and that he'd done it without turning it into a big to-do.

"She didn't know what she was missing," I said in all seriousness.

Ruse flashed another smile at me. "How kind of you to say."

"I mean it." And driven by an instinct I couldn't deny, I leaned in to kiss him.

I half expected him to pull back from the kiss, to confirm the disinterest I thought I'd picked up on earlier. I couldn't have been more wrong.

The second my lips brushed his, Ruse pushed himself up to better meet me. His mouth seared hot against mine, and his fingers teased into my hair to urge me closer. I found myself gripping his shirt, lost in the wave of sensation he could provoke so easily.

"You're perfect," he muttered against my lips. "Don't let any mortal prick convince you otherwise."

There were other pricks I was much more interested in paying attention to right now—one in particular, behind those fitted slacks. As he claimed my mouth even more scorchingly than before, I let my hand trail down his chest to his fly, just to be completely clear that I was up for more than a quick make-out.

My fingers grazed the erection already hardening behind the smooth fabric, and Ruse groaned low in his throat. The sound of his desire—his desire for *me*—sent a tingling rush through my chest. His grip on my hair tightened, the pressure drawing sparks through my scalp.

He rolled us so he was nearly on top of me, and right then I'd have happily welcomed him on top of that plaster mountain or up against it, or any other way he wanted this to go down. My worries about him using his abilities on me, messing with my mind, seemed absurd now.

No wonder he'd been nervous enough to break his promise and take that one peek inside my head that he had, if the only other time he'd believed a woman might want more than his sexual talents, he'd had *his* heart broken.

Ruse delved his tongue between my lips and eased his thigh between my legs to pay back some of the friction I'd offered him. I gasped, arching into him automatically.

My hand came up to find one of the curved points of his horns where it protruded from his hair just above his ears. He'd seemed to enjoy it when I touched those. I curled my fingers around it, his tongue twined with mine, and for a few seconds, nothing else in the world existed.

Only a few seconds, though. Without warning, Ruse's shoulders tensed. He drew back, his breath momentarily ragged while he gathered himself.

"Not the best place for this," he said, a twinkle dancing in his eyes. "And I *really* shouldn't be keeping you from your sleep anymore. Darkness knows Omen will be whipping us off on some new quest first thing in the morning."

I sat up, my giddiness fading. As we climbed down from the fake mountain and headed back toward the camper van, I couldn't shake the impression that those excuses hadn't been the whole truth, or maybe even most of it.

Ruse had told me more than he'd admitted to any of the shadowkind tonight, but there was something else going on with our incubus—something he didn't want to say to anyone at all.

16

Sorsha

Occasionally, my dreams were pretty damn delicious. A three-foot-high stack of waffles layered with custard and blueberries and drizzled with enough syrup to give Snap a spontaneous orgasm? Who cared if it was obviously unreal?

I searched the table for a fork, and suddenly in that way dreams had, it wasn't waffles but all three of my trio stretched out before me. Mouth-wateringly naked. Eyes come-hither. Still being drizzled with syrup.

Um, yes please, I'd take a bite out of *all* that. I leaned in to lick a trickle of sweetness off Thorn's massively muscled chest—and fuck all that was just and juicy if some asshole didn't yank me awake before I got even a taste.

A harsh voice was rasping by my ear. "Sorsha!" My pulse stuttered, and I thrashed aside the blanket I'd curled up under on one of the camper van's padded benches.

Omen loomed over me in the thin dawn light, his brimstone scent sharp around us. He hauled at my arm again. "Get up, they're on us—get out of here unless you want to be barbeque."

A crash and a metallic crunching reverberated through the air from somewhere beyond the van walls. My blearily sleep—and syrup—deprived mind couldn't quite process what was going on other than it was something very bad and apparently staying here would make it even worse. I lurched off the bench and dashed out the back of the van with the shadowkind boss.

He leapt up the funhouse's steps, tugging me with him, and propelled me through the entrance into the darkness. "Go, go, go!"

Go where? I sprinted through the shadowy halls, his urgency spurring me on even though I had no idea why it made any sense to be running away in here. Was this another dream? If so, I really needed to have a chat with my subconscious about appropriate transition points.

A figure sprang out of the darkness, hurtling right toward me. I flung myself to the side—and slammed into the cool glass of a mirror. The figure in front of me heaved sideways and winced too.

Oh, that was my reflection. Not looking so hot on three hours of sleep.

I whirled around in the hall of mirrors, barely able to make out more than blurred impressions of movement in the darkness. Were those shapes all me?

No—that one darted at me with a slash of some glinting blade. I threw myself past it, smacked my hand against a nearby mirror to push myself around a corner, and nearly pinged off another reflective panel.

An explosive sounding *boom* echoed through the walls, rattling the glass. My heart thudded faster.

As my breath stung in my raw throat, I dashed on. Something thwacked my shoulder. A searing hiss wound through the air from somewhere overhead.

I veered around another corner and pelted at full speed into a room full of hanging punching bags painted with smirking clowns. Welcome to heart-attack land! I pummeled my way through the dangling obstacles, the bags battering me this way and that as they swung back into me.

A metallic screech from behind me made my nerves jump. I bashed my way past the last of the freakish clowns and bolted into the next room, only to find myself swaying back and forth as if I'd careened onto a raft on stormy water.

The floor—the floor itself was warped into weird undulations, bending this way and that under my feet. I teetered to my left and almost fell to my knees.

Omen's voice rang out from somewhere in the distance. "Sorsha, hurry! Get to the roof!"

Then a distinctive squeal sounded almost directly above me. Panic raced through me with an icy jolt.

Pickle! What were these fuckers doing to my little dragon?

I scrambled onward across the topsy-turvy floor. By

the time I reached the far end, I wasn't just exhausted but woozy too, as if I'd had a couple of shots too many.

There was a stairwell. I pounded up the spiral steps to the second floor, ignored the rest of the wacky gauntlet for the door that must guard the route to the roof, and rammed my heel into the knob. To my momentary relief, the door burst right open.

Another squeal reached my ears, even more terrified than before. I hurtled up the steps to an open doorway where the faint dawn sunlight shone across the staircase. Before I'd even reached the top, the prickly scent of a fire flooded my nose.

I burst from the doorway into the wavering heat on the concrete plane of the roof. Pickle was perched on an overturned plastic bucket several feet away, flames crackling in a ring around him. His clipped wings fluttered in terror.

If I'd been thinking clearly, I'd probably have noticed that it made no sense at all for my shadowkind creature to be here or for a fire to have somehow flared up around him like that. But at that point I was running on pure adrenaline, and all I knew was I had to rescue him.

I raced toward the fire with a swipe of my hand, willing it away from him with all my might.

And just like that, the flames parted. They bowed to either side of a blackened patch they'd marked on the concrete in front of me, and Pickle sprang through the opening into my arms.

As I skidded to a halt, four forms shimmered out of the shadows along the edges of the roof. The nearest one,

Omen with his cold blue eyes gleaming bright, slashed a pocket knife across my forearm where I'd wrapped it around the dragon.

I yelped as much from surprise as the shallow sting of pain. As I moved to leap backward, Omen caught my wrist, wrenching me into place and turning the cut to the light in the same motion. My eyes caught on the narrow, red line—and all I could do then was stare.

The line *was* red with the blood welling up across the wound, but that liquid wasn't all that was seeping from my skin. A thin but unmistakable trickle of black smoke snaked up from my arm into the air.

Smoke, like shadowkind bled.

My heart had outright stopped for a few beats. It revved up again with a tremor through my veins, but the adrenaline rush was already fading. With fatigue closing in on me again, the smoke dwindled and disappeared, leaving only a streak of proper human blood across my pale skin.

"Well, fuck," Ruse said from where he was standing by my other side with Snap and Thorn. Even the incubus didn't seem to know what to say after that.

"We all saw it," Omen said, his voice taut. "Both the fire and the smoke."

"But I can't— It isn't *possible*," I said. My voice sounded hollow. As Pickle clambered onto my shoulder, I brought my arm close to my chest to inspect the cut. My entire abdomen felt hollowed out. "None of *you* would bleed actual blood like this if you were cut. Shadowkind never do."

"No human would bleed like smoke, though," Thorn said, his stern face frozen in an unusually stunned expression.

I guessed he should know from all the epic battles he'd fought long, long ago. I swallowed thickly. "I don't understand."

Omen flicked the pocket knife shut and tucked it into his pocket. "Neither do I, but you can't deny the evidence any longer. There's *something* about you that goes beyond normal mortal bounds. I don't think it's just a spell laid on you either, with it twined that deeply with your essence. It seems to only come out when you're particularly worked up. At least, for now. We'll see if we can work on that."

My idea of who—and what—I was had just been unavoidably flipped upside down, and he was already making plans for how he'd put me to use? "I don't—I've got to think about this."

"What's there to think about?" he demanded. "You have power. We need all the power we can get if we're going to take down the people intent on ravaging the entire existence of shadowkind. You've already wasted enough time with your refusals to admit it."

"Well, maybe I'd be a little more interested in exploring the possibilities if you had any idea what this means. But you don't, do you?" I glanced from him to my trio. "None of you knows how the hell this could happen."

The three pairs of uncertain eyes that gazed back at me held no more answers than Omen had offered.

I let out a ragged breath. "Right. I assume we're not actually under attack, and this was all just a ploy to freak me out enough to run your little test?"

"For now," Omen said. "The Company of Light *could* attack at any—"

"I *know*. But they're going to have to wait too. I need at least a few minutes to process this identity crisis. Just—just leave me alone."

I spun on my heel and stalked to the stairwell. Hurrying back through the funhouse, I barely registered the punching bags brushing against my shoulders or the warped reflections showing me only my own wan face. As I stepped out of the building by the camper van, my legs wobbled. Once I'd climbed inside the back of the vehicle, I tugged the door shut and burrowed under my blanket, cuddling Pickle against me.

The tiny dragon squirmed around and nuzzled his scaly head against my chin. I gave his neck a comforting rub. "The boss man was awfully mean to you, sticking you in that fire, wasn't he?" I paused, and a lump lodged in my throat. "Is that why you like me so much, Pickle? Because somewhere inside me I've got smoke for blood?"

Had Luna known and simply never told me—was that why she'd been willing to raise me? What did it mean about my parents? *Were* they even my parents? Did I have parents at all? I'd never heard of a shadowkind of any sort being born rather than simply coming into existence out of the ether of their native realm—never heard of a single mortal-shadowkind pregnancy despite the many liaisons between the cubi kind of both sexes and their lovers-slash-meals.

But of course, I obviously wasn't a shadowkind, at least not much of one. It was only a fragment of my being that emerged in tense situations.

I'd never heard of anything like that before either.

Even under the blanket, I felt it the moment another presence wavered from the shadows into the van.

"Sorsha?" Snap said, his voice tentative.

I forced myself to uncover my head. The devourer sat on the bench opposite me, his golden curls glowing with the rising sun but his moss-green eyes dark with concern.

He probably didn't even understand why any of this bothered me. Working supernatural voodoo and bleeding smoke was business as usual for every being he'd spent much time around before me.

"Can I do anything?" he asked, softly and simply, and somehow that was exactly what I'd needed to hear. He couldn't *really* do anything, but—maybe I didn't actually want to be left alone right now, not completely.

"Come here?" I said, scooting as close to the wall as I could to make room on my bench.

Snap smiled and moved to join me. Pickle scuttled away with a little snort, presumably deciding he wasn't interested in being the filling of our cuddle sandwich.

There was even less room on the bench than we'd had on the bunk back in the cabin, but Snap managed to lie himself down beside me without toppling over the edge. He slipped one arm around my waist and tucked his chin against my forehead, cocooning me in his bright warmth.

"Omen wanted us all to make it seem like there was some kind of attack, to scare you," he said. "I told him I wasn't going to help, but he went ahead anyway. He gets very... determined sometimes."

I leaned into his embrace. "I guess he wouldn't have gone to those lengths if I hadn't been so stubborn about insisting I couldn't do anything magical."

The devourer was silent for a moment. "*That* scares you. That you could influence fire in some magical way?"

Okay, so he could understand more than I'd given him credit for. It was fair to say I was scared. Possibly even terrified, not that I wanted to admit that out loud.

"And that there might be other powers I don't know about. Just... not knowing what I might be capable of, what I even *am*, and what else from my past must be either a lie or a total mystery."

"I think it's amazing that you have a force like that in you. You're even more special than I already realized." He pressed a light but possessive kiss to the top of my head. "But not knowing if you can control a power, one that could also hurt people... It feels pretty horrible, doesn't it? I believe Omen only wants to help you learn how to find that control. Or I could help, if you'd rather that. I'm not sure how to, but I'd try."

The lump in my throat returned with a pang of affection. I hugged him even tighter. "I appreciate that. I've never been scared of *you*, you know. No matter what power you have that you've decided you shouldn't use, it's obvious *you* can control it. I've never worried that you'll hurt me."

"I'm glad," Snap said, "but I hurt people before, and I can't forget that. That's how I make sure it doesn't happen again. I don't think you would in the first place, though."

His faith in me made my heart ache even if I couldn't say he was right. There'd been plenty of people I'd *wanted* to hurt over the years. In the heat of the moment, if I knew I could with barely any effort at all... but then, that was all the more reason to learn what the hell I was doing from beings who were experienced in the supernatural arts, wasn't it?

Maybe dealing with this puzzle wouldn't be so bad with Snap by my side. And Ruse... and Thorn...

My thoughts slipped back to the delicious dream Omen had woken me from, and then to last night when I'd been ready to give myself over to Ruse yet again. Was my greediness fair to the guy holding me right now and all his passionate devotion?

"Snap," I said. "Does it bother you that I might hook up with Ruse again, or even Thorn? It's not that I don't want you—I do, a hell of a lot. I just..."

I wasn't sure how to explain it. But Snap seemed to already understand that too. He shifted against me, fitting me even more perfectly against his body.

"I've seen you with them," he said. "And I can tell— the energy you have with them is a little different than with me. There's something you *get* that's different." He paused, his embrace tightening. "I wish very much that I could give you every conceivable thing, but I'm not sure that's possible. And if it's not, I don't want to take anything away from you. That would be incredibly selfish, wouldn't it?"

"For a lot of people, wanting to keep a lover to yourself would be a pretty normal feeling."

His hum reverberated from his lean chest into me. "I'm not a person, and I don't want to be like those sorts of humans. What I like the most when I'm around you is seeing you happy, and if they bring extra happiness that I can't, then that's a good thing." He ducked his head, his lips grazing my forehead. "As long as you're still mine."

I wouldn't have thought I'd ever agree to that kind of claiming, but who was I kidding? The possessiveness in his tone only set off a warm glow around my heart. The devourer had made an indelible mark there, one I suspected no supernatural voodoo could ever erase now.

"You've got me, all right," I said.

I felt his smile against my skin. "At least I know the two of them—I know they're worthy of having you too."

A better question would be whether I was worthy of any of them. Snuggled up against Snap, I wanted to be. I wanted to be a woman who could not just stage jailbreaks and sway fire to my will but also handle the hearts of those who cared about me with the care they deserved in return.

That kind of cherishing might be hard, like Ruse had suggested last night. It might even be impossible. But an hour ago I'd thought it was impossible that a human being like me could manipulate fire with my mind, so maybe I shouldn't draw any conclusions just yet.

If I was going to be that woman, I knew where I'd need to start. Hiding under a blanket wasn't going to cut it. I couldn't stand by my lovers properly if I was denying who I even was.

"Let's hope you're right about that," I said, tugging Snap upright with me. "I'd better see what Omen thinks he can teach me."

17

Sorsha

Saying my first official training session didn't go well would be like saying the Pacific Ocean was a teensy bit damp.

Omen marched me out into the deserted yard next to the funhouse, where a stray Ferris wheel car had been pummeled almost out of recognition. I guessed that was how Thorn had produced the crashing noises I'd taken as part of a Company attack earlier this morning. A rusty old delivery truck parked nearby seemed to hold a look of relief that it'd been spared in the slant of the dust smears on its windshield.

Omen clapped his hands together. "All right. We know you *can* work this power. Let's see if we can get you working it on purpose."

I thought of last night's failed experiment with the

popcorn bag. "I'm not sure I can, at least not out of the blue with no real reason to. Didn't you say it's activated when I get 'worked up'? I can't make myself panic over nothing."

The hellhound shifter's expression suggested he thought I'd been pointlessly overwrought plenty of times already, but he managed to keep at least a little of his disdain to himself. "You'll need to get familiar with the specific feeling of manipulating—or producing—fire until you can summon it up without a bunch of panic around it. But for now, we'll start by triggering it first."

He gave me a thin smile, and then he started pelting me with beanbags he must have found at an abandoned game stall.

Having the bags smack into my chest and legs—oh, and that was the side of my head—definitely pissed me off. I snatched one out of the air and flung it right back at Omen. It clocked him in the nose.

"That's not what we're looking for," Bossypants snapped. "Focus on the projectiles, not on me. They're what's hitting you. If you light one up, I'll stop."

"Promises, promises," I muttered, not really believing him, but it didn't matter anyway. I squinted at the beanbags as they whipped toward me until I thought I was going to go cross-eyed, but my irritation didn't come with the rush of energy that'd coursed through me a few times in the past. If that even was the feeling I was looking to stir up. I hadn't exactly been meditating on my inner state while I was dashing to save Pickle's life.

After a while, Omen gave up on that tactic and ushered me back to the funhouse rooftop. He shoved a slip of paper into my hand and motioned for me to get up on the low railing that circled the roof's edge. "Walk along there and see if you can get the paper burning."

I took a brief glance at the ground a couple dozen feet below. No biggie. With nimble steps, I crossed from one end of the building to the other in less than a minute. I looked back at Omen, my heartbeat barely elevated. "This is supposed to work how?"

He was glaring at me, a few tufts of his tawny hair poking up from the smooth surface he'd slicked it into. He swiped his hand back over them, failing to tame them, and stalked over. "Most people would be a little unnerved walking along up there."

I rolled my eyes at him. "You watched me pilfer that flower pot for you, and you still thought I might be afraid of heights?"

"Come on then, Disaster," he said in a growl. Apparently that was my new nickname—oh, joy.

After several more exercises that all seemed to involve battering or tripping me in some way, Omen resorted to getting into the camper van and roaring toward me at full speed. I watched him come with a slight hiccup of my pulse, but even as my body tensed, nothing supernatural woke up inside me.

He hit the brake just in time to screech to a halt a foot from where I stood. I waved my hand with the slip of paper that was now grayed and creased, and it proceeded to remain as unburnt as it'd been when he'd handed it to me.

The shifter threw open the van's door and loomed on me. "What the *hell* is wrong with you?"

I stared right back at him, my jaw clenching. It wasn't as if I'd been having a ball with what he'd put me through over the past several hours. "I thought we'd already determined that none of us has any idea."

"That's not what I— For fuck's sake, can't you get a little nervous even with that thing barreling toward you?" He waved toward the van.

I shrugged. "I knew you weren't going to actually run me over. That would kind of go against the whole 'use Sorsha to turn the tables on the baddies' plan, wouldn't it?"

An inarticulate noise of frustration spilled from his mouth. "How are you so fucking aggravating?"

The retort shot from my tongue automatically. "Because you're fucking infuriating and it's contagious?"

But this wasn't just some annoying jerk at the office. This was the highest order of shadowkind with multiple centuries of honing his might. He really did growl then— the sort of dark, grating sound I'd have expected his houndish form to emit, with a flare of his eyes from blue to scorching orange and a baring of his teeth to reveal fangs that hadn't been there a moment before.

I'd almost forgotten just how much coiled power that compact human frame contained before it hit me. A slap of otherworldly heat lashed my skin, and my pulse really lurched for the first time since I'd leapt to save Pickle.

So naturally, I did the thing any sensible person would have done: I set Omen's shirt on fire.

It was only a little fire—a flicker of flame that shot up from the hem and disappeared the second he'd whacked it with his open hand, leaving only a tiny scorch mark on the maroon fabric. It happened so quickly, like always, that I couldn't have said what exactly I'd been feeling when I'd done it, other than both incredibly frustrated and abruptly sure the guy was about to rip my head off, grand plans thrown to the wind.

When Omen raised his head from examining his shirt, his shoulders had come down, though they were still rigid, and his eyes had returned to their usual piercing blue. His voice came out tightly controlled. "I don't suppose you have any idea how to do that again, preferably to something other than me."

I splayed my hands in a helpless gesture. "It just... happened."

Running his fingers over his hair, which was now utterly ruffled, he let out a brusque huff of air and turned away. "Take a breather. I suppose you need to eat something by this point anyway."

I had wolfed down a few snacks here and there in between his various torture sessions, but I wasn't going to argue with the chance to indulge in a proper meal, even if I didn't totally understand his decision to retreat. Maybe he'd decided I was hopeless after all.

I clambered into the back of the van in its new location, murmuring a few soothing words to Pickle, who scuttled back and forth with his wings trembling. What did I have left in the stash I'd grabbed during our last gas station stop?

As I dug into the bags, Ruse appeared by the open door, a box balanced on one upturned hand. A pizza box. The second the combined smells of melted cheese, rich tomato sauce, and spicy pepperoni hit my nose, I was salivating. I could have jumped him in gratitude, except I was hungry enough that I'd rather jump the pizza.

I hopped back out, Pickle at my heels. To no one's surprise, Snap materialized out of the shadows a second later, his eyes eagerly intent on the pizza box. "What is *that*?" he asked.

Ruse chuckled. "And this is why I got a large. The mortal realm has plenty of fantastic food beyond fruits and sweets." He caught my gaze. "I'd have gotten you a spread of Thai, but that would have been much more unwieldy."

"No complaints here! Pizza is my second favorite." And definitely much more suited to digging into when you didn't have much in the way of furniture... or utensils.. or, well, anything.

Ruse stacked a couple of crates into a makeshift table and opened the pizza box there. Soaking up the fading rays of the late-afternoon sun while chowing down on a crisp slice gooey with mozzarella was the perfect combination. From the speed with which Snap downed his first slice and his euphoric expression as he reached for his second, he agreed.

"While you and the boss were busy playing, we heard back from our hacker," Ruse said. "She traced that address your friend got to a shell company—and some of those photos are buildings that company or some connected shell owns. We'll have to scope those out."

"Great, I'll pass the info on to the Fund too so they can make their own inquiries." I swallowed another tasty mouthful and glanced around, not wanting to exclude the third member of my trio from the meal. "Where's Thorn?"

The incubus waved his hand dismissively. "He got one of his 'feelings' and went off patrolling, as if he doesn't feel the need to patrol every second hour regardless. They've never attacked us by daylight before, but try telling the lunk that."

I glanced toward the funhouse, where the final member of our larger quartet was looking at something on the cellphone he'd picked up during our recent travels. I didn't feel particularly inclined to invite Omen over to our impromptu dinner, and anyway, if he'd wanted a piece of it, he'd have marched over and demanded it. Still, as I took in his frown at whatever he was looking at, some of my lingering irritation faded.

He was a hard-ass and a beast—literally—but it was mostly in the service of saving all shadowkind, something most of the rest of his kind weren't willing to put in any effort to accomplish at all. And... as much as my trio had glommed onto me and become fond of me, none of them had picked up on the hints of powers even I hadn't been ready to acknowledge. Probably because they couldn't conceive of a mortal *having* that kind of power.

Omen had noticed when he'd barely even known who I was. For all his disdain of humankind, he'd been open-minded enough to keep me around and push me—however obnoxiously—toward uncovering those powers further. He'd spent all day doing whatever he could think of to help me control them. It might not have been fun, but I doubted he'd considered it a laugh riot either.

With a little less generosity, he could have written me off as a hopeless mostly-human being. It wasn't as if the four shadowkind didn't have plenty of supernatural voodoo between them without me contributing.

Omen raised his head as if sensing me watching him, and I jerked my gaze away—just in time to see Thorn leaping out of the stretching shadow of the camper van.

The warrior strode toward us, his voice ringing out with a force that thrummed through my nerves. "We've got to go! There's a squad coming this way—it looked like they were—"

Before he could finish that thought, something shrieked through the air behind him to crash into a side window of the camper van.

Ka-boom!

An explosion shattered the van's other windows with a burst of fire that rocked the tires. Another one biting the dust. Sweet scorching salamanders, these people *really* meant business now.

For a second, I stood frozen, stuck in the uncertainty of where to run when our expected means of escape had

just gone up in flames. One frantic thought hit me
—*Pickle!*—but at the same moment, the little dragon
brushed against my ankle with a quavering squeak,
having followed the pizza brigade over here. Then a
volley of shouts and the rattle of gunfire from the
direction the missile had flown from spurred me into
action.

I scooped Pickle into my purse—which I'd picked up
out of habit, thank God—and whirled toward the only
other vehicle I'd noticed anywhere nearby: the rusty old
truck by the funhouse. My backpack with my cat-burglar
equipment was still in the van, but it'd be ashes in
another few heartbeats if it wasn't already. Losing the
scorch-blade I'd spent three robberies' worth of ill-gotten
income on hurt, but not as much agony as if one of those
missiles hit *me* going back for it.

My feet pounded across the pavement. Snap
vanished into the shadows, as Omen appeared to have
too, but Ruse dashed alongside me in physical form so he
could speak. "I already checked it—there are no keys. So
unless you're as good at hotwiring as you are at breaking
and entering..."

"Nope." But I did have some idea. My thoughts had
slipped back to the winter years ago when Malachi's car
battery had kept dying and we'd gone to a guy down the
hall to jump-start it four or five times. I'd watched them
hook things up; I had a basic idea of where the power
needed to flow. A little jolt was all it needed.

A little jolt like a flash of fire.

I had no idea whether it would work, but jumping on

a carousel horse wasn't going to get me anywhere. I sprinted faster, hoping Snap and Omen would head to the same destination too in their shadowy way.

Just as I reached the truck, Omen appeared in the driver's seat. He groped along the dash in search of a key, clearly not prepared to rewire the thing either. I turned as I yanked the passenger side door open—and my stomach flipped over with a surge of horror.

Thorn was charging after us across the lot. He'd stayed in his physical form too, no doubt expecting he could fend off any attacks that came his way and shield the rest of us from them at the same time. But the mercenaries who'd just come into view back by the burning van weren't looking to capture any shadowkind they got their hands on this time. No, from the size of the machine guns they raised, we'd made enough trouble that they were perfectly happy to wipe us all off the face of the earth now, even if it was a waste of experimental subjects.

Thorn hadn't looked behind them—Thorn didn't know. If the machine gun bullets were the same silver the guards in the toy store had fired, they'd tear him to pieces.

My heart pounding, I threw myself forward to catch his attention. "Thorn, into the shadows!" The words tore from my throat, and my hand slashed through the air at the same moment in a gesture of pure desperation.

The gunmen had just pressed their triggers. The rat-a-tat of machine gun fire pealed out—and cut off just as abruptly as the van's flames roared out at them. Fire lashed across the yard in a vast billow. The gunmen scrambled away with cries of pain, a hell of a lot more than their shirt hems on fire.

Thorn had vanished. I had to assume he was on his way to us and not fatally wounded by those first few shots. I leapt into the truck, slammed my palms against the dash without letting myself second-guess or really even think, and pictured another flare of heat setting off a spark deep beneath the hood.

The engine sputtered to life. My chest hitched with it. "We're all in," Ruse said from the cramped back bench, and I found just enough wherewithal to tug my door closed as Omen hit the gas.

The truck tore around with a groan and rattled toward the fairgrounds entrance. Snap formed on the seat behind me. "Thorn's hurt," he said in a stricken voice, and my pulse lurched all over again.

"I'm *fine*," the warrior said gruffly a second later, emerging into being on the back bench so abruptly his massive form shoved Snap and Ruse toward the windows. Which was all well and good for him to claim, but smoke was trailing off his back as if someone had set *him* on fire. At a jostle of the truck's rickety undercarriage, he winced.

Oh, hell, no. I grabbed my purse, which did have a few useful bits and bobs in it, set Pickle on the floor, and motioned Thorn back through the door that led to the truck's cargo area. "You're not bleeding out—or up, or whatever—on my watch. Get back there where we've got more space to work before you keel over."

"I need directions, stat!" Omen added. As I got up

from my seat, Ruse leapt through the shadows to take my place. He snatched up Omen's phone, and I followed Thorn into the dim cargo area.

The boxy space was swaying so violently that I nearly tripped over my feet. Thorn sank down against one bare wall, and I dropped down next to him with as much grace as I could manage, which wasn't a whole lot. More shots stuttered behind us, but they sounded farther away now. At least, I hoped I was judging that right.

"Let me have a look," I said—briskly, to cover up the panicked thumping of my heart. A little light seeped through the small window on the cargo door at the back. The space around us was empty except for a few crumpled cardboard boxes and a couple of canvas sheets that I could cut up into bandages if need be.

"I *will* be fine," Thorn insisted as he twisted at the waist to show me his back. "You warned me in time—they only clipped me. And I heal quickly."

He wasn't lying. I'd known about shadowkind resilience already, but it was still a little startling to see it in action. I knelt beside him, taking in the tatters of his tunic—and the already closing wounds that dappled the edges of his shoulders and back amid numerous scars of all sorts of shapes and sizes.

The streams of smoke had slowed to a trickle. By the time I made a single bandage, the gouges where the bullets had caught his flesh would probably be closed completely.

He was okay. Not dying, not even that badly injured. My breath whooshed from my lungs in a rush. Thorn shifted so his back rested against the wall again, and I tipped my head against the warrior's broad shoulder.

The muscles there had tensed, even harder to the touch than usual. Thorn's voice came out in a low, terse rumble. "You shouldn't have needed to warn me. I should have been more aware of our enemies' movements."

"You can't be looking everywhere at once. Anyway, none of us had any idea they'd up the ante that far."

"I should have considered it—it was to be expected after we'd proven ourselves such daunting opponents."

I tucked my hand around his massive bicep. "It doesn't matter. We got through it. I'm just glad I *could* warn you."

The frustration in Thorn's tone didn't fade. "It matters because you had to put your energy toward protecting *me* when my job is meant to be protecting you —and the others. Yet again, I have—"

He cut himself off, glowering at the opposite wall, but I thought I could fill in the blanks. He'd told me a little about the long-ago war he'd fought in and how ashamed he felt that he hadn't been there to battle to the death alongside so many of his fellow wingéd when he might have made more of a difference.

Did he really think he'd *failed* just now, even with all of us alive and no longer bleeding smoke all through the atmosphere? I wasn't sure whether to be more sad or offended about that.

"Hey," I said, and waited until he shifted his gaze to me. "You need to loosen up on yourself. You did enough. If you hadn't gone patrolling, they'd have caught us completely by surprise. And it shouldn't be only your responsibility to keep me—or anyone else—safe. Aside from the fact that I can look after myself just fine lots of the time, we're a team. That means we all look out for each other. We've got a much better chance of making it through *this* war that way. You watch my back, and I'll watch yours too—as well as I can, anyway."

Thorn blinked at me. His eyes slid away, his expression still so solemn I braced myself for further argument. But after a stretch of silence, he said, "I don't believe you need to worry about your capabilities. That was quite the blast you sent at the mortals who were shooting at me. I'm honored to have such a valiant warrior on my side."

I sputtered a laugh at both the idea of being valiant and being a warrior myself. "Don't count on me ever pulling off something on that large a scale again, at least not when we actually need it." The only way I seemed to be able to use my power was by not thinking about using it at all, just doing it... which was hardly a reliable strategy.

The truck jostled, and Thorn tucked his arm around my waist to hold me steady. It stayed there, his thumb tracing a gentle line up and down my side. "You did save my life, m'lady. Quite literally this time."

"Please don't tell me you now have another huge debt to repay."

An unexpectedly light note entered his voice. "Oh, I do. But I swear I won't mention it except under exceedingly urgent circumstances." He paused, and his usual serious demeanor returned. "Thank you. I wouldn't have expected—but I should know by now not to underestimate you."

"You really should," I agreed, and eased back to look at his face. "Just so we're clear, I *will* be looking out for you, but I don't think I'm ever going to live up to your standards as a warrior. Stealthily making sure I'm never even seen is much more my thing than direct combat."

The corner of his mouth twitched upward. "Maybe so. It doesn't change the fact that I'm still here because of your quick eyes and action. I suppose I can admit there's something to your point about teamwork, but there's no need for you to be a warrior when that's not your nature. It's not the incubus's or the devourer's either, but they have their own strengths I can't match."

"Because you're so strong at being strong." I poked him in the pec. "I do wish that me being mortal—however much I am, which seems to be a fair bit—wasn't such a liability in a battle. I guess there's not really any getting away from that, though." My fingers lingered on the muscles of his arm just below the sleeve of his tunic, trailing over the pale scars that marked his tan skin there too. "How far do these go back?"

"To my very first battle. Any time I'm wounded badly enough to draw out the smoke, the reminder is etched in my physical form. I haven't added many to it in centuries, though."

"Not since the wars way back when. Until now." I grimaced and, to distract myself from morbid thoughts, teased my fingers up to his neck and along his jaw where even more pale nicks and notches told the story of his valor. As hard as his features looked, his skin was warm and smooth, only lightly textured by the scars. I let my hand venture farther, into the thick fall of his hair.

Thorn made a rumbling sound from deep in his chest. His voice came out even lower than usual. "When you touch me like that, I'm glad for your body's softness."

My pulse kicked up a notch, but there was nothing fearful about its pounding now. My skin warmed where his arm still held me close. Gazing into his near-black eyes, I found I couldn't come up with anything cleverer to say than, "You'd better be." Then he was drawing me to him, his mouth claiming my lips before anything more inane could fall from them.

In that moment, the shudder of the truck's walls and the battle we were fleeing fell away. I gave myself over to the firm heat of his mouth and the stroke of his hand along my abdomen. It rose until his thumb skimmed the curve of my breast. Need condensed, sharp and hungry, between my legs, even though this wasn't the ideal place to indulge that desire.

"For the record," I said, my lips grazing his, "I think you're good at a few things other than fighting. And I'm *very* glad about that."

"Is that so?" Thorn said, and tugged me back to him with a kiss so demanding that glad wasn't the half of it.

At the screech of the tires and the jolt of the truck stopping, we pulled apart from each other. Thorn glanced toward the door that led to the front of the truck with a regretful air. "I suppose we'd best see where we've found ourselves—and where we're going from here."

"Yep." I heaved myself to my feet, but as he stood up beside me, I couldn't resist giving his cheek one last caress and saying, "To be continued. So please do your best not to get shot any more before I can make good on that promise."

18

Ruse

I might not have shared Omen's contempt for most things mortal, but the community center where Sorsha's Fund had gathered for their current meeting definitely wasn't the highlight of this realm. The stale sweat smell reached my senses even in the shadows, and the pounding of the basketballs in the gym next door filtered through the conversation so loudly I couldn't make out some of the words.

It did beat the smell of burning camper-van upholstery and the blare of machine-gun fire we'd left behind at the fairgrounds yesterday—I'd give it that.

One thing was clear without hearing any of the words: most of the members weren't happy. The leader with the black hair and sharp eyes had her hands on her hips as she spoke to Sorsha. "That was your apartment, wasn't it—that building that caught fire, where they found those dead bodies? And the victims found by that mini golf—they were smashed up the same way..."

Her wife and co-leader with the frizzy hair grimaced. "I saw the photos. Those injuries look like they were caused by shadowkind strength. What are these beings you've gotten yourself involved with?"

Sorsha was standing on the other side of the room's long table, only her friend Vivi next to her while they faced off against not just the group's leaders but the several other members who'd shown up and appeared equally disturbed. Clearly those people had no appreciation for Thorn's skill with his fists. What was he supposed to have done—tied up our attackers with a silk ribbon and asked the police to pretty please toss them in the clinker?

Our mortal—or whatever exactly she was, unexpected powers taken into consideration—looked as stubbornly stunning as ever, even though she'd had to rush off here with barely any notice. Her hands had clenched where she'd rested them against the table.

"We've been attacked," she said, dodging the question. "Repeatedly and violently. The people the Company of Light has sent after us have practically killed *me* at least half a dozen times at this point. Anything you've seen in those reports was self defense."

The ones that hadn't been strictly necessary, like the dope Omen had asked Thorn to off after we'd questioned him, we'd been able to dispose of more carefully since we hadn't been fleeing for our lives at the same moment. I could tell from the tension in Sorsha's jaw that she hadn't forgotten those deaths, even if she wasn't going to mention them to her fellow Fund members.

The Company assholes would have seen all shadowkind tarred, feathered, boiled in oil, and hung for good measure if they'd gotten the chance. Why should any of us be wracked with guilt over their loss of life? Mortals and their tender hearts.

Not that I minded Sorsha's. She had plenty of steel in there too... and if that heart hadn't been at least a little tender, she'd never have forgiven me for my broken promise.

"We've only got your word on that," one of the other members said. "None of us has seen any evidence that this 'Company' is doing anything at all to shadowkind."

"*I* saw what they did to one of their own guys," Vivi piped up. She might have screwed us over a little with her initial nosiness, but the flash in her dark eyes as she defended Sorsha earned her plenty of points. "They killed him and mutilated the body—these aren't anyone you'd want to make friends with."

"Do you even know for sure it was mortals who killed that guy?" asked the stout young man with the soft, gloomy face. "Or did you need Sorsha to tell you that too?"

He was the one Sorsha had once had some brief dalliance with. Not the massive asshole who'd vanished on her with a brief note about her vague inadequacies, whom I'd have liked to tar and feather myself, but the almost-as-massive asshole whose emotions churned with resentment and indignation—but not a hint of regret about his *own* behavior, funnily enough—whenever he'd looked at her. Leland something-or-other.

It'd been a pleasure to trip him in the movie theater where the group had met a couple of weeks ago. I slunk closer in case I got another chance to poke a foot from the shadows and knock him face-first onto the floor.

Vivi gave him a look as if she were contemplating doing the same thing. "Are you suggesting that Sorsha— the Sorsha who's worked with the Fund for more than a decade without getting into trouble—is suddenly orchestrating some kind of huge conspiracy that includes murdering random men, all to take down a bunch of people who've actually done nothing wrong?"

Leland shrugged, his expression turning even more sour. "She might not know either. The shadowkind *can* be manipulative."

Oh, I'd show him manipulative. I'd like to see him licking his own ass after I'd had a little charmed chat with him. From the emotions clouding his mind now, I didn't think he was even considering that Sorsha's story about the Company *might* be true. As far as he was concerned, she'd snubbed him and that meant she must be misguided in all things—just a dupe of vicious shadowkind.

He'd gotten to share all those bodily intimacies with her, but he didn't know her at all.

"Yes, some can look to mess with ours heads. That's why I wear this." Sorsha tugged down the neckline of her blouse to show the silver-and-iron trinket pinned to her undershirt. Probably for the best that she didn't mention the few times she'd taken it off—and what she'd gotten up to with me and sometimes Snap during those times. "Believe me, I'd like this fight to have a lot less blood in it, but that's not on us. The shadowkind just want to survive."

The first of the leaders had raised her pointed chin. "I'm afraid that given the evidence we've encountered, none of us feel comfortable pursuing this issue any further. And I think it'd be best if you got yourself out of whatever you've become mixed up in too."

Sorsha's mouth tightened. *You don't need these putzes*, I thought at her, but some part of her seemed to believe she did.

"*I'm* not willing to walk away from the shadowkind when they're facing this kind of threat. Did you find out anything else with all the digging you obviously did?"

"Yeah," Vivi said. "What about the addresses Sorsha passed on—did you get anywhere with those?"

The addresses our hacker had uncovered from us thanks to Vivi's efforts. The twitch of the older woman's eyes told me she knew something, all right, but she locked it away with a purse of her lips. "The matter is closed. We'll resume our regular meets at the usual time and place this weekend. You're both welcome to join us for our regular business there—it's up to you."

"Huyen," Sorsha protested. "Ellen. Please. I swear—"

The frizzy-haired woman was shaking her head. Sorsha took in their expressions and must have come to the same conclusion I had about ten minutes earlier: this bunch was useless. With a curt sigh, she stalked out of the room.

"Really?" Vivi said, glowering at her colleagues, but the other Fund members held steady. She flounced out after her best friend.

Which was why it was a good thing Sorsha had agreed to let us stake out this place—me inside the rec center and my three companions patrolling the neighborhood around it. You couldn't get a more perfect spy than a shadowkind lurking in dark corners.

Ellen rubbed her mouth, the only one who looked at all conflicted about what had just gone down. She turned to Leland. "We should keep an eye on the activity around that building in the docklands, as much as we can, just in case. I wouldn't have thought Sorsha would get involved with anything disturbing. If there *is* an organization hunting the shadowkind on this scale..."

Leland snorted. "All I found was a record of some trucks arriving at the place ten days ago. No way of knowing what was in them—and it's not like trucks are a strange sight on Wharf Street."

Ten days ago—that'd be right after we'd stormed the facility to break Omen out. Exactly when the Company would have needed to move its other captives. And one of the addresses our charmed hacker had matched to the Company's shell organization was on Wharf Street. Thank you so much for the tip, my glum friend.

A little more muttering followed between the various Fund members, but nothing of much interest. I slipped along through the shadows after them as they left. They wandered off in different directions, Leland heading across the street in the same general direction as the spot where I was supposed to meet up with Sorsha and the others. I followed right beside him, watching for a good moment to send him stumbling.

He rounded the corner—and stopped in his tracks. I peered through the slightly blurred view of the world beyond the shadows to make out what had startled him.

Oh. Sorsha's red hair was just visible down the alley where we were meant to meet, as were Snap's golden curls. The devourer had just leaned in to steal a kiss.

Leland's hands balled into fists at his sides. He couldn't have known from that glimpse that Snap was shadowkind—but maybe he could guess it, knowing what sort of beings Sorsha had been canoodling with lately.

Before he could move again, the two figures headed deeper into the alley where I'd need to join them. A scowl twisted Leland's lips. He strode on by with an aura like a storm cloud, fury and betrayal radiating off him so thickly I barely had to reach out my powers to taste it.

As if she owed him anything at all at this point. *I* had far more reason to wince at the sight than he did, and I barely had any at all. I'd told her to take all possible pleasure wherever she could receive it, after all.

But I did wince a little as I flitted toward the alley. Not because of the kiss with Snap. Not because I'd sensed the closeness between her and Thorn continuing to develop as well. Hell, at this point I didn't think even Omen was unaffected by her presence.

That would have been fine. She could have been kissing thousands of shadowkind, and I'd have said, "The more the merrier"... If I'd been letting myself kiss her too.

Okay, so I might not have exerted the greatest self-control in that area. My lips had stumbled into hers once or twice despite my best intentions. But every time they did, the deeper longing inside me welled up more potently.

If I couldn't have the fun without the pain tagging along, I had to go cold turkey on the whole endeavor. Let the longing be just a pang at moments like this rather than a full-out heartache. Who the fuck ever heard of an incubus with an aching heart anyway? Much more of this and I'd be a disgrace to my kind.

If there'd just been a way to enjoy her without those other desires creeping in as well...

I told the little voice in the back of my head to shut up and sped through the alley's shadows to our meet-up spot. The other four had already reached it. As I materialized next to Thorn, setting my mouth in a triumphant smile at the thought of the news I had to share—and shoving all other feelings down as far as they would go—Sorsha looked up from her phone.

"I just heard back from the shadowkind Jade said might be up for joining the cause. They're ready to meet us. Why don't we go see if they'll be more help than our mortal allies?"

19

Sorsha

The first words Omen muttered when our potential new allies came into sight by the looming wood-and-metal mass of the Finger were, "Fucking tourists. Of course."

We paused on the opposite side of the street from the courtyard, waiting for Thorn to give us one final signal that the coast was definitely clear. After the Company had managed to find us on the fairgrounds, we weren't taking any chances even when it came to other shadowkind.

I glanced over at the hellhound shifter. "Tourists?"

The two shadowkind hanging out by the fountain didn't look like my stereotypical image of tourists: no Hawaiian-print shirts or cameras dangling from neck-straps. They would have fit in pretty well at Jade's bar, actually. The guy was a burly teddy-bear type with a glossy chestnut mane of hair that spilled over his scalp from a loose mohawk. The girl, slim and doe-eyed, had dyed her spiky bob with streaks of so many hues I couldn't tell which was the base color. Their casual but well-tailored clothes gleamed with even more color and, in the girl's case, a heavy dose of glitter.

I suspected she and Luna would have gotten along well. If Thorn hadn't already identified the two as "equines" when he'd reported back to Omen, I'd have pegged her for a fae like my former guardian.

"Easy to tell from the look of them," Omen said with a hint of a sneer. "The type of shadowkind who come mortal-side like it's a recreational endeavor: take a little trip, indulge in the mortal lifestyle for a week or two when it suits their fancy, then back to the shadow realm before any of the logistics get too difficult. They don't care about anything other than enjoying themselves."

I could think of worse reasons to come to the mortal realm, but given Omen's general attitudes, I wasn't surprised that sort of cavalier traveling irked him. "Well, these two care enough about something else that they told Jade they wanted to take action. That's more than your gang buddies offered."

"I told you before, they're not my bud—" Omen started.

He cut himself off at a flash of a signal from Thorn by the other end of the courtyard. The warrior and our other two companions were going to stick to the shadows, ready to spring out as need be, while Omen and I talked with the newbies. We'd picked this central location for our meet-up hoping that it'd be way too public for the Company to stage any sort of attack here with all the human tourists around.

Omen started forward. "Come on. Let's see what these doofuses you dredged up think they're getting into."

The two shadowkind had been leaning against the wooden base of the statue, seemingly oblivious to the passersby who'd stopped to try to read the plaque they were blocking. As we approached, they straightened up, probably recognizing Omen's otherworldliness with just a glance and a sniff.

"Hi," I said with an awkward little wave. "I'm Sorsha. This is Omen—he's sort of—"

"I'm the one who calls the shots," Omen broke in, staring down both members of the couple in turn. "I don't know what you heard, but this isn't fun and games. There won't be any prancing around or sight-seeing or whatever else you usually get up to on this side of the rifts."

"Obviously," the girl said in a voice that practically twinkled, her doe-eyes growing even rounder. "You're after the jerks who took Cori, aren't you? We're not going to mess around when it comes to getting him back."

"Cori?" I asked.

"Coriander," the guy said with a droop of his head and his voluptuous mohawk. "Our best bud. We've partied all across the mortal realm with him, but just a few weeks ago, these dudes in silver-and-iron clothes grabbed him out of nowhere." His expression turned sheepish. "That night, we were all high on the LSD a little more than was really good for the reflexes."

Ah, so we were talking partying hardcore. Omen's mouth flattened at the mention of drugs, but his tone stayed even. "Who—and what—are *you*?"

"Bow," the guy said, pronouncing it so the W at the end of the name was obvious. His gaze flicked to judge the distance of the nearby mortals, and his voice lowered. "I'm a centaur, sir."

"Glisten, unicorn shifter," said the girl with less concern. "I prefer to go by Gisele if you don't mind."

She held out her hand in an offer to shake. As I accepted the gesture, I noticed the shimmering braid of what appeared to be hair wrapped around her wrist—hair that was growing from the underside of that wrist? Found her shadowkind trait. And I was guessing Bow's mohawk was literally a mane.

Fantastic. I knew of centaurs and unicorns, obviously, but the way all kids do from storybooks. I'd never met the real deal in the flesh before. What were the chances I'd get to see either of them in their shadowkind forms?

Possibly pretty low if Bossypants here had anything to say about it. Omen adjusted his stance, looking as though he wasn't sure whether to be more mollified by the "sir" or offended by the fact that Gisele had taken on a mortal name. "And what exactly do you think you can do for us?"

"Whatever you want, sir," Bow said eagerly. "I'm pretty strong, and Gisele is awfully fast and fierce when she's shifted, and, well, we'll try just about anything if it helps us get Cori back from those hunters or whoever they are."

Gisele nodded. "And if we need a getaway vehicle, there's plenty of room in the Everymobile."

Omen raised his eyebrows. "The 'Everymobile'?"

"You'll see! Come with us."

As Gisele bounded off across the cobblestones, Omen shot me a pointed look. I held up my hands. "Let's see what they've got. There's strength in numbers, right?"

"Depends on what those numbers are made up of," he grumbled.

The vehicle Gisele stopped at, parked half a block from the courtyard, looked for all the world like a typical city bus, though empty with a *Not in Service* message blinking on the display over the windshield. Gisele swiped her palm across a spot next to the door, and it hissed open for her. "All aboard!" she called out, and glanced at the shadows around us. "And I do mean all of you, unless you'd rather creep around in the dark spots out here instead."

The trio took the hint. As we tramped onto the bus, they reformed just inside—in a space that was several steps up from any public transportation vehicle I'd ever ridden on.

Behind the front seat with its violet velvet covering, the bus opened up into an immense RV. We were standing at the edge of a living room-slash-kitchen with a full sink surrounded by slick counters that sparkled like Gisele's blouse, hardwood cabinets, and a semi-circle of padded pearl-gray sofa-bench large enough to seat eight, which curved around a sleek table. A narrow hall led from there to a few other doorways, the open one offering a glimpse of a four-poster bed.

"Holy mother of manticores," I said, taking it in. "You've got yourself a mansion on wheels. It has a glamour on the outside?"

Gisele swept her hand toward the dashboard. "Programmed with multiple variations!"

The multi-colored buttons were carefully labeled. There was *City Bus*, naturally, as well as *Tour Bus*, *Cargo Van*, *School Bus*, and some particularly unexpected options like *Train Locomotive* and— "Military Submarine?" I couldn't help reading out loud in disbelief.

"We've never had the opportunity to use that one so far," Bow said from where he'd shut the door behind us. "It's too bad. It looks pretty amazing."

"Very slick," Ruse said with approval, and promptly sprawled out on the leather sofa cushions. "I approve. We did need new digs."

"Assuming our walking disaster here can manage not to get this latest vehicle blown to smithereens too," Omen muttered, but even he couldn't hide a glimmer of awe as he took in the space. "How did you two manage to get yourselves a ride like this?"

Gisele shrugged. "We already had the RV. Mortals have a tendency of wanting to make me happy. Cori crafted it bigger than it was before with his magic. But we were getting into trouble finding places to park it around the cities where we usually wanted to hang out. Then we helped a fae lady through a bad trip, and she repaid us with the glamouring."

I guessed knowing your way around psychoactive substances could have its benefits too.

Bow peered into one of the cupboards. "Do you all want anything to eat?" Beside me, Snap immediately perked up. The centaur licked his lips. "We've got grass and hay and a little clover with the flowers still on it..."

The devourer's expression fell again. Bow glanced back and caught our lack of interest in what I guessed were delicacies to equine types. A slyer smile crossed his lips. "We do also have the *other* kind of grass, that's not actually grass. Good stuff."

"None of us except the lady need physical sustenance," Thorn put in.

"Oh, the point of smoking this stuff isn't to fill your belly. Although I've made some pretty good brownies with it before."

I guessed Omen had decided the vehicle was too useful to pass up even if its owners weren't his cup of tea. He cleared his throat. "We're glad to have your assistance, but I think we'd better hold off on addling our minds until we've decided on our next course of action. Ruse, you mentioned a solid lead on our way over here."

"Yes!" Ruse straightened up with a clap of his hands. I dropped onto the sofa next to him, and Snap squeezed in beside me. Our hosts settled in across from us.

"That dark cloud you call an ex spilled the beans after you left," the incubus said with a tip of his head toward me. "There's a factory on Wharf Street that had a bunch of trucks arrive the day after we broke into the facility where they were holding Omen."

Thorn's attention jerked to us from where he'd been studying the street outside through the window. "One of the addresses the computer adept gave us lay on Wharf Street, didn't it?"

"Right you are, my friend."

For the first time since we'd fled the fairgrounds, Omen's mouth curved into a smile. "We'll have to scope the place out surreptitiously to confirm, of course," he said. "That's work for tonight, when we can hope at least some of the employees will have gone home for the day. But now we've got the perfect cover for cruising through the neighborhood."

He patted the Everymobile's sparkly counter and, shockingly, deigned to turn his smile on the tourists he'd snarked about less than an hour ago. "I'd bet the Company of Light has your friend there too. I think it's time to crash *their* party."

20

Sorsha

"**A**nd then while we're getting the prisoners out of there, the virus your hacker programmed can be spreading all through their computer systems, erasing their data!" Gisele bounced on the RV sofa, her eyes sparkling with enthusiasm. "It's the perfect plan."

I thought her confidence might have been a little overboard, and Thorn appeared to agree. "We still have many details to determine," the warrior said from where he was standing propped against the back of the driver's seat.

"We'll get there," Omen assured him with the restrained smile he'd been showing more often over the last day. "It's all coming together."

It'd better be. After scoping out the docklands building as well as we could around the Company's protections and surveillance, we'd spent most of the last couple of days piecing together how we could best break in and unleash the many shadowkind they held captive. The contribution from Ruse's hacker friend meant we could also destroy any hazardous information their experiments had uncovered so far—if we got the chance to use it. But having nearly twice as many people on our side this time around and significantly more experience tangling with Company guards made the mission feel less daunting.

"I just wish I still had my scorch-knife," I said, making a face at the thought of the blasted camper van.

Omen was close enough to jovial to give me a playful pat on the shoulder. "Maybe we'll find you a new one, Disaster."

"It's time to celebrate, then!" Bow sprang up from where he'd been chowing down on a salad of clover and strawberries and beckoned to Gisele. "If we're not storming the gates until tomorrow night when the next delivery comes by, it should be safe. Where's the good stuff we just picked up?"

As they pawed—or hoofed?—through the contents of their cupboards, I glanced up at Omen, who despite his good cheer hadn't relaxed enough yet to actually sit down. It was hard to resist needling him, so I didn't. "Still pissed off that I talked to Jade about getting help?"

He glowered at me, but only for a moment. His expression lightened again as his gaze traveled around the RV. "It didn't exactly bring us a heap of seasoned warriors... but I'll concede that I'd rather have these two joining us than be going it alone. Especially since I doubt Rex has any more camper vans for you to get blown up."

I elbowed him in the hip, which was as high as I could comfortably reach from the sofa. "I had even *less* to do with that act of destruction than I did with Betsy."

He hummed to himself as if to say we'd see about that, but the glint in his eyes might have been actual amusement. Even if I hadn't tamed the beast, I'd at least gotten him wagging his tail.

Before that thought could lead to me ogling his ass again—just to check whether he had a real tail at the moment, nothing more, shut up—I yanked my gaze back to our hosts. Gisele had produced a caramels tin she popped open to reveal a hefty stack of joints.

Ah. The other kind of grass indeed. No surprise that was how these two celebrated.

"Who wants in?" Bow asked, grabbing one. "We're happy to share."

As he lit the joint, sending a whiff of that pungent musky smoke into the air, I shook my head. "I'll pass. Not really my thing." And even though we were parked in a lot of city buses looking very city bus-y ourselves, I didn't totally trust the disaster Omen had been teasing me about not to descend on our heads.

Apparently our hedonistic incubus wasn't one for the MJ either. Ruse waved off the offer with a crooked grin. "Even the good stuff makes me queasy. Believe me, no one's sadder about that than I am."

Snap considered the rolled papers with tempered curiosity. "I've never tried this before."

"Go ahead," I said, tapping his calf with my foot under the table. "Just take it easy."

As he accepted the joint Bow passed him, Thorn loomed closer. "What possible purpose does this serve?"

Gisele smiled at him. "It's just for fun. Helps you relax and gets your mind thinking in creative ways. Maybe we'll figure out those details that are missing while we're flying high."

Or maybe they'd only be inspired to make a run for Cheetos and French fries, but I was willing to wait and see.

Thorn paused, his gaze shifting to me for a second. Thinking about my suggestion that he needed to loosen up? At his evident wavering, Bow added, "It's easy to shake off the effects if you need to. Popping into the shadows and back eliminates the chemicals from your system." He giggled, the weed's effects appearing to have kicked in. "As long as you can remember that you *can* pop into the shadows. Oh, that *is* good stuff."

"I certainly wouldn't become so muddled as to forget that," Thorn said with sudden resolve, and held out his hand. Son of a jacked-up jaguar, I wouldn't have predicted that, but I was plenty interested in discovering how it'd pan out. What could possibly go wrong?

Snap took one drag from the joint and shoved it back to Bow with a hacking cough. "That is—that is enough," he said weakly as Ruse clapped him on the back. "I don't suppose you have any more strawberries?"

Thankfully, the equines did. While Snap made short

work of those, Thorn sucked away on the spliff with a slight flush creeping across his tan skin.

"I can't see that it makes any difference at all," he announced after a few minutes, but a few minutes after *that*, he was chuckling to himself while he peered at the sparkly countertop. "I never realized it before. It's as if you could connect each glint to find the source," he informed us, whatever that was supposed to mean.

Pickle scampered across the table, his head weaving as if he'd gotten a bit high off the atmosphere too. Omen rolled his eyes and went up front to study the maps on the Everymobile's GPS some more.

By the time Thorn was lying on the floor beside the cabinets discussing horse feed, favorite forest terrain, and the slant of the evening light across the ceiling with our hosts—all with equal enthusiasm—the stink of the smoke was getting a bit much for me. Snap stirred restlessly, eyeing Thorn with obvious bewilderment, and Ruse... The incubus was smirking at his companion's newfound state of levity, but there was something muted about his glee at the situation. It could be the smoke was getting to him too or more of that odd reticence I'd noticed coming over him.

A burst of confidence rushed through me that might have been a tiny bit bolstered by a slight second-hand high. We knew where our enemies were. We had a plan to smash them tomorrow night. Even with new allies on our side, it was going to be absurdly dangerous. We all deserved to enjoy ourselves thoroughly before then.

I stood up. "Ruse, Snap, come on. I think we should have our own non-smoking celebration."

Snap leapt up, an eager glow brightening his face. Ruse's smirk took on a sly slant, but he got up more slowly, maybe with a little hesitance?

Well, we'd see what we could do about that. He'd only ever hesitated before because he'd thought *I* wasn't fully committed. How could I have forgotten that?

I motioned for them to follow me and sauntered down the hall to the RV's second bedroom, where I'd slept the past two nights.

You could tell the current owners had been responsible for decorating the space. The comforter had a dreamy purple cloud print; the built-in wardrobe had received a coating of silver glitter. The gauzy curtain over the small window sparkled with matching spangles in the afternoon light. The only other illumination came from a circle of fairy lights fixed to the ceiling.

Not really my taste in décor, but when our hosts had managed to provide me with a double bed in a freaking *RV*, I had no complaints.

Especially now that I might get to share that bed with not just one but two of my new lovers. As they came in after me, I sat down on the edge of the bed, my heart beating faster.

I'd never done anything like this before—but wasn't that all the more reason to try? If Thorn could get high, I could handle a threesome.

If the men involved could handle it, that was. Snap

beamed at me but then glanced uncertainly at Ruse. "How did you want to celebrate, Sorsha?"

I reached up to grasp his hand and turned my own gaze on Ruse, who looked oddly uncertain too for a creature whose natural habitat was bedrooms. "I think your soundproofing ability would come in handy right about now." One of his supernatural skills allowed him to ensure the sounds of lovemaking didn't escape a given room, thank all the glitter around us.

"And then I'll play voyeur?" he asked.

I kicked him—lightly—in the shin. "That wasn't what I was thinking. Haven't you offered on half a dozen occasions to teach Snap a few advanced techniques? No time like the present."

The incubus and the devourer considered each other. I couldn't tell which of them was more torn—or why Ruse was torn at all when this had been his idea to start with. Oh, well. If he left, that was up to him. Snap and I could still enjoy ourselves perfectly well.

"If it helps your decision any..." I said, and tugged off my blouse and undershirt together to remove my protective badge as well. Might as well put the assets on display. I leaned back so my boobs perked up even more in my demi-cup bra.

Snap made a hungry noise low in his throat and moved to join me without another second's hesitation. He trailed his fingers down my back, kissed my shoulder, and peered up at Ruse again. "I *would* like to know what you can show me. For Sorsha."

"Looking to put me out of a job, huh?" the incubus

joked, but his roguish face had softened. When he met my eyes again, the gleam in his brought an unexpected flutter into my chest. "I did offer, didn't I? I suppose a tutoring session can't hurt anything."

Did he think some other kind of hook-up *would* hurt? I wasn't sure how to ask that question, especially in front of Snap. And then Ruse leaned in to capture my mouth, and questioning his exact phrasing was the last thing on my mind.

He kissed me with such intensity it left me breathless, all my nerves quivering in anticipation of what would follow. He nudged me over on the bed so all three of us could sprawl there side by side and glanced across at Snap.

"The first and most important lesson: explore. There are no perfect spots or motions that get every woman off. You caress here and kiss there to see how she responds. The sounds she makes. The speed of her pulse. The heat of her skin." His smirk came back. "For your first round of homework, put that advice to test while I enjoy these lovely lips a little more."

He claimed another kiss, easing us both right down on top of the comforter. The intoxicating pressure of his lips turned even more potent with the stroke of Snap's hand up my side to my chest.

The devourer had already proven he was an intrepid explorer during our previous encounters. He unhooked my bra and, attentive to Ruse's advice, teased his fingers not just over the sensitive peaks of my breasts but all along the curves, across my ribs, down my spine, as if he were charting every plane of my naked skin.

His lithe fingers woke up tingles of sensation everywhere he touched, but when a particular spot made me hum, he lingered there a little longer. Soon it felt as if my whole body was thrumming with awakening pleasure. When Snap finally returned to my chest with a flick of his thumb over one nipple, I gasped into Ruse's mouth.

"The student learns quickly," the incubus murmured, and dipped his head to attend to my other breast.

Snap scooted higher, and I turned my head to meet his softer but no less passionate kiss. His forked tongue slipped between my lips, drawing lines of bliss inside my mouth.

I dug my fingers into his silky curls, into Ruse's shoulder as the incubus swiveled *his* tongue to urge the peak of my breast even stiffer, wondering what miracles I'd worked in some past incarnation to be worthy of this moment.

Snap kissed me harder and tweaked my nipple again. As he left my mouth to nibble along my jaw, Ruse slid his hand lower. When he reached the waist of my jeans, a sharper heat jolted between my legs. My hips canted upward of their own accord.

"Patience, Miss Blaze," Ruse teased, jerking my zipper downward. "We'll set you alight in all sorts of places."

Snap paused in his attentions to watch Ruse help me

squirm out of my pants. The neon glint came into his eyes.

"You tasted her here before," he said, his fingers gliding down my abdomen to the hem of my panties. "I want to try that—I want to learn how to make her feel as good as when you did it."

"Hmm." Ruse branded my breast with another scorching kiss. "I'm sure that could be arranged, if our mortal has no objections."

I let out a laugh that turned into a gasp when Snap grazed his fingertips over my clit through the thin fabric. With just that light touch, my entire sex woke up with a pulse of pleasure. "No objections whatsoever," I managed to say. "Instruct away."

As he pulled my panties down, Ruse trailed his lips across my belly and over my hip. Each point of contact lit a giddy glow beneath my skin, just as he'd promised.

Snap bent by my thighs and pressed a tentative kiss just below my belly button. He inhaled deeply, and my nerves tingled at the way he appeared to revel in my scent.

"The word of the day is still 'explore'," Ruse said in that chocolatey voice of his. "Sample every bit of the terrain to see where she reacts most enthusiastically. Soft or forceful; lips, tongue, teeth, and fingers—make use of every tool at your disposal in every way. But carefully until you're sure you're onto something. Even the strongest of women have some rather delicate pieces down there." He waggled his eyebrows at me.

Snap's head dipped lower. He slicked his tongue over

my clit, the forked tip encircling it for an instant, and an even giddier heat rushed through my core. A whimper shuddered out of me.

As he suckled me harder, I returned my hand to his head, tangling my fingers in his hair and expressing my pleasure with both the pant of my breath and the tug of his curls. The latter became more important when Ruse eased up beside me and reclaimed my mouth.

Within moments, I really was blazing everywhere. Between my legs, Snap coaxed more and more pleasure with each increasingly confident swipe of his tongue and nibble of his teeth. He delved one finger right inside me, his other hand stroking my hip down to the sensitive back of my knee. As bliss spiraled up from my sex, Ruse's mouth on mine and his skillful fondling of my breasts drew out even more to join it. My body practically vibrated with the heady waves.

I jerked at Ruse's shirt to get at the sculpted muscle underneath. He nipped my earlobe before stripping it off. As he leaned over me again, Snap's long finger hit just the right spot inside me, in perfect concert with his lips on my clit.

"That's it," I said, unable to stop my hips from arching up. "Right there. Oh..."

And then I couldn't speak at all with the flood of bliss that rose up over me, surging higher so swiftly it stole my breath. With one more swipe of his tongue, it crashed in a burst of ecstasy that knocked all thought from my head. My hand clenched in Snap's hair.

As I lay there, momentarily jellified, he peered up at

me. A hopeful smile curled his glistening lips. "That was a good one?"

A laugh tumbled out of me. "They're all good ones, but that one definitely makes at least the top five." A different sort of hunger gripped me, gratitude and desire mingling. "Get up here. You should find out how good being 'tasted' can make *you* feel."

Snap scooted up the bed, and I sat up, yanking at his Henley shirt. He let me tug it off him, but when I reached for his pants, he blinked, and the rest of his clothes vanished in the same trick he'd used in the cabin. Even if there was no syrup to be had here, my mouth watered at the sight of his long, lean frame on display, cock jutting eagerly from his slimly muscled hips.

Ruse chuckled. "I guess this is where I take my leave."

I grasped his wrist before he could get off the bed and caught his eyes. "I want you too. If you're up for it, I mean."

His hazel eyes glimmered with a hint of their unearthly shadowkind glow. "Always," he said softly. "How do you want me?"

An eager shiver shot through me at the thought of the possibilities. "Inside me. I'll leave the rest up to you. I know I'm in good hands." I grinned at him and turned back to Snap.

I kissed the devourer on the mouth first, taking my time to revel in the passionate intentness with which he returned the gesture. As I made my way down his trimly toned chest, pecking more kisses against his smooth skin,

Ruse knelt behind me. The incubus ran his hands down my back, over my sides, and up my torso to cup my breasts. His squeeze of my nipples left me growling for more.

When I circled the head of Snap's erection with my tongue, the devourer's chest hitched. "Oh, that is—That is *very* good."

"It gets even better," I assured him, and took his cock right into my mouth.

The tender skin there held the same fresh, sweet taste as the rest of him with its darker mossy undertone. Delicious. I pressed my tongue to the veins on the underside and swiveled it around. Snap groaned. Then I was groaning too, as Ruse tested my slit with his fingers and slid his own cock inside me in one practiced thrust.

We moved together in an erratic rhythm that slowly came together: Snap's hips jerking up and his hand squeezing my shoulder, my head bobbing over his cock while I sucked him farther down, my body rocking as Ruse plunged deeper into me. Every eagerly desperate sound that escaped the devourer's mouth, every ecstatic stutter of the incubus's breath as he drove us both toward release, sparked my own bliss even hotter than the delectable friction inside me could generate on its own. The whole room seemed to have lit up with our pleasure. Well, maybe the profusion of sparkles had something to do with that too.

When Ruse sped up his thrusts, his fingers slipping around my hip to stroke my clit, it wasn't just sparkles but twinkling stars that formed behind my eyes. I moaned around Snap's cock, sucking harder.

We all careened into release together. Snap's head tipped back into the pillow as his salty cum flooded my mouth. I swallowed and gasped with my second orgasm pealing through me. Ruse bent over me with a satisfied sigh and a few last lazy pumps of his hips to extend the bliss a little longer.

I slumped next to Snap, and Ruse sank down at my other side. The devourer looped an arm across my waist, the incubus rested his hand on my thigh, and for a few minutes as we lay there in the afterglow, we felt perfectly connected. Like a single being, no push or pull of competition. I didn't figure it would last, but I'd enjoy it while I had it.

Snap was just shifting closer to kiss my temple when my ringtone carried from my purse. I grimaced but waved at Ruse for him to retrieve it from the floor. No one much called me, so if someone was bothering, it might be important.

The number on the display was Huyen's. Maybe the Fund's leaders had come to a change of heart? But when I squirmed onto my back and raised the phone to my ear, it was the voice of one of the other members that spilled out.

"Sorsha? I don't know what the hell you've gotten into now, but I thought you should know—Ellen was attacked this evening."

21

Thorn

As soon as we arrived in view of the tall, white hospital building, my combat instincts shot a twinge through me. I materialized on the vehicle's sofa by the driver's seat and thumped the back of that seat. "Keep driving past. Someone's watching. We don't want them realizing there's anything odd about this vehicle."

Bow nodded, the centaur's hands tight on the steering wheel. Had it only been minutes ago that we'd been chuckling and exclaiming over... I couldn't remember what now, only the exhilaration that had come with the supposed brilliance we'd stumbled on. Diving into the shadows and back out again had felt like leaping through the frigid flow of a mountain waterfall, wiping my senses clean.

That "grass" the equines had given me had been potent in its effects. It had certainly loosened up *something* in my mind while I'd inhaled the smoke, but the uncertainty of what I'd actually been thinking in that loosened state left my nerves on edge. Perhaps not a substance I'd partake of again.

Sorsha sat rigid at the other end of the sofa, her fingers curled around the edge of the leather seat. "Did you see Company people out there?" she asked.

"I'm not sure of the exact threat, but someone hostile toward us is monitoring the place. Several someones. And I can't imagine what other party would match that description."

She shifted her weight. "I have to get in there. I have to see her and make sure she's okay."

"What good will that do?" Omen demanded, his posture tensed where he was leaning against the kitchen counter across from us. "You aren't a doctor, and your powers have nothing to do with healing. You can't help her with her injuries. Company people have seen you before—they'll notice if you go in. And given how thorough they are, I think we can assume they're watching every entrance."

"It's my fault they attacked her," Sorsha said. I didn't fully understand why this meant she needed to visit the woman—wouldn't it be more sensible to steer clear and avoid drawing further danger?—but her voice was so raw it squeezed my heart.

Omen did not appear to be similarly affected. He motioned sharply at her. "So, get whatever details we might need to inform our plans over the phone, and leave it there. She abandoned our cause. You don't owe her anything."

Sorsha glared at him. "Maybe not in shadowkind terms, but humans don't work like that. I've known Ellen for more than a decade—she and Huyen helped me get back on my feet after Luna died. I owe her a hell of a lot more than the last few weeks can decide. I'd be an actual monster if I didn't make an effort to show I care."

"Well, it looks like you'll have to do *that* over the phone. Because you're not walking through any door on that building."

I glanced back toward the hospital, taking in the rows of glossy windows all the way up its dozen or so floors... and the neighboring office building, darkened at the end of the day, standing right next to it. The memory of Sorsha snatching the flower pot from the apartment balcony flashed through my mind.

"Maybe she doesn't need to use a door," I said before they could keep arguing. "I could slip into the place through the shadows, find a room that faces the building next door where I can open a window, and she could jump across." I looked at Omen. "I'd make sure our mission remains uncompromised." I wasn't sure how well I could hold to that statement, so I didn't make it an outright promise.

Omen's jaw worked, but Sorsha had perked up a little from her despondence. "That's perfect," she said. "I'll just pop in, see if there's anything I can do or anything they can tell us that'll help us crush these bastards, and pop back out. You know Thorn would never let me get up to anything ill-advised." The smile she gave me was both sweet and a little sly.

"I could drive around the other side of the block and park there," Bow offered. "The tour bus guise is pretty multipurpose—we can stop just about anywhere without looking strange."

Omen threw his hands in the air. "Fine. A quick 'pop'-in. But if you're not done in half an hour, we're leaving without you and you can find your own way back."

Bow brought the bus to a surprisingly smooth stop less than a minute later. Sorsha sprang up immediately. "Be careful," Snap said with a worried frown.

Ruse moved to stand. "It might be easier with more than one of us—"

"Everyone else stays put," Omen said in a cutting tone. He jerked his head toward the doorway as he fixed his gaze on Sorsha. "Your half hour has started. Get a move on."

Sorsha mouthed a quick "Thank you" to me on her way out, already opening up the pack of lock-picking tools Ruse had gotten her this morning to replace her old ones. Our lady was so sure of herself and so stubborn. By the realms, I hoped I hadn't made a mistake in offering to orchestrate this surreptitious entrance.

Whether I had or not, the thing needed to be done swiftly. I stepped back into the shadows and trailed behind her out through the general haze of the dusk across the street. She ducked down an alley to weave toward the office building out of view, and I raced straight to the bright walls of the hospital.

It wasn't, I realized once I'd squeezed through the shadow around a doorway, the most ideal environment for a shadowkind. Stark lights glowed all across the hall ceilings and reflected off the pale walls. I leapt from one thin patch of darkness to another until a trolley of operating equipment carried me the rest of the way to a stairwell. It was fortunate that the size of my physical form had no bearing on how I filled out the shadows.

The caller who'd notified Sorsha of the attack had told her that her injured friend was on the fifth floor. I rushed up that far and then dashed through the patient rooms on the side of the building that faced the offices. Finally, I entered a darkened room where the bed lay empty. I emerged from the shadows by the window, yanked out the screen, and shoved the lower pane high.

Sorsha spotted me from a fifth floor office room farther down. She gave a quick wave there, vanished, and reappeared directly across from me in a matter of seconds.

The buildings had only a five-foot gap between them. I stepped to the side, and she threw herself across that space with only a slight *oomph* as she caught the window ledge with both arms. She scrambled inside, bobbed up to peck me on the cheek, and hurried out to the hall.

I had the distinct impression that I'd hardly go unnoticed with my broad human body in the clothes I'd chosen for comfort several centuries ago, but I wasn't going to let her charge off completely undefended. With another leap into the shadows, I followed her to her friend's room.

A few figures from those meetings of hers stood outside the doorway. They all stiffened at the sight of Sorsha.

"What are *you* doing here?" asked a young man whose soft face didn't show any of the strength he'd built up in his musclebound body. During my time on the battlefield, that would have marked him as easy pickings, barely worth the time it'd take to knock him off his feet. I might have judged it worth the effort anyway after his sneer at the lady.

"I had to come," Sorsha said, her back stiffening. She glanced past him to the other figures. "How's she doing? Is she awake?"

"Huyen's in with her now," one of the women said flatly. "From what she said, Ellen is still pretty out of it. They hit her hard—concussion, broken ribs, all that."

At that moment, another woman strode out of the hospital room, her face tight with worry. Her mouth pulled even tighter when she saw Sorsha. Without a second's hesitation, she grabbed our mortal's arm and yanked her farther down the hall. The soft-faced man slunk closer, presumably to listen in, which only increased my desire to punch his face in.

"You have to get out of here," the woman snapped in a harsh undertone. "This is all because of you and your crazy crusade."

Guilt flashed through Sorsha's expression. "I didn't mean—I tried to make sure we were careful."

"Obviously not careful enough."

"I'm so sorry, Huyen." Sorsha set her jaw. "I know it doesn't make up for the attack, but—you can tell her we're going to bring down the assholes who did this tomorrow night."

The woman sucked in a sharp breath. "Are you kidding me? Do you want to screw us over even more? The people who attacked her asked her to pass on a message: to tell you and your friends to stay out of their business. They nearly *killed* her, you know. I didn't even want you coming here—Lila shouldn't have called you."

Sorsha swallowed audibly, her shoulders drooping. "I'll go. I just wanted to see—when I heard—" She shook her head. Then her gaze jerked back up with a flicker of concern. She raised her voice so it would carry to the cluster by the door. "Did anyone call Vivi?"

The woman who'd spoken to her earlier nodded. "I tried. Went straight to voicemail. Either her battery's dead or she was on the subway or something."

"Okay. Okay." Sorsha looked as if she wanted to make a run for the injured woman's room after all—I collected myself in the shadows in case I needed to clear the way for her—but then she spun around and hurried to the other room where she'd entered.

As soon as she'd shut the door, she pulled out her phone. I emerged into the physical realm next to her.

She answered my question before I had to ask it. "They went for Ellen—why wouldn't they go for my best friend too? If they've identified the Fund members, they're not going to buy Vivi's phony story about her grandma's car getting stolen anymore. Shit, shit, shit." She grimaced at the phone, which I supposed hadn't connected with Vivi, and shoved it back into her pocket. "I've got to go to her place. They jumped Ellen right outside her apartment. Vivi would usually be working late today—if I can get there first—"

"Where are we going?" I asked as she clambered into the window.

Sorsha glanced back at me. "I don't expect you to come. Omen was pretty clear that he didn't approve of getting even this involved. You can let the others know I'll meet you all at the bus lot on Lincoln Road."

If she made it back to the lot at all. Did she really think she could tackle a band of attackers on her own—or that I'd let her attempt it?

"No," I said firmly, striding over to join her. "We have each other's backs—isn't that how you put it? We'll do this together. Omen can wait."

"Are you—oh, fuck it, there isn't time. Thank you." She shot me a smile and leapt back to the office building.

I flung myself after her, stretching myself to cross the entire space as little more than a blur of thicker darkness in the hazy evening dimness. On the other side, Sorsha dashed straight for the door she must have jimmied open.

"Thank heavenly heathens Vivi just had to live right in the middle of downtown," she said, racing toward the stairs. "Her apartment is only six blocks from here." A wild laugh hitched from her chest. "We might even make it back before Omen's thirty-minute deadline is up."

We sprinted through the alleyways and along a busy

street lined with restaurants and shops, Sorsha's sneakers smacking the sidewalk and me soaring through the shadows where I could move faster and without obstruction. She only slowed on the fifth block, with another jab at her phone's screen. I hurtled ahead of her but stopped where I could still hear her voice as it pealed out with relief.

"Vivi! Please tell me you're not home yet. Oh, geez, if you squint you'll probably see me down the street." She started walking again at a brisk clip. "Don't come any closer. We've got to—"

I'd already peered ahead to where a familiar figure with a puff of black curls and a sleek white outfit stood outside a shop at the other end of the next block. Or rather, she was standing outside it when my gaze first located her. An instant later, two figures in plated vests charged from around the side of the nearest building.

Sorsha's voice cut off at her friend's shriek. She propelled herself forward as fast as her mortal feet would carry her.

I reached the attackers even more swiftly. Leaping from the shadows at the last second, I plowed my fist straight into the nearest miscreant's throat.

The man fell with a sputter of blood, but the other attacker hauled Sorsha's friend through the doorway next to him. Sorsha and I charged after them—and two more Company combatants rushed in after us, the first raising a gun and the other flicking one of those whips of light that made my entire being twitch with discomfort.

A thick, meaty scent filled my nose. We'd barreled

into a butcher shop. I managed to kick the gun from the one man's hand with a snap of the bones in his wrist. Then I raced after the man who'd grabbed Vivi, who was now hauling her through another doorway at the back.

Sorsha and I burst into a room of hanging carcasses, vibrant red and pink etched with paler lines of fat. The smell rolled over us in a thick wave, but Sorsha didn't hesitate even as she coughed. She launched herself straight at her friend's captor.

My first instinct was to hurl myself after her and take the fellow down for her, but I forced myself to stop and quite literally have her back instead. I ripped a thigh off one of the cow carcasses and slammed it into the man who'd come in behind us before he could slash either of us with that unnerving whip.

The strategy worked out well enough, as Sorsha clearly had her side of the battle under control. She dodged to the side at the last second and heaved an entire carcass into Vivi's attacker, pummeling him in the head with the raw meat.

The man grunted and teetered; Vivi tore free with a yelp. When the man lunged after her, his hand jerking upward with a pistol in its grasp, Sorsha tackled him.

Sparks shot up. The waft of heat she'd conjured browned the carcasses above them, turning the raw meat stink into barbeque.

Our attacker with the whip hadn't been dissuaded yet. He flung the arc of light toward me, and I dove under it, ramming into his legs. As he toppled, I threw myself around both the weapon and the venomous plates of his armor. I rammed the beef thigh into his mouth hard enough to puncture the back of his throat.

"Eat that, villain," I said, and swiveled around to discover that Sorsha had managed to bury her foe under three of the heavy carcasses. The cords they'd been hanging from dangled with blackened ends where they'd been burnt through.

She caught my eye, and I found myself smiling at her, a rare sense of elation filling my chest. I hadn't *enjoyed* combat in eons. But this... this had been good. What a battle was meant to be: comrades conquering evil side by side. Protecting each other wasn't all it came down to. I had to give my companions room to be the warriors they were capable of becoming too.

Perhaps I could make sure *this* war was won the right way after all.

Vivi was braced against the far wall, breathing hard, her sleek white outfit now streaked with blood. "Sorsha?" she said tentatively, her eyes wide.

The lady held out her hand. "Come on, Vivi. We're getting you out of here."

22

Sorsha

"Well, this is... something, all right," Vivi said, taking in the walls in the low-ceilinged living space, which looked—and smelled—like they were pasted with dried algae. From her face, I suspected she was resisting the urge to wrinkle her nose.

Gisele pranced around the room, which otherwise held an odd collection of rattan furniture with cotton cushions that at least appeared to be cozy. The unicorn shifter's perky voice gave no sign that she'd noticed Vivi's hesitance. "Kaiso said we could drop in and use the place any time. He's got houseboats all over the world, so he's not here that much."

"A big fan of water living, huh?" I adjusted my balance as the floor rocked under us with the shifting currents of the river.

"It makes sense. He's a kappa, after all."

Vivi's eyebrows shot up. "Um, are you totally sure he won't be back while I'm staying here?" Temperaments really varied even across shadowkind of the same sort, but kappa did have a reputation as tricksters at best and murderers-by-drowning-mortals at worst.

"Oh, I'm sure it won't be a problem even if he does," Gisele said. "Just tell him you're a friend of ours."

Vivi didn't look any more certain about that strategy than I felt—who was to say the water spirit would ask for introductions before getting down to drowning—but Omen stepped into the boat's interior then. *He* didn't hesitate to wrinkle his nose as he glanced around.

"You should be safe from any shadowkind who come wandering this way," he said. "I've marked the place with my power as a warning. There aren't many who'd purposefully risk the wrath of a hellhound."

Marked the place? What, had he peed on the deck in hound form to leave his scent? The image made the corners of my mouth twitch, but I decided it was better not to risk his wrath right *now* by sharing it. Too much gratitude was tickling up through my chest.

I hadn't expected Omen to even participate in finding Vivi a safe place to hide out, let alone use his influence to protect her.

"Thank you," I said, meaning it.

He shrugged and stalked back out without another word. "I guess the other guy got all the friendliness on offer when they came into being, huh?" Vivi said with a quirk of her lips. Ruse had been by a few minutes earlier to drop off food and a couple of changes of clothing he'd gathered for her, which he'd presented in his usual charming fashion.

"Something like that." I glanced at Gisele. "This is great. Thank *you* so much too. Can you give us a little while to talk?"

"Of course!" The unicorn shifter bobbed her head with its rainbow of hair to my best friend. "A pleasure to meet you." She trotted out after Omen.

Vivi flopped down into one of the rattan chairs. "My God, what a night. Out of the frying pan and into a five-alarm blaze."

The comment pinched at my gut. I knew she only meant it as an expression, but I also wasn't sure if she'd noticed the spurts of heat and flame I'd been able to produce while I was taking down her attacker in the butcher shop. She hadn't brought it up, and I'd figured it was better not to heap any more craziness on her than she was already dealing with... and also I wasn't super keen on seeing how our friendship might change if I revealed I might not be completely human after all.

"Ruse will bring more supplies around if you need them," I said. "And I'll always have my phone on me. But hopefully what we're going to do tonight will get us a huge step closer to taking down the Company of Light completely, and then we won't need to worry about them coming after you again."

"You think so? They're a hell of a lot more organized and vicious than any hunters we've tangled with before."

"Well, if we can free a bunch of higher shadowkind they've been torturing, that's tons of new allies right there. And we're going to get all the info we can out of the people working there, whatever files they have on site, and then hopefully erase everything on their end so all their experimental data is kaput... We're a lot better prepared than we were before."

"You had things figured out well enough to get to me before the jerks strung me up or whatever the heck they were planning, so I have all possible faith in your plans." Vivi reached to pat my arm as I sat down beside her, but her usual energy was still dampened.

A sharper jab lanced through my stomach. If I hadn't pursued the Company and kept helping Omen and the others work out how to take them down—if I hadn't gone to the Fund asking for help—right now, Ellen would be at the theater getting everything ready for the day. Vivi would be able to go back to the apartment she'd decorated with so much flair. Neither of them, or any of the other Fund members, would be living with the fear of murderous psychopaths in silver-and-iron armor rampaging into their lives.

"I'm sorry," I said. "I didn't realize—I thought taking this to the Fund would be safe with all the precautions we took. The last thing I wanted—"

Vivi held up her hand. "I'm going to stop you right there. I *begged* you to let me be a part of this, Sorsha. Ellen and Huyen made their own choices too. The whole point of the Shadowkind Defense Fund is supposed to be to stop assholes who treat the shadowkind as worse than vermin, and these Company people are clearly the worst of the lot. Do you really think it'd be better if we stepped back and let them run their experiments and murder anyone else who stumbled onto their scheming? Because I don't. I'm still 100% on team Crush Those Assholes To Smithereens."

I had to smile at that, but my fingers tightened against my pocket where my phone formed a flat, silent lump. "You're the only one out of the Fund who feels that way, as far as I can tell. The only people who answered when I tried to reach out this morning didn't have much to say other than to fuck off."

"Aw, they'll get their heads on straight when you expose everything the Company has been up to. And those who don't are just chickens."

Her vehemence eased my guilt a little. I sank back into my chair with the rocking of the boat. Thankfully it was docked far down the river from the place we'd be crashing into tonight.

"So..." Vivi prodded me with her index finger. "How many shadowkind groupies do you have now?"

I rolled my eyes at her, ignoring the faint flush that crept into my cheeks. "Still just the three. You don't think that's enough?"

"Why stop there? That Omen guy is pretty hot in an I'll-rip-your-face-off sort of way."

I was pretty sure Omen had literally ripped plenty of people's faces off, but maybe Vivi realized that. "We can barely have a conversation without wanting to punch one another. I think I'll stick to three." I rubbed my face. "It's weird enough that I'm having any kind of relationship with a bunch of monsters in the first place, isn't it?"

Vivi shrugged. "Nothing wrong with having unusual taste in men. Leaves more of the typical hotties for the rest of us. Now that I've met them, I can definitely see the appeal." She shot me a wide smile.

"Believe me, they're more trouble than they look," I muttered, but the complaint was half-hearted. I couldn't say I regretted that the trio had barged into my apartment and my life those weeks ago—not even a little bit, the loss of that apartment and just about everything else I'd counted on notwithstanding.

And we had much bigger trouble to tackle tonight. I'd have loved to linger there on the plump cushions, ignoring the algae smell and chatting with Vivi as if this were some unexpected aquatic holiday and not an attempt to save her life, but I really should get back to our final preparations.

I pushed myself off the chair. Vivi got up too so I could squeeze her in a hug. She hugged me back just as hard.

"You lay low completely this time, all right," I ordered, wagging a finger at her. "Don't set one foot off this boat—unless the bad guys set foot *on* it, of course."

"Aye, aye, captain," she said with a cheeky salute. Then a cloud crossed her expression, a hint of the fears she was suppressing. "Ditto."

"Ditto."

As I crossed the houseboat's deck, my own fears swelled inside my chest. I'd only just barely protected Vivi this time. If the Company tracked her down here...

We'd just have to make sure they didn't get the chance to so much as try.

As I headed for solid ground, I spun a lyric around and sang the newly mangled version under my breath to bolster my spirits. "Stand up and burn 'em down, never let them see us frown. Ne-eh-ver. Ne—"

I stopped in my tracks when I saw Omen waiting for me on the road. The Everymobile had vanished, leaving just him—and the motorcycle he'd apparently retrieved when I wasn't looking. He straddled the old but well-polished Harley, one foot on the ground and one propped on the footrest. All he'd need was a beat-up leather jacket, and he could have driven straight out of a '70s biker flick.

Not my decade, but I could appreciate the vibe all the same.

I ambled over, crossing my arms. "Decided it was time to lean into the bad-boy persona, did you? This does look more your style than good ol' Betsy."

He grimaced at me. "You will not besmirch Betsy's good name. She gave us her all. This is Charlotte."

I swallowed a guffaw. "Do you name all your vehicles?"

"All two of them that I used to have, yes. Do you think you can manage not to get this vehicle blown up, Disaster?"

"The other ones weren't even my fault," I felt the need to point out. "Why are you letting me near dear Charlotte if you're concerned about that?"

His gaze sharpened. "Thorn mentioned that you

used your powers again to fend off your friend's attackers. You seem to be getting better at bringing them out—it's just the control bit that needs work. It occurred to me that the bike might be a good way to get some concentrated practice."

"How so?"

"You can't drive, so I'm going to guess you're not quite as confident *on* a speeding vehicle as standing in front of one. And I've got plenty of tricks to get your heart thumping. Get on." He tapped the seat behind him and then a strip of paper he'd taped to the end of the right handlebar. "When you're agitated enough that you can feel your power, see if you can light *this* on fire—not me. I've got more where it came from once that one's good and crispy."

It actually sounded like a reasonable plan... except I wasn't only hesitant about the whole riding on a speeding motorcycle thing but also having to cling to the man in front of me while I was doing it. I couldn't exactly hope to perch daintily on the back—no, this was going to require full body contact.

I wasn't going to let Bossypants see that hesitation, though. "Fine," I said, and hopped on.

As I settled my knees against his hips and wrapped my arms around his waist, Omen turned to face ahead. His entire abdomen was packed with solid muscle. This wasn't a man I'd ever expected—or wanted—to be embracing, but I couldn't say it was an entirely unpleasant experience. Here was hoping I didn't, like, drench him in sweat in the summer heat or something.

"No helmets?" I asked.

He chuckled. "And here I thought you had a hard-on for danger. We're going to do a little death-defying today."

Without another word or any warning, he sent the bike roaring forward.

My arms jerked even tighter around Omen's frame in an instinctive bid to, y'know, *not die*. My legs pressed in too, my body shifting forward to meld against him for security's sake. Well, now I could say I'd had the fourth member of my shadowkind quartet between my thighs, even if it wasn't in the way Vivi had been teasing me about.

As we tore down the street and around a corner, the shifter's hellish scent filled my nose, plenty dangerous in itself. His muscles flexed beneath my fingers. My heart was thumping all right, but it might have partly been because my jerk of a brain couldn't help wondering how Omen would react if I dipped my hands a little lower and found out what *he* would get a hard-on for.

Then the hellhound took another turn with a rev of the engine and a lurch of the bike to one side, and all thoughts of anything other than surviving fled my mind. Seconds later, he whipped around a curve dipping so low I'd swear my hair grazed the pavement.

My pulse stuttered. With his shadowkind strength, he'd probably recover from a high-speed tumble. Did he comprehend how easily *my* head would crack open?

Yes, yes, he did. That was the whole point of veering so close to this guardrail that I could see the traffic passing below the bridge as vividly as my life flashing before my eyes. For one specific purpose.

Focus, Sorsha. I *wanted* to master this force in me.

With my next jolt of panic at a risky maneuver, I trained my attention on the strip of paper now flapping wildly in the wind. Heat flared in my chest alongside the clanging of adrenaline. I narrowed my eyes—and the paper went up in a burst of flame.

Omen slowed at a traffic light and fished another slip out of his pocket. "Good. Let's do it again. After a few times, we'll see if you can manage it when you're slightly less terrified."

"I'm not *terrified*," I objected, and lost the rest of my protest and probably all of my credibility when the bike took off again with a squeal of burnt rubber that shocked a yelp from my throat.

As much as I was tempted to whack Omen across the head for the wild ride, it did work. By the time I'd fried my fourth slip of paper, the surge of power from my gut to my chest was becoming familiar. True to his word, the hellhound shifter eased up on the stunts, and even with the—okay—terror dwindling to a tamer uneasiness, I managed to summon enough sparks to burn up a few more strips by dredging up that sensation.

I hadn't realized he'd swung around to arrive at the bus lot until he parked just outside it. I pulled myself away from him and clambered off the bike, figuring a little space was in order now, but the smile he shot me— the brightest and most genuine one I'd seen from him so far—brought back that pulse-thump of attraction.

That was okay, wasn't it? I didn't have any plans to actually jump his bones or anything. Why couldn't a gal simply have unusual taste in men, as Vivi had put it?

"You're getting a handle on it," he said.

"Maybe not such a disaster after all?"

"We'll see how it goes tonight." He said that part dryly, but his gaze didn't feel quite as icy as usual as it lingered on my face. "You have kept up all right so far."

Coming from him, that was the highest of praise. Had I brought the hound to heel?

I found myself grinning back at him. "And you only took a *little* convincing."

He snorted, but then his good humor seemed to fade. He motioned me toward the lot. "I've got to stash Charlotte. See if the others have made any progress with the final details. We've wasted enough time getting your issues sorted out already."

Then he drove off without another word, leaving me caught in a different sort of whiplash.

23

Sorsha

Our hosts only looked a little put out when Ruse opted to make a run for Thai take-out instead of the rest of us digging into their stash of actual grass and other fine greens. "They make a great salad too," Bow said, holding up his plate of foliage. He studied the containers of rice noodles and creamy curries with a puzzled expression as if he couldn't work out why anyone would choose to put those things into their bellies.

"I need protein for brain food," I said. "It's... a mortal thing." It seemed politest not to mention that eating grass and clover wasn't a human thing in any scenario I was aware of.

Omen was flipping through the photos and blueprints we'd gotten for the Wharf Street building on a tablet Ruse had charmed out of our hacker-on-call. "Don't feel bad for her," the incubus had told me. "She has a stack of them twice as tall as your dragon." Snap tucked his arm around me on the RV's sofa.

I gave in to the urge to feed the devourer a tidbit of green curry chicken off my fork. His tongue flicked over his lips to absorb the lingering traces of spice, and his pupils dilated.

"It has a sweetness, and also so much heat." His smile took on a sly slant. "I can see why you like it, Peach."

"Shut up," I said, and kissed him on the cheek so he'd know my light tone meant I was joking.

Ruse had tucked himself in at the table by my other side, not quite as cuddly as Snap but with more of his usual laidback air. Whatever he'd been tense about before, our recent interlude of three must have cured it. His eyes twinkling, he swiped his thumb over a speck of sauce at the corner of my lips and sucked it into his own mouth.

Oh, yeah, I was made of heat. A wash of it had pooled between my thighs before he even rested a teasing hand on my leg under the table.

"The best place to get some fiery action going would be here," Omen said, zooming in on an image. "How close do you think you'd need to get, Sorsha?"

If I *could* get the building burning in the first place? I sucked my lower lip under my teeth as I considered. "I don't know. I moved the flames on the camper van from something like fifty feet away, but that was just propelling what was already there—plus I was trying to stop those guys from murdering Thorn. I don't think I'd like to go at this with the same inspiration. But maybe, if we come down this alley, I could get a lot closer than that without getting caught anyway."

"While the rest of us stay in the shadows. That could work. And where would you dodge to—oh, let me guess, that window wouldn't be too much of a scramble for you?" The corner of his mouth curved upward.

"You've gotten to know me so well," I said with amusement, but something *had* transformed in the dynamic between us since this morning, his brusqueness after the bike ride aside. We'd been bouncing ideas back and forth all afternoon with a familiarity that was starting to feel almost comfortable. Not an adjective I'd ever thought I'd associate with Bossypants here.

Snap, as always, was looking out for my well-being more than I tended to do. "We don't know what guards might be stationed on the second floor there. Sorsha could end up jumping right into their midst."

"I'll take the same route she does," Thorn said, shifting his shoulders as Pickle galivanted from one to the other. He shot the little creature a glower, but that didn't stop him from reaching up to scratch Pickle's chin. "They won't be expecting us, and it'd be poorer tactics than the Company has ever shown to have many guards grouped at the same point without reason to anticipate entry. Between the two of us, we'll tear right through any there."

"As soon as we've got our brethren free, we'll have even more strength in numbers," Omen said.

I drummed my fingers on the table. "But remember, we don't want to stick around long enough for the Company to bring in reinforcements, and we need all the data we can get about their operations. As soon as Ruse has the virus uploaded onto the first computer we find, we'll want to grab any other computer equipment we see before he activates it. We can figure out what we'll get out of their records when we've hauled the equipment back to the Everymobile."

Omen nodded. "Snap, you determine which equipment is the most vital if we have to prioritize. Bow and Gisele, we'll want you two wrangling the escapees and making sure they stay on track. But I think this should pull together well." He paused and then lifted his gaze to catch my eyes. "You do understand that we won't be leaving any humans alive in that place if we can help it, don't you?"

A chill ran down my spine at the coolness with which he made that statement, but I'd been prepared for it. Slaughtering the building's mortal occupants was the easiest way to ensure our own safety both during the attack and afterward. The more we reduced the number of people working for the Company of Light, the harder it'd be for the Company to keep running and the easier for us to disrupt any other parts of the organization we needed to destroy.

A quiver of queasiness passed through my stomach— and faded with the memory of the asshole who'd rammed his gun at Vivi, of the descriptions I'd gotten of Ellen's injuries.

Anyone working in that facility knew they were torturing conscious beings that had all the self-awareness humans did, and had been party to who knew how many horrors inflicted on actual humans as well. I didn't enjoy the idea of spilling their blood, but I wasn't going to shed tears over their deaths either.

"If that's what we've got to do, then we do it," I said firmly. "I'll fry a few of them if I have to." If I could.

The hellhound shifter tipped his head approvingly and started going over a few more points with Thorn, who leaned over to peer at the screen. I forced down another mouthful of pad thai, but it dropped heavy into my stomach.

The last time we'd stormed one of the Company's buildings, we'd had fewer people and less idea what to expect—but I'd also had less time for the enormity of what we were taking on to sink in.

I squeezed between Snap and the table to squirm off of the sofa, snatching a kiss from him as I passed. "Bathroom break. Don't leave without me."

As Gisele tittered at that unnecessary request, I ducked into the little RV bathroom and yanked the door shut behind me. The compact space was the only part of the vehicle its shadowkind owners hadn't expanded or spruced up, probably because they had little use for it. I sat down on the closed toilet seat, one knee bumping the sliding door to the shower stall, and dragged in a deep breath.

I could do this. I could generate fire out of nothing— I'd done it plenty of times before, and tonight I'd do it again, as many times as I needed to. That was all there was to it.

I tugged a square of toilet paper off the roll and held

it up in front of me. All I needed was to remember the sensations from that motorcycle ride. Stir up the emotions that brought the flare of heat into my chest. Think of Vivi being grabbed by those assholes—of that hall of cages in the experimental facility—of Snap's expression when he'd gleaned impressions of the pain the Company's experiments had caused. Of the hail of machine gun fire aimed at Thorn.

My lungs constricted with a hitch of my pulse. All those fuckers *deserved* to be burned to a crisp.

I glared at the square of floppy paper, and a flame spurted up along its edge.

Beautiful. I'd need a lot more fire than that to raze the Wharf Street building to the ground when we were through, but I'd have a lot more motivation when I was in the middle of the fray. And if my newfound powers faltered once I was in the building, I had a new lighter and bottle of kerosene to speed things along.

I doused the flaming toilet paper with a spray of water in the sink and stepped out to find Snap waiting for me in the hall just outside. His eyes took me in with unusual intentness.

"Are you all right?" he asked.

My most devoted lover was nothing if not attentive. I rested my hand on his chest, smiling up at him. "Absolutely. We've got this."

He brushed his fingers over my hair, gazing at me with such affection that my heart skipped a beat for much more pleasant reasons. "I'll look after you out there too. Not just Thorn. I won't let anyone hurt you again."

"Hey, if I take any more bullets or break any more bones, that dryad can always patch me up again, right?"

When his intensity didn't soften at my teasing, I leaned even closer, trailing my hand up to his shoulder. "Don't worry. I'll be fine."

He hummed to himself. "You can't always be fine. But when you're not, I'll be there for you."

That simple but determined statement sent an echoing rush of affection through me. I tugged him to me for a proper kiss, but it didn't feel like enough.

I had to make sure I had my devourer's back too, like the sort-of agreement I'd made with Thorn. Hell, any one of my quartet and our new companions might need protection at some point, supernatural powers or not. I'd be ready if that happened.

With all final loose ends tied as tightly as we could manage ahead of time, we drove the RV out of the lot. I did my best not to fidget in my seat on the sofa. Pickle curled up on my lap, bumping his head against my stomach as if sensing the tension and attempting to reassure me. Omen paced from one end of the living space to the other with only a slight sway when the RV turned.

I'd sat myself down so I could see part of the view from the front windshield. The Finger came into view up ahead, a looming F-you against the dwindling dusk. The ring of lights around the outside of the courtyard barely touched the enormous statue. Halfway there.

My phone chimed. Vivi? I tugged it out as quickly as I could.

It wasn't my bestie's number but one I didn't recognize. I hit the answer button, a new thread of uneasiness already winding through my gut. "Hello?"

"Sorsha? Oh, good, I got you."

It took me a second to place the voice with its odd wavering distance. She must still be woozy from the medications the hospital would have doped her up on. "Ellen! How are you? You have to know I'm so—"

"Don't worry about that. That isn't—" She coughed. "You're right. These people—we can't let it continue. But I overheard—Leland was talking near the doorway—he said something about making sure you don't get anyone else hurt. It sounded as if... he meant to do something... something he probably shouldn't."

Something that had troubled the Fund's leader enough that she'd reached out to me despite her injuries. My throat constricted. "Thank you. I—I'll keep that in mind. You get some more rest, okay? We need you better."

As I lowered the phone, the Finger slid by outside the RV's windows. I'd just opened my mouth to say we needed to stop and take stock with this new warning when the roar of another engine penetrated the wall across from me.

The RV jolted and lurched to the side with a crunch of steel ramming steel.

24

Sorsha

The crash threw me back into the sofa cushions, my phone spinning from my fingers. I threw my arms over my head just in time to shield it as the entire RV careened over.

I tumbled toward the roof, and the window next to me shattered. Metal screeched as the vehicle skidded on its side across the asphalt.

"It's them!" I gasped out over the throbbing where my recently healed shoulder had slammed into a ridge in the wall. "The Company. They knew we were coming."

My shadowkind companions whirled around me, flashing in and out of the patches of darkness. Footsteps were thumping outside. "Can you get up, Sorsha?" Thorn hollered, and I shoved myself onto my feet, snatching up a trembling Pickle as I did. Given the way the Company had blasted our last two vehicles, I had no reason to believe I was safer in here than out there on the street.

Omen had already bashed the door open in what was now the ceiling of the toppled RV. I ran to it, and Thorn heaved me up onto the steel side that still, miraculously, looked like a city bus.

The others had darted outside through the shadows. Maybe it'd be better if they stayed there. Figures in typical Company of Light armor were rushing all around the RV, spilling from the armored truck that must have rammed us. "Get back, get back!" more distant voices were yelling at pedestrians who'd been nearby.

Taking in the chaos in those initial few seconds, my first chilling thought was that the shadowkind should leave me. Get the hell out of here as fast as they could, and let the Company take out their frustrations on the one being who couldn't slip away through the shadows. There were too many of the mercenaries—they'd caught us too off-guard—

But Thorn leapt out of the RV in his solid form without any hint of considering abandoning me. The swing of his fist gouged out the face of one soldier who'd been springing at me. As another clambered onto the overturned vehicle, he slammed his heel into the back of the man's head.

On the ground, someone... rode by on horseback? Holy mother of a mongoose, no, that was *Bow*, charging at our attackers with a battle cry and an actual bow notched with an arrow that seemed to have appeared alongside his full shadowkind form. His human-like torso emerged from the shoulders of a chestnut stallion's body.

With a scream that was somehow silvery sweet, another horse charged into the soldiers' midst—a graceful ivory animal with tassels of hair sprouting above her slender hooves and a brilliant horn sparkling where it jutted from her forehead. At least, it sparkled for the instant I saw it before Gisele stabbed her horn into a man's gut. The equines apparently had no intention of giving up their Everymobile without a fight.

The unicorn jerked back with a squeal of pain as the man's armor banged her. The twined metals left a black mark just below the slick of blood dripping from the rest of her horn.

"Come." Thorn hefted me onto his back, presumably to make our escape, but he'd only just jumped to the ground when a barrage of attackers came at him. As he whipped around to fend them off, the jolt of the abrupt motion loosened my grip. I tumbled onto the cobblestones of the courtyard.

I scrambled up, spinning this way and that in search of shelter or, better yet, a clear direction to flee in. As long as I was vulnerable, my companions would make themselves vulnerable protecting me. My gaze caught Snap blinking out of the darkness for just long enough to slap the gun from one soldier's hands—a gun that had been pointed my way.

Another attacker came at me swinging one of those horrible laser-like whips. I managed to duck under it and hurled myself at the guy's legs. We toppled together, his helmet falling off with a clang as it hit the ground. Omen hurtled past us in hellhound form with a slash of his claws to open the guy's throat.

But there were still more—still way too many fucking more of the pricks. I grabbed the dagger my latest attacker had strapped to his hip and pushed away from him just in time to see a clot of the Company soldiers tossing one of those glinting nets around Bow.

The centaur staggered to a halt with a clomping of his massive hooves. His captors closed in around him, and a jolt of horror rang through me. Without hesitating, I sprinted toward them.

The centaur shuddered in the toxic metals' grasp, and a furious heat surged through my body. I threw myself between two of the men holding the net, grasped one silver-and-iron strand, and propelled the searing sensation out through my hands with all the force I had in me.

The soldiers around the net yelped or barked with pain. Their hands jerked from the bindings, whiffs of burnt flesh reaching my nose. I wrenched at the net and managed to yank it off Bow before they recovered.

The centaur staggered away, shaking himself, and then wheeled with renewed resolve. As a couple of the men whose hands I'd barbequed launched themselves at me, Bow charged between them. One kick of his powerful hind legs shattered a man's hips. His fists sent the other reeling backward to meet Thorn's crystalline knuckles.

Was that the wail of a siren somewhere in the

distance? The Company of Light couldn't have stopped every spectator from calling in the crash and the following fight. Once emergency services got here, our attackers would have to skedaddle or start offering explanations I didn't think they wanted to. If they wouldn't give us room to make a dash for it, we just had to hold on that long.

I dodged one way and another, yanking off a helmet here, tripping an asshole there. My focus narrowed down to the flurry of combat around me and the thump of my pulse, hard but steady. Skewered lyrics to match its beat trickled through my mind and off my tongue. "Once I ran you through, now to stun some crew…"

The words buoyed my spirits. I tossed out a few more lines with the weaving of my body. An elbow to a nose here, with a satisfying crack. A knee to the balls there with an even more satisfying groan. "…And that's not nearly a-a-all!"

A mass of movement on the other side of the courtyard's immense wood-and-metal sculpture caught my eyes. A new wave of attackers was racing toward us from beyond the Finger. The streetlamp light glanced off their armor—and more nets, more knives, more guns. Shit.

My pulse hiccupped. Strength flared inside me. I shoved my arms forward, intending to hurl a tsunami of flames to stop them in their tracks.

What came out wasn't quite a tidal wave—more like a wavering. And that wavering firelight smacked mostly into the wooden struts of the looming statue rather than the attackers charging around it. Flames leapt up over the boards with a plume of smoke. I'd lit up one of the city's most beloved landmarks.

Oops.

Before I could attempt to summon any more of my fiery power, the second squad of Company soldiers was on us. Thorn, Omen, and Gisele ripped through the front lines, but more converged on us from all around.

Why the hell weren't those sirens getting louder faster? Couldn't they see the entire damn Finger was now blazing away, the flames licking higher than the buildings around the square?

Which, yes, was my fault, but do we really need to keep score here?

The shadowkind couldn't hold the front on all sides. An armored woman barrelled around the toppled RV straight at me. Her pistol shot went wide, but the next instant she was bashing the gun across the side of my head.

I stumbled but managed to punch her hard enough to compel a spurt of blood from her nose. Ruse flashed out of the shadows for long enough to kick her legs out from under her.

Another two attackers were already running at me. I knocked one back with an uppercut, but I wasn't fast enough to handle both. The second grasped my wrist and heaved me toward the blade he was holding—more silver and iron, it looked like, but those would sever my mortal soul from my body just fine if he filleted me with it.

I yanked away from him. The blade slashed across

my chest, slicing through my shirt and drawing a line of blood across my sternum and down my ribs. Pain spiked all across the cut.

I gasped and flailed again, but the man held on tight. My first punch dislodged his helmet, but he evaded my second and flipped the knife in his hand to plunge it straight into my heart.

Snap flickered out of the shadows in a flash of golden curls, his eyes wide and face pale with panic. "No!" He snatched at the blade and hissed through his teeth as it seared his fingers. My attacker landed a kick to the devourer's belly that sent him slamming into the underside of the Everymobile.

The mercenary spun back toward me. I lashed out with my free hand again, my fingers curled to claw out his eyes if I could, but he jerked me into the swing of his knee. It pummeled my gut so hard the world swam before my eyes. His blade rammed down—

And a sinewy figure loomed over the man with an unearthly shriek.

It was Snap. Even in my momentary daze, the golden curls and heavenly face were unmistakable. But his body had stretched, serpentine, to even greater heights. As I watched, his face stretched too, his chin lengthening to a sharp point. His eyes blazed neon green around the slits of his shadowkind pupils. Long, twig-like fingers clutched my attacker's shoulders.

Then his mouth yawned wide open, his jaw unhinging and dropping even farther to reveal rows of spindly gleaming fangs. With an audible creak that shivered through my nerves, he snapped them around the man's skull.

My attacker's eyes bulged. His own jaw dropped with what looked as if it should have been a scream, but the sound came out so thin and strained it barely split the air. It carried on and on as his face purpled. The scream got even thinner and higher but never ceased, as if the pain of whatever was happening was so great it'd seared through his voice. The hairs all over my body stood on end.

I'd gotten a front-row seat to the showing of why the shadowkind called my sweetly innocent lover a devourer.

25

Snap

T he kick to my gut and the slam of my back into the RV sent more shock than pain through my body. I'd kept to the shadows for most of our altercations before —I'd never felt what it was like to be tossed around in the fray.

An instinct shot through me to dodge back into the darkness where our enemies couldn't reach us. Then my gaze caught on Sorsha buckling at another blow from her attacker, his knife gleaming as he moved to stab it down into her—

No. The protest rang through my entire being. I'd promised to protect her; I'd promised I'd keep her safe. I couldn't let her loyalty to us bring her death.

She was *mine*—my peach, my Sorsha—and I refused to lose her.

I flung myself forward on a surge of alarm and

defiance. My hands clamped on the man's shoulders—and a very different instinct kicked in.

The shift into my full shadowkind form raced through me like a rough wind. Rising, lengthening, *sharpening*... I yanked the man backward into my hold and clamped my gaping jaws around his head.

The second my teeth pricked his scalp, a wallop of sensation drowned out the rest of the battle. I gulped flickers of memories full of color and sound and here and there a smell or taste: grass baking in the sun in a park, a scramble up the stinging surface of a slide, a party full of other children with flames dancing over a cake, a flush of shame as a presence—*Mommy*—snapped angry words.

Each shred flowed into me with an underlying quiver of resistance and agony as my jaws sheared the mortal's soul away bit by bit. That silent wail of pain was the seasoning on the feast, turning every moment I devoured more poignant. I drank it in with an answering clang of satisfaction all through my limbs.

It'd been too long. Years and years since I'd indulged like this that one time. How had I ever given it up?

More and more impressions flitted through me, now with little spasms of anguish through the man's body. I wrenched more and more from him, tearing away at his being particle by particle, swallowing it all down. A spilling of notes from a long, thin instrument under a spotlight on a stage. A kiss and a hot fumbling in a darkened parking lot. A lacing of heavy boots while a curt voice barked commands. All mine now—*mine, mine, mine.*

Slivers reached me of how he must have come to stand with the Company in their silver-and-iron armor. He'd brushed up against some sort of shadowkind creature—a man had spoken to him of a grave threat in tones that both soothed and terrified him. The promise of destroying the things he thought of as monsters pealed through him like joy until I tore it away.

I ripped more and more from him as if peeling off his skin in curls. The pain that mixed with the cocktail flooded faster in turn. That was mine too. None of it belonged to him any longer, not now that I had him in my grip. I would ravage him until nothing remained but a black hole of emptiness and the vast well inside me overflowed.

His soul was dwindling. The impressions had a tang of recency to them now, a little clearer and more vivid. Standing in a room with several humans who awed him— a sense of elation as someone said, *We'll hollow them out. Hollow the danger out of those beasts and make them ours* — the perfect sweetness of a summer plum, its juice dribbling down his throat—*It'll spread and claim them all. There'll be no stopping it once we have it right*—a looming mansion of gray brick with a turret rising from the righthand side, a place he was honored to protect— wind whipping past him as his legs pumped a bicycle— fading, fading, into a spiral of searing torment.

The torment *I* was causing. As the flow of sensations ebbed, more of my broader awareness crept back in. The physical stomach I'd nearly forgotten I had turned with a fit of nausea.

All the agony and horror reverberating through the final moments of this being's existence—I'd brought that on him. I'd wrung it through his *entire* existence, from his very first memories onward, as I'd savaged my way through them.

Even then, I couldn't will my jaws to open. I couldn't let go of that delectable thread until it petered out completely, leaving my prey nothing but a husk.

My jaws unlocked. The man collapsed as if boneless. I contracted back into the human form that fit this world better and found myself staring at Sorsha... who was staring back at me.

She'd fallen to the ground when I'd pulled her attacker off her. Her hands had tensed where she'd braced them against the pavement, the knuckles white. There was so much white in her eyes too, gleaming starkly. Her throat worked with a thick swallow.

Any pleasure I'd gotten from the devouring shattered into a thousand icy shards. Oh, no. That wasn't—I'd *sworn* I'd never again—

And yet underneath the chill, a tiny part of me wondered what it would be like to consume her existence too, every morsel that made her the fascinating woman I'd only barely scraped the surface of. The keening hunger pealed through me. I felt my tongue flick against my sharpened teeth before I could catch it. *Yes.*

My gut lurched, and the impulse vanished under a fresh wave of horror. A shout reached my ears alongside a blare of sirens—flashing lights at the other end of the courtyard.

The men in their poisonous armor were racing back to their truck and wherever else they'd come from. Thorn charged past me with a bellow to Omen. "Help me push!" He glanced at us. "Snap, Sorsha, get out of the way!"

I didn't know what he meant, but I scrambled in the other direction. Sorsha heaved herself to her feet and followed, her gaze sliding away from me. But I could still see her expression in my mind's eye: the shimmer of the whites of her eyes, the stiffness of her features.

She'd been looking at me as if I were a monster.

With a creaking and a thud, the RV righted itself. Or rather, Thorn must have pushed it upright with Omen's help. Ruse appeared at the window by the driver's seat. The engine growled, and he flashed a grin, but it faltered when he glanced outside.

Thorn and Omen had dashed back around the RV. As they rushed across the cobblestones, ignoring the hollers of the uniformed workers streaming out of the flashing vehicles beyond the blazing statue, Sorsha sprinted over to join them.

Bow was swaying toward us, smoke streaming from his injuries—but even more billowing from the crumpled form he held in his broad arms. Gisele lay limp, her shadowkind essence draining away into the night air in great gusts that showed no sign of slowing.

I leapt forward and then hesitated, torn about which direction it'd help more for me to go in. Omen solved that problem an instant later by waving me toward the RV. "Get on. We've got to take off, *now*."

I darted through the shadows to the living area, which had become a jumble of shattered window glass, leaves from the cupboards, and takeout cartons. Pickle huddled in one corner, shivering. When Sorsha dashed on board, she spotted him immediately and scooped him up. As she cuddled him against her, the others materialized on board.

"Go, now—go!" Omen yelled at Ruse.

More sirens were screeching nearby. The roar of the RV's engine couldn't drown them out, but it could carry us away from them. The vehicle heaved forward and tore down the street.

Sorsha's gaze followed Thorn and Bow as they rushed Gisele's battered form into the main bedroom. "Is there anything—"

"We'll do what we can, which might not be much," Omen snapped, barging past. "Too many hands will only make more confusion."

I guessed that applied to me too. I watched the door slam behind them and glanced down at Sorsha. Her face drawn, she slumped onto the sofa with the dragon. She was bleeding too in her human way from a cut partly visible through her slashed shirt. Her nerves had apparently calmed enough that her wound wasn't smoking, if it even had been before, like that time on the roof. It'd been hard to make out details in the dusk—and I'd been so caught up...

I wavered, wanting to reach out to her, afraid she'd cringe away from me.

Before I'd decided what to do, Sorsha extended her

hand to grasp mine. She tugged me down onto the sofa next to her and rested her head against my shoulder. "Thank you," she said. "For— That guy would have killed me."

Even with her saying that and with a pang of longing radiating through me to absorb even more of her warmth, I couldn't bring myself to put my arm around her. I'd saved her, yes, like I'd meant to do, but the way I'd done it— And there'd been a piece of me that had wanted to inflict the same torment on her for my own satisfaction.

She'd looked at me like I was a monster because I was one.

That thought filled my head, blotting out everything else. I'd tried so very hard to exorcise the ferociously hungry side of myself. The one time it had happened before, I hadn't known where the instinct would lead. I could have believed it was a mistake. Now I knew that wasn't true.

I was a devourer. I couldn't stop being one, no matter how long or thoroughly I denied the hunger. Sorsha was in danger while she stayed with us, yes, but not because of our enemies. Because of us.

Because of *me*.

I could hurt anyone around me if I was pushed the wrong way at the wrong time. Not just her but her friends, her colleagues... Maybe even my own companions. I had no idea how my power would work on a shadowkind, but that didn't mean it wouldn't.

The windows darkened as we left the brighter streets

of downtown behind. Omen and Thorn emerged from the bedroom, and Sorsha straightened up.

"She's not well, but she seems to have stabilized there," Omen said before she had to ask about Gisele. "We stemmed the bleeding. She hasn't regained consciousness yet. I'm not sure if she will."

As Sorsha muttered several colorful swear words under her breath, our leader's gaze shifted to me. Before he'd even spoken, the cool glint in them told me he'd seen my performance of my full powers.

"This might not have been a *total* catastrophe, thanks to Snap. Did you get anything useful from the one you devoured?"

I'd taken in so much. My mouth opened and closed again with the rush of memory and the sickening mix of relish and guilt it stirred up. I wanted to lick my lips and also to vomit.

"I think he was someone fairly close to the important people in the Company," I ventured. "It seemed as if he was there for meetings, hearing about some of their plans... something they're going to do to take away our powers, maybe?"

Sorsha's head jerked around. "That could be what the experiments are for—to figure out if they can destroy your abilities somehow."

"There was something else they said..." It was all a jumble now, and it hadn't totally made sense to me even as it was careening through my head. "Something they wanted to spread and 'claim'—but maybe that wasn't about us. I don't know." I paused. "I saw one building a few times that he was honored to have the chance to guard. Big with gray bricks and a turret on the right side, a lot of grass around it. I think a tall fence?"

"We didn't see anything like that when we looked at the places connected to the shell company," Ruse said, clearly following our conversation from where he sat behind the wheel.

"I don't know how it fits in," I said. "There might be more I'll piece together. It all comes so fast."

Omen squeezed my shoulder. "Let me know if anything else comes to you that stands out. More of it might make sense as we make additional discoveries via other avenues." He folded his arms over his chest. "They knew we were coming. They knew what bus to look for."

Sorsha tipped her head back against the sofa with a groan. "It was Leland—my ex, from the Fund. Ellen tried to warn me, but it was too late."

Thorn's expression managed to darken even more. "He told the Company our plans? I should have—He was listening at the hospital. He must have heard you tell the other woman we were making a move tonight. And then we were talking in the other room after. If he came over to the door, he might have heard some of that too."

"I think I mentioned the lot where we'd been staying with the bus. Shit." Sorsha's mouth pulled tight. "From the things Leland was saying at the last meeting, he figured *we* were the real villains, beating up on innocent humans. He must have decided he had to protect the Company from us."

"Mostly because he resented you caring what anyone

other than him wanted with you, not out of the goodness of his heart, I'd imagine," Ruse said in a disdainful tone.

A fiery sheen had lit in Omen's eyes. "Mortals," he spat out, and then raised his chin, his posture rigid. "We won't return to the same lot, then. What else did—"

"Sorsha's wounded too," I broke in. "Before you ask her any more questions, someone should see to that."

Not me. Someone who posed less of a threat.

While Thorn sprang to inspect her and grab bandaging supplies, Omen paced, and Ruse shouted suggestions from the front, I slipped away into the shadows. The mishmash of voices from the devouring still jostled in my head, but one fragment pealed clearer than the rest.

Hollow the danger out of those beasts.

My focus curled around the words as if they formed a lifeline. Could the Company do that? Could they carve out the pieces of me that made me truly a monster?

If they could, wouldn't it be worth the torture that came with it? It wasn't as if I didn't deserve to face the same agony I'd inflicted on my victims.

I pulled deeper into the darkness, stitching together a path through the impressions I'd devoured that might take me someplace where I wouldn't be a threat to anyone.

26

Sorsha

I woke up to a spray of grit pattering against my cheek. As I swiped it away, the morning sun seared my eyes through the broken window above me.

I'd fallen asleep on the RV's sofa, one arm cradling my head and the other tucked against my bandaged belly. I couldn't remember deciding to forego the actual bed—everything after the ramming of the armored truck into the Everymobile had turned into a blur.

Birds were chirping outside, and the next gust of wind brought a wash of pleasant warmth along with more grit. I sat up and squinted at the scene outside.

Right. Somewhere during our hasty flight last night, Ruse had switched the RV to its school bus setting. We'd parked in the lot outside a sprawling rural elementary school well outside the city limits. A stretch of trees beyond the lot blocked any view of the nearest buildings. On a Sunday, no one would be bothering us here.

At least, that should be the case. Leland might have overheard us talking about the city bus lot, but I didn't see how he could have figured out what glamours the RV held unless he'd developed some unexpected supernatural power too. The best we could figure, he'd directed the Company to keep an eye on the Lincoln Road lot last night, and they'd tracked what would have looked to them like a city bus until they'd been able to get into a suitable position to ambush us.

Lord only knew what the people around the square had thought of the chaos afterward.

Pickle leapt up from the floor and tucked himself close to me, resting his chin on my thigh. As I scratched between his ears, three of my higher shadowkind companions materialized in the living space around me. Ruse took a glance into the kitchen cupboards and appeared disappointed with his findings. Thorn surveyed the inside of the RV as thoroughly as I suspected he'd just been investigating the grounds outside, his expression typically grim.

Omen brushed his hands together. "We appear to have evaded any additional assaults for the time being, but I don't think we should count on that luck holding."

If you could even call what we'd experienced so far "luck." My gaze darted to the door to the master bedroom. "How's Gisele?"

Thorn grimaced. "Still unconscious. I've seen shadowkind in a similar coma a few times before when they're badly wounded... Sometimes they manage to regain enough energy to restore themselves, and sometimes they fade utterly into smoke in a couple of days."

"At least we had the RV to drive off in before the mortals ended her completely." Omen patted the wall. "You managed not to get one of our vehicles destroyed, Disaster. So far, anyway."

I wasn't in the mood to return his snark with more of the same. Bow must still be in the bedroom watching over his—friend? Wife? They'd never really clarified their relationship.

Shadowkind didn't tend to pair up in a romantic sense in their own realm, but for mortal-side enthusiasts, who knew what human customs they might have gone in for beyond the horse feed and the other kind of grass. Whatever the case, the centaur and the unicorn shifter clearly cared about each other a lot.

My stomach clenched at the thought that next time it might be one of my trio who drew the short straw in facing off against the Company. And speaking of that trio...

I glanced around. "Where's Snap?"

"Dozing in the shadows to sleep off that big meal, apparently," Ruse said with amusement. "Hey, devourer, time to rejoin the physical realm!"

No slim figure emerged to answer his call. Ruse cocked his head and vanished into the dark patches himself. When he returned several seconds later, still alone, the clenching sensation crept up to the base of my throat.

"He wouldn't have gone far," the incubus said. "He's always stuck close to the rest of us before. And we've all seen he's particularly stuck on you." He shot me a smile, but it was tense along the edges.

Thorn was frowning. "I didn't encounter him during my sweeps of the area around the school. Where would he go?"

"Perhaps he heard there was a country fruit stand nearby," Omen muttered, but his cool eyes betrayed more concern.

I got up to check the view from the windshield as if the others might have somehow missed him shooting hoops in the school yard. "When was the last time anyone saw him? I know he was in the RV with us when we took off from the square."

I'd held onto him briefly then, confirming to myself that he was still the same passionately gentle man I'd found myself welcoming into my bed and my heart—and doing my best to reassure *him* that I knew it. I might have been startled by seeing his full shadowkind powers in action, and what he'd done to that guy hadn't been pleasant to watch, but he hadn't used them lightly. His regret over taking that step had been written all over his beautiful face afterward.

Ruse's brow furrowed as he thought back to the previous night. "We talked about what he saw during his devouring. Then you two started patching up Sorsha's wound, and I don't think I heard anything from him after that. When we parked here for the night, I assumed he'd taken to the shadows to get some rest."

"We were focused on helping Sorsha and finding somewhere safe to pass the night." Thorn rubbed his chiseled jaw. His frown deepened. "I don't recall taking note of him after that initial conversation either. It never occurred to me that he might leave."

Fucking hell. A lump rose in my throat, almost choking me. "He was so ashamed of his power. You all saw the way he would react when it came up. He was so adamant that he'd never use it again, and then for him to feel like he had to..." Because of me.

It was all because of me, wasn't it? Leland had tipped off the Company because of his grudge against me. The shadowkind had stayed by the RV instead of escaping into the shadows to protect me. I should have been paying more attention to Snap after—I should have noticed he was slipping away from us.

I dropped my head into my hands. Pickle nuzzled my arm as if sensing my distress, but the gesture didn't give me much comfort. "Where would he have gone?" I asked the RV at large.

"I don't know," Ruse said. "I don't think he's been mortal-side long enough to have regular haunts."

Omen's voice had turned even flatter than usual. "If he isn't in his right mind enough to stay with us, he'll be easy pickings for any Company hunters prowling around. Let's hope we find him—or he finds his way back to us—before they do." His shoes scraped the floor as he swiveled. "You two take my bike back into the city. Try to follow the same route we took and watch for him. We also need to check the Wharf Street building so we know whether it's still a valid target."

I glanced up at him. "You're letting *Ruse* drive 'Charlotte'? What are *you* going to do?"

As Ruse and Thorn tramped out to detach the motorcycle from where Omen had clamped it to the back of the RV yesterday, hidden under the glamour, the hellhound shifter fixed his narrow gaze on me. "I've got to see how much more power we can drag out of you, mortal. If we've lost the element of surprise *and* Snap, we're going to need you outright blazing to take the Company down and get him back."

The last thing I felt like doing at this particular moment was tap dancing to Bossypants's tune, but the look he gave me warned off any arguments. And he might have a point. It wasn't as if I'd be doing Snap any good by sitting around and moping.

I marched after him out into the parking lot. He ushered me toward the school yard. Chalk marks from the previous week's recesses colored the pavement in pastels: creamy hopscotch boxes, jagged pink and purple flowers, a mint-green abomination of a kitten. That kid better not have any dreams of art school.

The yard gave us plenty of space to work with. The sprawl of pavement stretched all around the brick school building and out to a larger stretch of grass, where football goal posts jutted toward the clear blue sky. I rolled my shoulders and shook out my arms, trying to shed the guilt twisting through my innards.

"Okay, here we are. What crap are you going to put me through this time?"

Omen had turned to face me. His eyes flashed. "I hardly think you can call it 'crap' when it's gotten you this far. You could barely summon a spark to save yourself before, and last night you started a bonfire. It'd just be ideal if next time you could light up our enemies instead of random civic sculptures."

He motioned to a piece of blue construction paper the breeze was nudging across the ground, doodled with gawky stick figures. "Let's see if you can get a blaze started now without an immediate crisis hanging over you."

He didn't think Snap's disappearance was a crisis? Maybe I should try setting his shirt on fire again. But as much as my emotions were churning inside me, it wasn't the sort of distress that got my heart thumping. I glared at the shifter and then the paper, but no heat stirred beneath the gloomy funk that had come over me.

"What does this even matter?" I demanded. "We should be out there looking for Snap too—covering as much ground as we can."

"It appears he's been gone all night. He's got too great a head start if we head out on foot, and we only have one vehicle I feel comfortable sending back into the city to simply meander around, thanks to this friend of yours and his loose lips."

That provoked a flare, but of my temper rather than any voodoo. "He's not my friend. He's fucking *nothing* to me." Which was exactly what had pissed Leland off. How had I ever been attracted to anything about him?

He'd seemed normal. Safe, as long as there were no strings attached. Look how wrong I'd proven to be about that.

"Nonetheless, my point stands." Omen jerked his head toward the field. "Let's at least get your pulse going, then, and see if that's enough to jump-start your inner fire. Sprint between the goal posts a few times."

To my irritation, my feet started to move automatically. I caught myself and planted them on the pavement. "No."

The ice in Omen's gaze hardened. "No?"

"You heard me, Luce. N. O. You ran me ragged at the fairgrounds, and that got us diddly squat. The only thing you've actually tried that worked was dragging me around on your motorcycle, which you've already sent off with someone else—oh, and getting all houndish up in my face, if you want to see if I'll light *you* up again."

He sneered. "I'd like to see you try. Is that what you need—for me to get in your face? Rain a little hellfire down on you and see what catches?"

He stalked toward me, all controlled aggression, everything from his stance to his predatory expression setting off a clang of warning bells in my head. Maybe I should have taken the sprint while I had the chance.

Fuck that regret to Fiji and back. I wasn't letting him terrorize me, no matter what kind of deadly beast he was.

I backed up, but slowly, my hands rising as they clenched. "What do you think you're going to do to me, huh? Take a few swipes with those puppy-dog claws? Gnash your great big fangs? Somehow I'm not shaking in my boots yet."

"You should be," he snapped with a hint of a snarl that chilled my blood. Then he socked me right in the shoulder.

His fist wasn't chilly—it slammed into my body with a blast of otherworldly heat. Apparently *he* could blaze just fine even in human form.

I stumbled, clamping my teeth against a gasp as the impact radiated through the still-healing cut across my abdomen. Then I lunged right at him.

I wasn't totally sure what I was hoping to accomplish. I just wanted to pummel something or someone, and Omen was there acting like such a dick it was hard not to see him as an ideal target. I lashed out with my own fist, skimming his jaw as he dodged to the side. He gave me a shove—not too hard, just enough to send me staggering backward.

"Come on then, little mortal," he taunted. "Where's your fire now? Am I going to have to thrash it out of you?"

I didn't think so. As I circled him, my heart was thudding like the rhythmic pumping of bellows raising flames from a furnace's embers. My inner fire burned through my gut and trickled through my veins, turning me molten.

"Such a fantastic teacher," I shot back at him. "Five minutes in, and you're beating up on your only student."

"If it's the only lesson that'll work..." He feinted and snatched at me. His fingers bruised my arm as he yanked me toward him and spun me around. I barely wrenched myself out of the way of the kick he aimed at my ass. "Seems like you need a little more toughening up, anyway."

I swung at him, and he caught my knuckles. With a chuckle and a heave, he sent me stumbling sideways. "Nice try. Is that the best you can do?"

"You haven't seen anything yet. Let me remind you that I've done more for *your* people in the last few years than you've managed so far."

That blow landed even if the physical ones hadn't. An orange light flashed in his eyes, but his voice stayed tight. "If you think that, then why are you so afraid of giving this battle your all? Let that fire out, Disaster. Show me what you've got."

He came at me then like a hound unleashed, no sign that he intended to stop until I forced him to. His first smack across my cheek whipped my head to the side. The next sent a lance of prickling pain through my collarbone.

I did my best to block him, to dodge him, but I'd never fought anyone like this. My self defense classes had focused on a few quick moves to disable your attacker so you could run for the hills, and I couldn't land a single one of those against the onslaught of this shadowkind.

He must have been able to tell he was overwhelming me, but he didn't let up. A fist to my jaw. A heel to my toes. Fresh jolts of pain marked my body with every huff of breath he released.

The flames inside me flared hotter on the combined fuel of frustration and panic. I slashed my hand at him, and his sleeve caught fire. He slapped it out and pushed me toward the school building. "Not enough. Let's see more of that. I want to see *everything*."

The welling sense of power was starting to sear right through me from the inside out. Why couldn't he lay off me for one fucking second?

Why did Leland have to be such a vengeful asshole? Why hadn't I steered clear of him to begin with?

How could I not have realized Snap needed more from me last night?

Such a fucking mess. Burn it down. Burn it all down.

The urge rolled over me in a wave so visceral it brought a jab of terror with it. The certainty gripped me that if I gave Omen what I was asking for, if I let loose everything that was raging inside me, I could burn even this man with all his powers to a crisp.

A flare of heat slipped out—a flame shot up from a tuft of his hair that had risen from the slicked-back strands. He shook it away and punched my other shoulder. "Still not seeing what makes you so great."

"I don't think you want to. I don't think you'd survive it."

"Oh, ho, big talk from the mortal." He swiped at my temple, hitting me hard enough to send my thoughts reeling. "Try me, then."

The heat scorched my throat. I couldn't swallow it down. My rising terror flickered higher alongside those flames. "No, Omen, I really don't think—"

"Come *on*, Disaster! Why can't you do this one thing? Or were all those grand rescues before, letting out the collectors' prizes, only about the glory of pulling the capers off? Don't you care whether you can help any more shadowkind? Or whether we ever see Snap again?"

"Don't *you*?" I burst out. "All I see is a fucking bully who doesn't have a clue what he's doing if he can't badger everyone around him into falling into line. As far as I can tell, you're the problem here, not the solution."

A growl escaped him, and suddenly he was *really* on me, hurling me into the wall with a slam that spiked pain all through my back. He pinned me there, the thrust of his hands nearly shattering my wrists, his eyes burning and his teeth bared. His hot breath spilled over my face.

There—there was the beast I knew was in him. Somehow seeing his cold front fall away dampened the fury in me.

Not so much for Omen. He wrenched himself back a step a moment later, cursing under his breath. His hair had bristled; his chest was heaving. He blinked, but the orange haze wouldn't quite clear from his eyes.

I let my arms drop to my sides. He leaned in again, his palm against the bricks just inches from my head, his conflicted gaze holding mine.

"What is it about you that you always have to bring out the worst in me?" he asked in a ragged voice.

"I don't think this is the worst," I said honestly. "Right now? You feel like you're being real. I *like* you angry— way better than I like the ice-cold prick who orders people around from his high goddamned horse, anyway."

He guffawed, the sound equally raw. "You like me

better when I'm on the verge of literally biting your head off."

I shrugged, my shoulders scraping the wall. I might have liked him better, but I still valued my life too much to try to push past him right now. My anger had dwindled, but fear was alive and well, thrumming through my pulse. "It's become increasingly clear to me that I have unusual tastes. But yeah, I do. Although I'd also prefer that you didn't actually bite my head off, if it's all the same to you."

Omen's own head bowed, dipping closer so his forehead almost grazed mine. The heat of his body radiated over me. It wasn't entirely unpleasant, to tell you the truth.

Yep, the poster girl for unusual tastes, right here.

"If you had any idea how hard I've worked to get here..." he muttered.

"Get where?" I asked. "The state of being an asshole?"

"See, that— You—" He let out another growl, but it was a subdued one this time. Then he eased back just a little. A flicker of something I hadn't seen in him before crossed his expression. Was that... concern?

He fingered the side of my shirt, his fingertips brushing my side for the briefest of seconds. "I opened your wound again."

I glanced down, more surprised than I should have been by the streak of bright red spreading across the center of the bandage. The sight of it brought the sting of the wound into sharper awareness. My mouth twisted.

"Well, hey, what's it matter if another mortal is spouting blood, right?"

Omen's tone was gruff but firm. "You know you're more than that."

I supposed I did. And that was clearly the only reason he cared—because of my superpowers and how they might help his cause. "I'm sure I'll survive, because or in spite of that."

"No doubt." He hesitated, still looming over me by the wall, as if he couldn't quite tear himself away but also didn't know what he was doing there. "I was taking out frustrations I shouldn't have directed at you, at least not entirely. I wish... that I'd been less of an 'ice-cold prick' toward Snap lately. Maybe he thought he'd crossed some line I wouldn't abide by, and I'd made him feel he couldn't even check with me to see where he stood."

I would have laughed if I hadn't been so shocked that Omen was lowering himself to admitting any regrets at all. "You think I haven't been beating myself up as much as I tried to beat up you? If I'd been more careful what I said around my ex—if I'd paid more attention to the state Snap was in last night—"

Omen interrupted me with a hoarse chuckle. "Suffice to say there's plenty of blame to go around. Maybe you didn't send me up in flames, but you put up a pretty good fight."

I guessed that was a high compliment coming from him. I wasn't completely comfortable with the flames that *had* been surging through me just minutes ago, though. If

I'd let myself hurl the full force of them at him, just how bad would it have been?

Then he raised his hand to my hair, and those thoughts fell away. My awareness condensed to the warmth of his knuckles grazing my cheek as he fingered a few stray strands—not so different from how Snap had the first morning we'd met.

Omen's gaze slid from his hand against my face to my eyes. The fiery light had faded from his, but the pale blue didn't look quite so icy now. I found my hand drifting forward to rest against his chest, taking in the slowing rhythm of his breaths beneath the taut muscles.

What the hell was I doing? I couldn't tell you. Whatever it was, it seemed to draw Omen nearer. He leaned in, his fingers sliding down to stroke across my chin, and a new pulse of heat flared in my lips. I wet them, my pulse kicking up a notch, not entirely sure what I wanted but wanting it *very* much at the same time.

His breath tickled over my face. Then he shoved the hand he'd leaned against the wall to push completely away from me, his gaze jerking toward the RV.

"We should get you patched up again before you make any more of a mess of yourself, Disaster," he said, back to business as usual.

I peeled myself off the wall with only a smidgeon of disappointment. Whatever line *we'd* come close to crossing just now, I couldn't help suspecting it might be better if we stayed on this side of it.

"And then back to training?" I suggested.

Omen shook his head. "No. I think we've both had

enough of pushing you around. I know you'll fight as well as you can when the need is there."

I wasn't sure whether to be relieved or insulted by him throwing in the towel. I was trudging after him toward the Everymobile, debating just how suicidal I'd be to put up an argument, when the door flew open and Bow stared out at us.

"Please—Gisele—I think she's getting worse."

27

Sorsha

O ther than a glimpse as the other shadowkind had hustled her onto the RV, I hadn't seen Gisele since the start of the battle. At the sight of her lying crumpled in the master bedroom, horror overwhelmed any sense I'd had of my own discomforts.

Her slim, graceful body had deflated, limbs limp and cheeks sunken. What skin I could make out had lost its pearly sheen to a creeping gray undertone, as if her entire being had clouded over. Most of her, though, was covered with rough fabric wrapped tight and dappled with yellow-green smears.

From what the shadowkind had said, those bindings had stabilized her before. Now, thin trails of smoke were seeping through the cloth. Omen took one look at her and made a noise of consternation.

As he grabbed a jar off the bedside table, Bow

hovered uneasily nearby. "I wasn't sure if it was a good idea to put on even more..."

"We do this and give her a chance to recover, or she leaks away into nothingness," Omen said. "It's not much of a choice."

I didn't understand why there was any debate at all until he started slathering the pale green paste from the jar onto the bandages. Gisele's face remained flaccid, but her arms twitched, her shallow breaths stuttering. Bow winced and turned away as if he couldn't bear to watch.

"It's hurting her?" I asked quietly.

"The herbs in the salve are toxic to shadowkind," the hellhound shifter said without looking up from his task. "Normally we'd avoid them—they'd weaken us. But in a case where someone is already severely weakened and in danger of wasting away, in small amounts they can repel our essence back into the body. The hope is that before too long, that body can heal itself enough to stem the bleeding on its own."

The treatment was poisoning her as much as it was curing her. My stomach turned. But Omen's efforts had clearly accomplished their goal—the wisps of smoke faded away. A tremor ran through Gisele's body, and then it sagged even more lifelessly into the mattress.

Bow was swiping at his eyes. He sat down onto the bed next to her, the haggard expression on his usually jovial face almost as painful to look at as his companion was. Omen set down the jar with a sharp rap. He stalked out of the room to wash his hands with a hiss of the faucet and returned a moment later, brushing his reddened fingertips against his pants. The stuff had burned his skin too.

"Next time, you start applying the salve the moment you notice any seepage. She can barely afford to lose the little essence she still has."

The centaur's head drooped more, but he nodded. "I'm sorry. I—I panicked. We've never gotten more than a scratch here before. I didn't know what it would be like."

"This is war," Omen said. "Don't imagine it can't get worse." His tone softened just slightly. "We'll continue doing what we can for her. I've put a call in to a dryad with healing skills—if he's willing to stick his neck out this far after we've become such a target. I'm not sure how much even he'd be able to help her at this point as it is. She seemed strong. She may manage to pull through."

He spun around, and I followed him back to the living area.

"If she starts bleeding again, I could put the salve on," I said. "It wouldn't hurt me at all."

Omen glanced at his fingers, where the flush of irritation was already fading. "It's a minor discomfort. Better that I handle it, or Thorn—we can judge what's a reasonable amount from how it affects us."

"I guess you have experience with this sort of thing from the wars before."

He gave me a sharp look. "Not something Thorn would want you discussing with anyone else."

I grimaced at him. "I figured *you're* safe enough, since he told me you were there. You already know what he is."

"That's hardly—"

An engine sounded outside, and he cut off whatever other criticism he might have added with a rough breath. "Enough of that. Charlotte's back—and let's hope our wingéd, our incubus, *and* our devourer are with her."

Had the others found Snap? As I hustled to the door, my heart leapt with more hope than I knew was sensible.

When I stepped out onto the pavement, Ruse was just driving the motorcycle into the lot. He parked it, and Thorn emerged from the shadows around the undercarriage where he must have been riding—alone.

"No sign of Snap," the warrior reported to Omen without preamble. "And no sign of activity at the Wharf Street factory either. I ventured inside, and it appeared to have been very recently gutted."

Omen swore. "They guessed that was our target."

"This Leland twerp could have told them everything the Fund was looking into on Sorsha's behalf," Ruse said. "Everything her friend discovered at the fundraising gala."

"Then we can assume that anything important they were keeping at the other locations under that shell company has been cleared out or will be shortly too." The shifter started to pace. "In some ways that could be good. We've got them on the run; they'll be getting short on property where they can carry out their operations and stash their prisoners. They may be having to cut corners on certain security measures to avoid places we might know about."

"Except they'll be cutting it at places we *don't* know about," I couldn't help saying.

"Yes, that is the primary problem."

Was that my fault too? We wouldn't have known to make that factory a target if I hadn't gotten Vivi and the Fund involved in the first place, so... maybe it all evened out on the scale of horribleness and personal responsibility?

That thought didn't exactly lift my spirits.

Thorn stepped forward, worry turning his expression even more somber. "Sorsha, you're bleeding again."

Oh, right. Gisele's much more urgent injuries had diverted Omen and me from the whole patching-Sorsha-up plan. I set my hand on the top of the bandage. "It just needs a change of dressing. I'll be fine. It only stings a little." And maybe there was a bit of throbbing in there too after all this bustling around, but he didn't need to know that.

Despite my reassurances, the warrior ushered me back into the RV like some kind of hulking matron. As he unwrapped the wound, he tutted under his breath. He added a few careful stitches where a couple Omen had sewn in last night had broken and dabbed antiseptic cream over the whole slash. When he'd wrapped a layer of gauze around the new sterile pad, Ruse set a paper bag on the table by the sofa. I straightened up, a buttery, cheddar-y scent reaching my nose.

"I liberated some breakfast for you," the incubus said, his tone jaunty but his hazel eyes darker than usual as they lingered on my face. "I know it's no substitute for our beloved devourer, but you do need to look after the inside of your belly as well as the outside."

I couldn't deny that—and on a better day, my mouth would have been watering at the savory smell. "Thank you," I said, unwrapping a breakfast sandwich of biscuit, egg, and melted cheese. It sure beat hay-and-clover salad.

As I took a bite, the two remaining members of my original trio stood on the other side of the table like stalwart guardians—or wardens, ensuring I didn't leave until they were satisfied I'd taken care of myself. The crumbly pastry dissolved on my tongue, and the cheese added the perfect amount of bite to the creamy scrambled egg. For a guy who used human sexual satisfaction for sustenance, Ruse was an excellent judge of actual food.

But each gulp stuck in my throat before dropping into the hollow in my gut. I'd only made it halfway through the sandwich when the lump expanding inside me felt almost too heavy to bear.

I set the sandwich down, figuring I could at least take a breather, and Thorn's brow knit. "You don't look well. Your sleep can't have been satisfactory lying on that bench all night. You should take some rest in your bed."

"I'm really not—"

"No arguments, this once," he said, and swept me off the sofa into his bulging arms as if I weighed no more than Pickle did.

"Thorn," I protested, ineffectually trying to squirm out of his hold. Exerting just enough strength to stop me from bending at the torso and straining my wound again, the warrior marched me to the second bedroom without a word.

"Sleep tight!" Ruse called after us with audible amusement.

Thorn set me down gingerly on the bed. When he moved to leave, a more piercing resistance shot through me. My throat closed up, and my arm darted to grasp the side of his shirt before he could get very far.

"If you want me to rest, you'd better stick around and make sure I do."

Thorn peered down at me. "Sorsha..."

I tugged on his shirt. "I'm not tired, just worried and upset and..." I had to pause to steady my voice. "I don't really want to be alone right now."

The firmness in the warrior's expression vanished under a wash of tenderness. He sank down onto the edge of the bed next to me and managed to make only a small disgruntled sound when I pushed myself into a sitting position.

I tucked myself against Thorn's broad, solid chest. His musky smell with its trace of smoke filled my nose, and when his arm came around my shoulders, his warmth enveloped me too.

Having him with me like this didn't make up for Snap's disappearance any more than the breakfast sandwich had, but in the power coiled through his brawny body, I could feel the certainty that he wouldn't give up until the devourer was back with us where he belonged.

Thorn held cautiously still for a moment and then allowed his hand to stroke up and down my arm from shoulder to elbow. He tipped his head so his chin rested against my temple. "Snap was incredibly dedicated to our cause—and, from what I saw recently, to you. If he can make it back to us, I doubt he'll stay away very long. And if those bastards have imprisoned him, we'll get him back. They didn't manage to break Omen in all those weeks."

"I know," I said. But Snap wasn't Omen. He meant so well, and he felt things so deeply. "I was startled... and maybe a little scared when I saw his full form. With how horrible he feels about devouring already, he might have convinced himself *I* think he's horrible."

Thorn grunted. "He couldn't believe that for very long if he's been paying any attention at all. I'm no expert in affection, but *I* could see how much you cared for him. He means a lot to you."

"You all do." As the words spilled up, the truth of them swelled inside me. When the trio had shown up out of nowhere in my kitchen, I'd seen them as nothing but a hassle. Now, it was hard to imagine going on with regular human life once this was over and never seeing them again.

Thorn's hesitance to accept the affection I was offering *him* even after I'd asked him to stay twisted me up inside even more. I raised my head to gaze up into his ruggedly handsome face. "You realize that, don't you? That if something happened to you—if you left or the Company hurt you—I'd be just as upset as I am over Snap."

He opened his mouth and closed it again as he appeared to gather his thoughts. His dark eyes held mine. "I don't have the gentleness and joy the devourer exudes

—I can't offer the incubus's skill with words or caresses. How could I expect to provoke the same fondness they do?"

I made a dismissive sound. My hand came up so I could trace my fingers over the faint lines of the scars that framed his face. "You know, *they're* the outliers. I never really went for cheerful sweethearts or suave smooth-talkers before. Give me a strong silent type any day."

He grunted doubtfully.

I tapped his cheek. "I've seen how much emotion you carry under that stoic front. I've never known anyone, human or shadowkind, half as resolute or loyal as you."

"Only to make up for where I failed in the past."

"I'm not convinced you actually screwed up so very badly back then in the first place, but believe me, an awful lot of human beings go through their much shorter lives totally disregarding the people they let down along the way." Or even lashing out at those people as if they were to blame. Thorn—and Ruse and Snap, and maybe even Omen—was worth a thousand Lelands. When you compared him and his vengeful sabotage to them, how could you say the shadowkind were more monstrous?

My tastes might be unusual, but why the hell should I want a generic jerk when I could have a magnificent monster—or, you know, three?

Thorn brushed a lock of my hair behind my ear, the skim of his fingers tingling over my skin. His voice dropped to a husky note that sent those tingles deeper. "You contain plenty of tenacity yourself, m'lady. A steely will and yet so much compassion as well. You were a worthy ally before we knew you had any unearthly power."

"Only an ally?"

His hand teased along my jaw in answer, tipping up my chin so he could claim my lips. I hadn't known how much I needed this until I was kissing him back, melting into the planes of his muscular frame.

His mouth branded mine, as determined as if he were pouring all the affection he had for me into that one kiss. His fingers trailed down my back, tucking me closer to him, and my knee slid up over his thigh. A rush of heat flooded me.

Yes. Yes. Just for this moment, I wanted to revel in what I still had instead of brooding over what I'd lost. I wanted to see that steely, compassionate woman Thorn took me for reflected in his eyes.

I shifted even closer, running my hand over his chest, and drew my lips from his just far enough to say in a voice so thick with need I barely recognized it, "Thorn, can we—"

The desire ringing through the words must have said enough before I even finished the question. Thorn grasped me and swung me right onto his lap, capturing anything else I might have said with another kiss. As I straddled him, he stroked my thigh while his other hand tangled in my hair.

I slid forward, and my sex settled against the substantial bulge of his groin. Even through the layers of fabric, the feel of that hardness was enough to make me groan.

I arched into him, extending the friction, and Thorn groaned too. His mouth plundered mine, but there was still a carefulness to the way he held me, even as the squeeze of his fingers around my thigh urged on my rocking against him.

He eased my face back an inch, still close enough that the heat of his breath flooded down my neck. His voice came out strained. "I don't want to hurt you, Sorsha. This body is made for fighting, not love-making."

I'd seen how large my warrior was in *every* area a few weeks ago when he'd sprung out of the shadows nude. The memory only spurred on the ache of need between my thighs. "I think it's made for whatever you decide to do with it," I murmured, splaying my hands against his abdomen. "Let me worry about how much I can handle. If anything's too hard or too fast or too... large"—my palm slid over his erection—"I'll let you know. But so far I have no complaints."

"As m'lady wishes," he breathed in return. It came out like a prayer, so different from the reluctant tones with which he'd once offered that term of respect that delight trembled through me.

I stripped off his tunic, eager to see all that sculpted flesh on display again, and he managed to tug my blouse open above the bandage on my stomach with surprising deftness, though his thick fingers fumbled with my bra. I unhooked it for him and gasped as his hands engulfed my breasts. The swivel of his calloused palms against my nipples raised them to points with a surge of bliss. The sensation shot to my sex, and the lingering pain of my wound hazed away in the wake of that pleasure.

I kissed Thorn again, still rocking against him, the heat between us turning searing. I'd waited too long to get this intimate with the last of my lovers—I had no patience left. My mouth skidded against his lips, a whimper tumbled from my throat at the powerful sweep of his thumbs over my breasts, and then I was groping at the ties of his trousers.

Sweet simmering symphonies, medieval clothing was a devil to unravel. At my muttered curse, Thorn let out a chuckle and flicked the knot loose as if it were nothing— through some supernatural voodoo, I was sure. I didn't spend much time worrying about it, because the next second I'd delved inside his underclothes to free that massive cock.

It was magnificent, thick and corded with veins and so fucking hard I thought he might explode as I gripped it. His erection twitched at my touch, and a ragged breath shuddered out of the warrior.

"M'lady," he whispered, and that time it sounded like a plea. One I was all too happy to answer. We could play around with more possibilities some other time.

There would be other times. I swore it by whatever was still true in my soul.

I scrambled out of my jeans and panties, and Thorn pulled me to him, the strength even in that controlled gesture taking my breath away. I ran my fingers up and down his cock. He kissed me so hard his teeth nicked my tongue, and then I lowered myself onto him with as much haste as my body allowed.

Just the head of his cock penetrating my slit stretched me more than I'd ever experienced. I stopped there, adjusting. Pleasure pulsed through me as my channel relaxed to accommodate him.

The warrior was a perfect gentleman, as torturous as the wait must have been for him. He kissed the side of my neck and massaged my breasts, adding to the blissful sensations coursing through me.

I sank a little lower and a little lower still, each inch stretching me farther with a burn that was increasingly ecstatic. My head tipped against Thorn's shoulder, sweat dampening my brow. "You feel so good," I said, my lips brushing his skin. My fingers teased over his belly, his pecs, his pert nipples, any way I could pay him back for the intense pleasure he was offering me with his patience.

Another groan slipped out of him. "As do you."

The impulse flitted through me to feel all of him pressing down on me, to lose myself in the surge of that massive body over and inside me, but I wasn't sure I was quite ready for that yet. I settled for dropping even lower, a pleased sound reverberating from my chest.

I felt full to bursting in the most giddying sense. The only question left was how well we could move together.

I eased up and down, up and down, a little more each time. The bond between us turned slick with my expanding arousal. As I hit a rhythm, Thorn found the confidence to raise his hips to meet me, gently at first and then, when he saw how I whimpered at the additional motion, with more force.

I bit my lip, struggling to hold in the louder cries of pleasure that wanted to peal from my lungs. The walls in the RV weren't thick enough to disguise those without Ruse's soundproofing magic.

I didn't have to hold them in very long. The ecstasy building inside me was spiking higher, racing me toward my peak with a momentum I couldn't rein in. I bucked against Thorn, clutching his shoulder, his side, and he was right there to meet me. His lips crashed into mine, the thrust of his hips sent me spiraling even higher, and I came so hard my vision whited out with the flare of bliss.

As my sex clenched around him, the warrior's fingers dug into my thigh. He jerked me to him, impaling me so deeply his cock set off a second orgasmic wave just as he spilled himself inside me.

I sagged into him, alight with the afterglow. Thorn cupped my cheek and kissed me with a softer determination. As I nestled against his broad chest, the doubts and self-recriminations that had gripped me earlier scattered into the distance.

I was strong—hell, yes, I was. Strong enough to take a legendary warrior as my lover. No shitty ex was going to beat me down.

Leland had used the conflict with the Company of Light to act out his resentment against me. Maybe it was time to turn the tables right around and see how we could use *him*.

28

Sorsha

O men watched me climb onto the motorcycle behind Ruse with obvious reluctance. I gave him an optimistic thumbs-up. "Don't worry! We'll take care of Charlotte."

"I don't think you'd enjoy finding out what'll happen if you don't," he retorted, but he turned away rather than continuing to stew about the situation. This plan required only Ruse and me, and as much as the hellhound shifter might have wanted to tag along to supervise from the shadows, it didn't really make sense to put anyone else at risk. The Company people were a hell of a lot more likely to notice us in the city than way out here in the middle of nowhere.

In my attempt to avoid drawing their notice, I fit the helmet the incubus had been kind enough to obtain for me over my head, where a black knit hat already hid my red hair. Ruse sported a helmet himself, a situationally appropriate way to disguise his horns. He gave Omen's retreating back a salute, patted my knee to confirm my position against him, and gunned the engine.

It was way easier to relax against the incubus's lean back than when I'd been clinging to Omen yesterday. For one, Ruse didn't drive the bike like a, well, demon. He might not have been the smoothest at lane changes, but he was concerned enough about keeping a low profile to stick to the same speed as the cars and avoid any flashy moves.

And considering how intimate we'd gotten on multiple occasions, I didn't have a whole lot of modesty left when it came to having my arms wrapped around his chest or my thighs pressed against his hips.

He followed the directions I'd given him to Leland's townhouse without a hitch. The sight of the narrow, gray building on the end of the row made my chest constrict.

How many times had I rung that doorbell ready for a quick jump in the sack—a dozen? Twenty? It had never felt like anything other than scratching an itch, and then even that enjoyment had turned sour with Leland's caustic disappointment in me.

My current feelings toward him went well past sour and into "raze it to the ground" territory, but I wasn't here to mess with his living space. At least, not yet. We'd see how this visit went first.

I knew my ex-friends-with-benefits's schedule well enough to have anticipated that he'd be at the gym on a Sunday afternoon. We left the bike a couple of blocks over and slunk into Leland's backyard, Ruse sticking to the shadows now. As I waited for him to slip inside and unlock the door for me, I set my shoulders, gathering my chutzpah.

We had a plan—one that should get us to Snap if the Company had grabbed him. No uncomfortable memories were going to shake me out of accomplishing that. Leland had no idea what he'd set himself up for.

Ruse opened the door with a little bow, and I marched inside.

Had the place always held this stale grease smell? Maybe I'd never been close enough to the kitchen before to notice it. Wrinkling my nose, I passed through the space with its tarnished steel appliances and into the living room off the front hall where I intended to wait.

I clearly hadn't spent enough time on the first floor in general, or the framed photographs along the mantel would have been a tip-off that this guy wasn't worth my time even as an easy lay. Each of those photographs was of Leland, on his own: posing at an amateur weight-lifting competition, leaning over beneath the open hood of a car I doubted he had the slightest idea how to fix, giving a victory sign on the deck of a speed boat. He might as well have built a little shrine to his ego—a testament to how much he thought the world should revolve around him alone.

Ruse ambled over to contemplate them closer up. "Such a catch," he teased. "What a mistake you made in letting this fine specimen go. At least, *he* clearly thinks he's the finest specimen around."

"No kidding." I socked him lightly in the shoulder. "No need to rub it in. I did find the good sense to move on to greener pastures."

The incubus wiggled his eyebrows. "And I've been delighted to plow you." As I choked on a laugh, one of those eyebrows arched higher. "Speaking of which... I take it you got something other than grumbles and glowers out of our Incredible Hulk."

My interlude with Thorn. A faint flush crept up my neck. "We tried to be quiet."

"Don't worry your lovely head about that. I have especially keen senses when it comes to my area of expertise. I lent a little magic to give you the privacy I figured you'd want to have."

"Oh. Thank you." I paused. "That didn't require you to be in the room, did it?"

Ruse held up his hands. "I enjoy participating in the act, not so much watching it from afar. Consider the favor my contribution to the public good. Thorn's needed a good lay for at least a few centuries, I'd estimate."

I socked him again, but his banter had helped distract me from my uneasiness in this place. When Snap and I had gotten close, the incubus had told me that he was happy for me to seek pleasure wherever I could find it. It sounded like that applied to the warrior as well, as much as their attitudes tended to clash.

The gaudy brass clock standing between the photos showed it was quarter past three. "Leland will be here soon," I said. "You'd better stay out of sight until I give the signal that his badge is off." I didn't know whether he'd be wearing it just to walk around the city, but after screwing us over as badly as he had yesterday, I wouldn't be surprised to find him extra cautious.

Ruse nodded and vanished. I prowled around the living room until I found an ideal spot where I could crouch beside a side table. The position gave me a clear view of the hall so I'd know what I was dealing with before I sprang into action, but should hide me from a casual glance. Then all I had to do was wait.

As the minutes ticked by, I twisted a lyric and sang softly into the silence. "Waiting for that final woe sent, you'll say the words that lie and prey." Leland would probably claim siccing our enemies on us had been a heroic act. Well, he'd lost any hope of screwing me months ago, and now he was going to lose any chance of screwing *us* over again.

Ruse blinked into the physical space just long enough to say, "He's coming down the street," and then vanished again. I tensed in my hunched pose. My fingers curled toward my palms.

A key clicked in the lock. Leland strode in, all puffed up on an endorphin high from the weights he'd have been hefting. As he tossed his gym bag to the side of the hall, his shirt shifted, and I caught a glint of silver at its V neckline. He was wearing his protective badge pinned to an undershirt like I often did. No other metallic gear gleamed on his person.

That was all I needed to know. I sprang up and leapt across the few feet between us.

Leland stiffened in surprise—wrong reflex, dude.

"Sorsha," he sputtered, and I was already on him, smacking his defensive hand away with a quick swipe while I yanked on his shirt. With one swift jerk, the badge snapped off the layer of cotton underneath. I flashed it through the air to signal Ruse.

"What the fuck are you doing?" Leland snapped, lunging at me. Too bad he spent all his gym time bulking up and not developing his inner Jack Be Nimble. I darted out of the way just as Ruse materialized in the space between us.

"Hello, my friend," the incubus said in his most cajoling tone, so strung through with supernatural power I could feel the vibration of it in the air. "As you can see, we're all going to get along here. We came out of concern for your well-being —you need to listen to us or you could be in grave danger."

Leland swayed on his feet, his boyish face tensing. The voodoo hadn't totally enraptured him in one go. "You're one of the shadowkind she's working with. I don't think you should be here. Either of you. You—"

Ruse held up his hands in a placating gesture. "We'll certainly leave as soon as we've settled things with you. You've been in contact with very malicious people, and we couldn't bear to see you get hurt because of that. I know you and Sorsha have had your differences, but can't you see how much she still cares for you?"

I fought back the urge to glare at him for that remark and gave Leland the sweetest smile I could summon. Which probably wasn't very sweet, since I was also inclined to puke on the jerk's shiny trainers at the idea of caring about him, but it appeared to be enough to smooth Ruse's spell along.

"I always knew she must, somewhere in there," Leland said, peering back at me with his own smile, which was so self-satisfied I nearly did puke.

Thankfully, Ruse stepped in before any expelling of bodily fluids became necessary. As he nodded, a sly thread crept into his voice. "And you must care about *yourself* enough to prioritize your safety, no? Look at this magnificent display of your past achievements." He motioned to the photos on the mantel.

Leland's gaze followed the gesture. "We have to celebrate our victories," he said. "Pep ourselves up to take on even more. Or to step in when other people are going too far." He glanced back at me, drawing himself up with a pompous air. "You were ruining people's lives. I couldn't stand back and let that happen."

I bit my tongue to avoid pointing out that *he'd* potentially ruined dozens of lives by enabling the Company's attack and preventing us from freeing their captives. As much as he'd pretended to care about defending the shadowkind, their lives clearly didn't mean all that much to him. Maybe he only saw them as worth protecting when they were small and inept. Maybe it'd always been about gaining a sense of magnanimity and never about kindness at all.

Ruse grinned. Confident he now had the other guy completely under his sway, he pointed Leland to the photos again. "I need to see just how dedicated you are to yourself before I know how we can help you. Take your favorite image and give yourself a kiss."

"*Ruse,*" I whispered in protest. We had more important things to do here than goof around with my ex on puppet strings.

The incubus ignored me, and it *was* kind of satisfying watching Leland rush to grab the photo of himself on the boat deck and give it a hearty smooch. My lips twitched despite myself.

Ruse applauded. "Perfect. Now, do you think you could show us a headstand? It's very important for ensuring we give you the most helpful strategies for protecting yourself..."

Leland was already bending over to set his head on the rug. He braced himself and heaved his bulky legs into the air. They flailed this way and that for a few seconds before he toppled over onto the rug with an audible *whoomph*. Then he was leaping up again as if ready for another go.

I elbowed Ruse. As much as I'd like to watch my ex make a fool of himself for hours, we were here on business, not pleasure.

"All right, all right," the incubus said, and motioned Leland over. "Just one more thing I'd like to check. If you wanted so much for Sorsha to offer you the full girlfriend experience, why didn't you romance her like a boyfriend would? An honest answer, please."

Leland's expression turned vaguely puzzled, but he was charmed enough to answer without balking. "Why should I have to put in that work first if she didn't appreciate what she already had? I didn't hear any complaints about our hook-ups. I've got a good job, I work out—I'm a goddamned catch. I'm not going to chase someone who can't be bothered to give me a foot massage or cook up a meal to pay back what they're getting out of me. She obviously has delusions about deserving all kinds of fawning. I bet that's how these creepy shadowkind sucked her in."

That time I bit my tongue so hard I winced at the jab of pain. What I'd been getting out of him? Last I'd checked, he'd gotten off at least as much as I had from our hops into bed. Was I supposed to have been so honored that he'd stuck his dick in me that I'd decide to play merry homemaker—and without a single indication he even wanted that until he started sulking that it wasn't happening?

Ruse had my back in his own way. "I see," he said. "You really are a prickish piece of work, aren't you?"

Leland faltered. "What? I—"

The thrum came back into Ruse's voice. "Say it—that you're a prickish piece of work. Like you mean it."

"I'm a prickish piece of work," Leland said emphatically.

"Wonderful! Now let's get down to work. These people on Wharf Street I assume you contacted—how did you reach out to them? It'll help us so much to know."

Any uncertainty that had crossed Leland's face with the past instruction faded. "I wasn't sure I'd get someone in charge if I just called. It seemed like the message should go to someone higher up. So I went right down there."

He'd gotten a look at the building? "What did they do when you got there?" I asked.

"They were pretty tense about the whole thing." Leland frowned. "I guess it makes sense they would be when I showed up out of nowhere. When I told them I had vital information, a different guy came out to talk to me in the yard."

Ruse's eyes gleamed intently. "You didn't go inside?"

"Nope. I told him that I had reason to believe a woman working with some hostile shadowkind was going to attack his operations tonight, and that they definitely knew about the Wharf Street location and a few others— the ones the Fund checked out. Do you think that's why they'd be out to get me now—because I was involved in doing that research, even though I realized what the right side was?"

"Could be," Ruse said sagely. "Although if you went back there now that they've foiled the attack and seen you gave them good intel, maybe they'd be more friendly and let you in on their plans."

Leland dashed any hopes we'd had of sending him out into the field as an unwitting double-agent with a chuckle. "Oh, they're not at that place anymore. They were pretty upset about what I told them, and I heard one guy say to another as I was leaving something about having nowhere to move now except Gorge Avenue. But I have no idea where on Gorge Avenue they were going. That wasn't an address the Fund had."

No, it wasn't. I hadn't seen or heard anything about Gorge Avenue before—but it sounded like that was where the Company would have taken their prisoners.

"Did you overhear anything else? Anything at all?" I pressed.

Leland shook his head. "They shooed me off pretty quickly. Even the guy who made that comment shut up really quickly afterward. And now they're after me? I was only trying to help them. I thought—" His forehead furrowed as he tried to connect what he'd believed before to what Ruse's charm was forcing him to feel. "Have they actually been hurting people? It wasn't just Sorsha getting caught up with the wrong sort of shadowkind who wanted her to think that?"

"Unfortunately for you, these people are the worst of the worst, and it turns out they didn't appreciate that help," Ruse said in his most apologetic tone. "But I've determined that there's a simple way you can ensure they don't interfere with your life one bit."

Leland breathed a sigh of relief. "Thank you so much. I was trying to take the hassle *out* of my life by cutting off Sorsha's false crusade, not add to it. She'd already gotten the Fund too tangled up in all that. I never should have started investigating... Well, I guess if this Company of Light really *is* part of some kind of conspiracy... But that's more than I'm prepared to deal with anyway."

Right, because God forbid *he* experience the slightest discomfort while shadowkind were caged and tortured. He didn't sound even slightly regretful that he'd turned us in to people I'd warned him repeatedly were up to no good. I glanced at Ruse curiously.

The incubus rubbed his hands together in a way that would have tipped off anyone not under the spell of his charm that he was up to no good. "It's very simple. You must fix a pair of your underwear on your head and keep it there like a hat for at least three days. Oh, and only drink coffee that's as dark as you can brew it with no cream or sugar, left to cool for two hours first. Finally, call in sick from work while you're undergoing these steps and be sure to tell your boss exactly what you truly think of him."

I had to clap a hand over my mouth to hold in a laugh. The puzzled crease returned to Leland's forehead, but Ruse's voodoo gripped him tightly enough that he didn't argue. "Thank you. These people work in strange ways, I guess. I'll do all of that."

"Excellent. Don't mention we were here or your visit to Wharf Street to anyone. And may you find a romantic partner who's everything you deserve!"

The stairs creaked as Leland headed up to his bedroom to obtain the boxers that would serve as a hat. Ruse held in his snicker until we'd reached the back door.

"I'd have come up with a more public humiliation," he murmured to me, "but I think it's best if we don't call attention to our magical meddling."

"You didn't have to do any of that," I said. "All we needed was the information."

He made a skeptical humming sound. "Just be glad the defending of your honor was done my way and not

Thorn's. I had plenty of my own bones to pick with the jackass at this point, you know."

"Fair." A twinge of affection shot through my chest. "And thank you."

"Think nothing of it, Miss Blaze. You're worth a hundred thousand of that putz." Ruse looked in the direction we'd left Charlotte. "What do you say we take a detour along Gorge Avenue?"

"Sounds like the perfect next step."

Once we'd reached the outer reaches of the suburbs where Gorge Avenue was located—nowhere near any actual gorges we could toss our enemies into, sadly—it wasn't long before we realized that Snap had left us with one last gift. The motorcycle crested a low hill, and at the sight of an estate that sprawled across the entirety of the next block, I squeezed Ruse's arm.

It was a mansion of gray brick with a turret on the right-hand side, the one Snap's victim must have guarded in times past. And from what Leland had overheard, the Company had nowhere left to run if we came for them here.

29

Omen

"We've got them," I said, tapping the RV's tabletop and looking around at my three associates. A sense of triumph rippled through me. "This puts us in an even better position than if we'd taken them on in that factory building by the river. We've backed them into a corner, and they'll have consolidated all their equipment and resources in that one building, ripe for destruction."

"They'll have consolidated all their security there too," Thorn pointed out, ever the man of practicalities and glasses half empty. "Especially if—you said you think the man who owns the property may be the head of the entire Company of Light?"

After Ruse had returned from his venture with Sorsha, he and I had driven out to see what further information his hacker dupe could unearth. With her charmed dedication, she'd found enough records to clarify the situation.

I nodded. "He's covered his tracks well, but we came across money trails that convince me that this Victor Bane is behind the biggest operations the Company has conducted in this city. Either that, or someone with immense influence over him was pulling his strings, which amounts to the same thing."

Restlessness gripped me, and I had to tense my legs to stop myself from pacing. This was only the first glimpse of our real victory. We wouldn't achieve the rest until we got down to action.

But Thorn was right. We couldn't charge in, eyes and fists blazing, like the wild fool I'd once been. I dragged in a breath. "And he'll have plenty of security, yes. But most of the guards won't be used to working there. We can still make use of parts of our original plan, like the various diversions to divide and conquer. It may be difficult, with fewer of us..."

My gaze lifted to the bedroom doorway down the hall. The unicorn had proven herself a fierce fighter—I'd give her credit for that—but even if her body healed, she'd be in no condition to leap back into a battle for several days at a minimum. I wasn't sure the centaur would join us in venturing that far from her bedside either, even to avenge her injuries.

And Snap... The day had crept into evening and then dusk with full night looming over us, and our devourer hadn't reappeared.

When I'd asked him to enlist in my team, I'd known

that he had lingering reservations about the most potent part of his nature, but I'd thought his eagerness to help save our kind would override that if he ended up needing to use his greater power. Evidently he'd been more fragile —or the Company's hunters swifter—than I'd anticipated.

"We'll make the best of what we have," I went on, and then, as I drew in my next breath, a knock sounded on the RV's door.

Both Thorn and Sorsha sprang up, but their demeanors couldn't have been more different. Thorn's muscles flexed, his body braced to meet an attack—as if our enemies would have *knocked* before attempting to blow us to smithereens.

As Sorsha obviously realized. Her face had lit up with hesitant but obvious hope. In that moment, I didn't see any of the mouthy mortal who pushed me to the limits of my temper or the cocky thief who laughed at deadly threats, only a woman whose heart was leaping at the possibility that our missing companion had come back to us unharmed.

The sight wrenched at me more than I'd have liked. When had I ever seen a mortal that earnestly dedicated to any of the shadowkind? But I didn't think it was Snap out there—I doubted it would have occurred to the devourer to knock with his return either. And perhaps there was also an incredibly small yet niggling sensation with the knowledge that she'd have looked nowhere near that enthusiastic if I'd been the one who'd vanished.

You didn't win wars by courting affection. My job

was to kick her ass into getting those powers up to speed —a job I might already have backed off on more than I should have today.

I strode to the door and yanked it open, my other hand balled at my side ready to launch my claws. With my first glance outside, my stance relaxed, but only slightly. "What are *you* doing here?"

Rex was standing just outside the RV's door, his arms folded over his chest and a particularly wolfish gleam in his keen eyes. "You put out a plea for help, didn't you, Omen? Are you going to let us answer it or not?"

As he said "us," he stepped close enough for his companions to converge around him. By brimstone and hellfire, it looked as if he'd brought his entire outfit along for the ride. The inner circle stood at his flanks—Birch the dryad, Lazuli the troll, and Tassel the succubus—and at least half a dozen of the gang's lower underlings encircled them.

"I remember reaching out to see if Birch would lend his healing abilities," I said. "Are the rest of you along to provide him with moral support?"

The werewolf rolled his eyes. "Why don't we discuss all this inside before some country-dwelling mortal drives by and wonders what's going on with the party at the school bus?"

He had a point, but my hackles rose instinctively at the thought of letting so many powerful and self-interested shadowkind onto the vehicle I was starting to consider mine. Of course, technically it belonged to the tourists in the back, and power was relative. In the grand scheme of shadowkind existences, Rex with his century or so of experience was still a gangling teen, and he was the most established of the bunch. Thorn and I would have stood a decent chance at decimating this pack between the two of us.

That was an evaluation the werewolf could likely make for himself with the experience he did have and his knowledge of me. And I *had* asked for at least one of them to make an appearance. I restrained my inner hound and stepped back to let them in.

The inner circle kept their physical forms, coming to join the four of us by the sofa. At Rex's gesture, the underlings flitted into the shadows as they followed. I could still sense their presence lurking around us, but at least we weren't being squashed into the space like sardines in a tin.

Both Thorn and Sorsha stayed on their feet. Maybe I shouldn't have been surprised that even faced with several shadowkind she barely knew, our mortal was the one to push them into action.

"You should take a look at Gisele right away," she said, motioning to Birch. "They hurt her really badly. Omen and Thorn patched her up as well as they could, but..."

Her voice faded as she led him to the master bedroom. Rex glanced at me with a slight arch of his eyebrows as if amused that I'd let the human call any of the shots, but he didn't remark on it.

"That was quite a ruckus you stirred up downtown last night," he said instead.

I grimaced. "Not by our choosing. We meant to ravage the pricks on their own turf, but they caught wind of our plans and ambushed us on our way there. We still managed to do plenty of ravaging, though, just not the rescue effort we'd hoped to include."

"They've moved their prisoners again," Thorn added with a grumble of frustration. "And they may have captured one of our own."

Rex's gaze skimmed over us. "Oh, yes, your ray of sunshine is missing, isn't he? What a pity."

A squeak sounded as if in agreement. Sorsha's shadowkind pet had been huddled in a corner of the sofa at the arrival of the newcomers. Apparently having recognized them now, the little dragon scampered across the floor to twine around Laz's ankle like a cat. The troll stared down at the creature with an expression of such anguish that I had to suppress a laugh. So much for the tough-guy front.

Sorsha slipped out of the bedroom alone, her face drawn, and moved to rejoin us. I tipped my head to Rex with all the authority I could emanate. "Why exactly are you all here, Rex? Does your dryad require this much protection or were you simply wanting to gawk at us? Because we have more plans to make and battles to carry out on behalf of all shadowkind that I'd like to get back to."

The werewolf chuckled, but the arrogance in his pose deflated a little in recognition of who was the greater alpha here. I didn't push the matter far enough to force him to outright cower in front of his associates. There might be times when it'd be useful to call in a favor from this man in the future. Aggression got you farthest in the long run when tempered by diplomacy.

"We're not here as bodyguards or to gawk," he said. "I got the impression last time we spoke that you wouldn't mind a little assistance with all this battling. Well, here we are. We can battle on our own behalf. Just point us at the bastards who need gutting."

I had to stiffen my expression to hide my shock. He was willing to step into a conflict that didn't directly involve him yet—and not just offering his own allegiance, but that of his followers as well?

"*I* got the impression you didn't give a shit what happened to the rest of the shadowkind as long as you and your comrades weren't affected," I said, keeping my tone dry. "What changed your tune?"

"Oh, we're affected now." A growl crept into the werewolf's voice. "This is our city, and those assholes think they can burn down the fucking *Finger*? Maybe I'm not going to join you on any epic quests to win justice for all, but they clearly need to be taught a lesson."

I managed to stop my gaze from twitching in Sorsha's direction. From the corner of my eye, I could see her lips had pressed tight. It seemed wisest not to mention that it was one of *my* associates and not the Company who'd reduced the better part of that monstrosity of a statue to ashes.

"So they do," I said without missing a beat. "And who better to deliver that lesson than you and your followers." A smile curved my own mouth. "I'm looking forward to seeing how much damage we can inflict on them together. If I have it my way, they'll never light so much as a cigarette around here again. Let's get down to work."

We'd just finished filling the gang in on what we knew and our plans so far—"Infecting their computer system," Tassel purred. "I like it."—when Birch emerged from the master bedroom. Somehow his nearly translucent skin looked even paler than it had when he'd gone in. His voice seemed to have faded too.

"The unicorn shifter will live," he murmured roughly. "She woke up enough to exchange words with her partner. It may take another day or two before she can even move around on her feet, though. I've suggested they retire to the shadow realm until she's fully recovered, as soon as she's strong enough to make the leap through a rift."

"You've got yourself a *unicorn* shifter?" Rex gave a disbelieving guffaw and then snapped his fingers at the troll. "That reminds me of something. Laz, fill Birch in on what he missed. Omen, a word?"

We stepped into the second bedroom—and damn if I couldn't still scent a trace of the passion Sorsha must have shared with at least one of my shadowkind companions in the past couple of days. I willed it out of my awareness before my thoughts could linger on the moment in the yard when her body, her lips, had drawn me in with a nearly magnetic pull before I'd broken out of the spell. "What?"

The werewolf rubbed his hands together. "On the subject of unusual and powerful allies... I don't remember many details—this was at least a couple of decades ago, though not so long it couldn't be relevant. The Highest were searching for a particularly virile and apparently unpredictable shadowkind in this realm back then. I got the impression this one had caused some kind of chaos they needed to settle. Can't remember the name they asked us about... A red stone of some sort. Jasper? Garnet?"

"Is this story going anywhere?" I asked, as though my interest wasn't already piqued.

"I'm getting there. From what I heard from my contacts, they were looking for this red-stone-name all over the country. Maybe farther out too. And they specifically told us not to engage with the shadowkind if we got any word. It was too great a risk, and we should let them handle it." He grinned. "I never heard that they caught that one. If *you* could track this Jasper or Garnet or whatever down... That'd be someone to have on your side in this war with the mortals, don't you think? Could be almost as much a rebel as you are."

I had a vague recollection of hearing murmurs about this subject, but I'd mostly been shadow-side during that time. As it probably had back then too, the first thought that flitted through my mind was of a being long-gone. I didn't think the Highest had ever taken issue with anyone more than they had with Tempest, my once some-time partner-in-crime, and she'd gone through guises like mortals shed clothes... but I'd watched the minions of the ancient ones batter her to a pulp centuries ago. The sphynx was long gone, and we were likely all better for it. I doubted she'd ever have reformed.

Whoever this newer rebel was, it certainly sounded as though they had energy and guts to spare. Stumbling on them would be a longshot, but a possibility to file away all the same.

"I'll keep that in mind," I said. "If we need the extra assistance in the first place. I say we crush the bastards tonight and end things there."

"That works for me." Rex bumped shoulders with me hesitantly, as if half expecting me to take a bite out of him for his forwardness. I settled on a simple glare. He hadn't needed to offer anywhere near this much help. I could allow a little chumminess.

And maybe not just with him. When we returned to the living room, my eyes settled on Sorsha—sitting cozied up to Ruse now, poking Thorn in his massive bicep without any fear of the wingéd's power, shooting a snappy response back at something Tassel had said. Like she belonged here.

Could I really say she didn't? Correct blame for the fire aside, I doubted *Rex* would be here at all if she hadn't laid into him about his self-centeredness.

Our mortal and her hope springing eternal.

I just had to keep a careful eye on all the other emotions her presence tended to stir in me. There was no room for distractions. We had a conspiracy of humans to destroy—and I intended to see them fall before the night was done.

30

Sorsha

In taking on the Company of Light, we'd faced old office buildings, modern lab facilities, and now what might as well have been a castle, set well back on its sprawling lawn. I wouldn't be surprised if the man who owned the old mansion figured he really was some kind of king. Victor Bane—that was a super-villain name if I'd ever heard one. If that even was his real name and not yet another layer of subterfuge.

Thanks to Birch's healing efforts just before we'd headed out, my no-longer-wounded stomach could rest against my thighs in my crouched position without pain prickling through it. I scanned the yard from my perch on the branch of an oak tree in Bane's neighbor's backyard. Thorn's initial scouting through the shadows had shown him about twenty armed guards on the premises outside the building, and I could make out several of them stalking along in their patrols.

No big deal. We were more than ready for them. Bane or whoever couldn't know that we'd more than doubled our numbers since the Company's last assault on us, or I suspected he'd have called in every man he could.

Of course, maybe he already had. Thorn, Omen, and the others had torn through quite a few last night.

We had to crash their party before they got the chance to find out about our latest plans. The Company had eyes and ears in too many places—nothing we did seemed to stay secret for long. The only times we'd really turned the tables on them was when we'd acted on our information right away.

I just wished this plan didn't depend so much on my powers kicking in when they should. Or on keeping those powers secret even from our new allies.

Omen had pulled me aside after we'd finished settling our strategy, in which he'd claimed responsibility for setting a few things alight once we were at the Bane property.

"You know which parts you were meant to handle," he'd said in a dark undertone. "Stick to the original plan on that count—I'll be with Thorn focusing on cutting down as many of the guards as we can. But don't let Rex or his lackeys see you at it if you can help it. Easier for us to keep you as our ace up our sleeve if word doesn't get out too widely."

I already didn't love the way Rex tended to eye me as

if speculating how he'd carve me up into steaks given the opportunity. Keeping any additional attention off me sounded just dandy.

I would hold my own tonight—I'd be more an asset than a liability, even if some of the help I offered went under most of our allies' radar. If we lost anyone else tonight because of my actions or my mortal limitations...

My jaw tightened. No, I wasn't even going to think that far. It wouldn't happen. I wouldn't let it.

To begin with, our main trick would be creating small enough diversions that the shadowkind could pick off one or two guards at a time without them realizing they were under attack. We'd rather no one clued in that an assault was underway until we'd reduced their numbers already. If we could make it all the way to wherever the Company was keeping its imprisoned shadowkind, even better—but I didn't expect our luck would stretch that far.

The shadowkind could pull off a hell of a lot of their own, but they were going to need me to open those silver-and-iron cages, and I couldn't waltz in through the shadows unseen. Without Snap to taste the locks, I wasn't even sure how long it'd take me to break into whatever cages the captives were currently being held in. We might have to rely on Ruse charming an employee who happened to know the entry codes or Rex's techie guy to find the details in the computer system.

So, yeah, the more of our opposition we picked off ahead of time, the better for all of us. Particularly, for me making it out of this alive and without taking anyone else down with me.

A light flickered on and off around the back of the Bane property. I tensed on my perch. That was my cue. I was supposed to wait ten seconds.

As I counted, I sang under my breath to bolster my nerve. "We'll laugh and flare, woo-oah, giving them a scare."

Holy mother of margaritas, did I wish I had Snap's upbeat presence by my side now. If these assholes had caught him in their nets and hurt him in any way... I'd happily join the shadowkind in the bloodier part of this rampage.

That thought sent a little spurt of adrenaline through me, just enough to kick my pulse up a notch—and to fuel my inner flames. With the narrowing of my eyes, I flung the energy out toward the electrical wire that cut across the sky from a nearby post.

Sparks leapt from the cable. Then a lick of fire spurted up, sizzling over the rubbery coating.

Shouts volleyed across the lawn. Some of the security force had noticed. My heart thumped even faster as I aimed my attention at the post itself. Another flame flickered into being where the cables hooked onto it.

Just a little electrical issue threatening to cut off the entire property's power. Wouldn't want to have to explain to the big man how they'd let that happen.

Someone was talking into a phone in urgent tones, and a few of the guards approached the front gate. That was right—just walk on out past the wall like it's an ordinary night, just a little hassle with the utilities...

The gate's metal bars clanged shut behind them, and

my perked ears caught the faintest grunt as a couple of the shadowkind must have toppled that bunch. I didn't have time to waste on wondering how the skirmish was playing out or how horribly my allies might be eviscerating the Company dudes right now. My gaze darted across the grounds to the trees closest to the utility post.

A little smoldering here, a little flare of heat there. At least, that's what I wanted to happen. The branches stayed dark and unburnt as ever.

Come on, come *on*. I gritted my teeth and thought again of Snap—of Snap on one of those metal tables where the Company did their experiments, pinned with silver and iron bindings so he was in too much distress to be able to shed his physical form, his body pierced with scalpels and needles and whatever other horrors these people inflected on their prisoners—

Flames darted across a few twigs at the top of the trees, as if they'd leapt from somewhere along the burning cable. I willed them higher until another round of shouts rang out.

A few more guards headed out through the gate to their doom, and a handful more hustled into the stand of trees near the northern wall by me, where monsters lurked in the darkness.

The distraction part of the plan wasn't *all* on me. A motor growled, and footsteps thumped around the back of the yard too, where Ruse would have activated the ride-on lawnmower. On the far side of the mansion, a few of the gang members would be standing on the other side of the wall hooting with laughter and smashing bottles against the stones like drunken hooligans.

How many of the guards had we drawn away between all our efforts? I edged farther along my oak branch, readying myself to spring onto the top of the wall and then down when I got a signal that the coast was clear.

Hardly any guards were in sight now. The two I could see striding across the lawn to check on their colleagues toppled abruptly under the impact of two burly shadowkind who burst from the shadows. Silver and iron might protect these people from shadowkind voodoo, but it couldn't do anything to stop those fists from smashing their skulls in.

A molten orange glow streaked across the grass toward the building's side door—Omen, making himself visible in hellhound form just long enough for me to see him. We were heading inside. Time for the hard part.

I threw myself onto the wall and then landed with a thump on the grass just inside the property. A voice started to bellow in alarm, but the sound was cut off with a bloody gurgle. Fickle fates willing, no one up at the house had taken note of that first sound the guard had barely managed to get out.

The grass whispered under my sneakers as I darted across the lawn. The side door swung open, its lock released, just as I reached it. Quieting my rasping breath, I ducked into the hall on the other side.

Thorn solidified completely just long enough to give me a nod and an encouraging squeeze of my arm. *We'll be right there with you,* he'd said when we'd discussed this phase of the mission, and the same sentiment was etched all over his face.

Here I was, the most essential piece in the plan and also the most breakable.

The shadowkind intruders had already gotten to work on clearing my way. I darted past a body slumped against the wall, her gut gouged open beneath her metal vest, and pushed through the doorway ahead of me.

In the first second as the wavering blueish light washed over me, I thought I'd stumbled on a mad scientist's lab already. Then my eyes adjusted to the dim light—and the stink of chlorine. The bastard had his own indoor pool, for fuck's sake.

I skirted the still water and the glow of the lights beneath it. I'd made it halfway around the pool when a guard pushed past the far door. From his stern but not frantic expression and the energy to his stride, he was concerned about whatever he'd come down here to investigate but not yet aware it was an all-out invasion.

At least, until he spotted me. "Halt right there!" he shouted, his gun hand jerking up.

He had better instincts than Leland, but not good enough. I'd already grabbed a life preserver that'd been mounted on the wall beside me. I hurled it at him like a massive discus in time to smack his arm to the side.

The good news: I remained bullet-free. The bad

news: His finger still squeezed the trigger, sending one of those bullets into the far wall with an unmistakable boom that echoed through the building around us.

There went our advantage of stealth. Our chances of victory were really ticking away now.

I dove at the guard's legs, aiming to stay out of the line of fire while I knocked him on his ass. Unfortunately, there are rules about running on pool decks for a reason. My feet skidded on a slick patch, and *I* tumbled over on my ass.

Ruse materialized beside me looking ready to come to my defense however he could, but at the same moment, Bow leapt from the shadows in full centaur form. "I can't touch your head in that helmet, but the diving board doesn't have the same problem," he declared, and spun so he could slam his hind horse legs into the guard's gut.

The man hurtled across the water. The back of his skull smacked into the edge of the diving board so hard the helmet dented halfway through his head. He dropped like a sack of potatoes into the pool. Bow wiped his hands together with an unusually vicious expression.

Possibly too vicious. "Maybe a little lighter on the hoof power next time?" Ruse said as we dashed to the door the guard had emerged from. "We need at least one of these fools alive—and conscious enough—for me to charm them into leading the way to their prison."

"Sorry," Bow said, not looking as if he meant the apology all that much. "I just—I think that's one of the guys who attacked Gisele."

"And payback was a bitch. Just remember the best payback will be getting the rest of our kind free *before* we cave in the rest of their skulls."

They both slipped back into the darkness. I hustled through a small change room, down a short hall on the other side, and burst through the next doorway into—a personal *bowling alley*?

Victor Bane must take plenty of time for his recreational pursuits in between attempts to destroy all shadowkind.

Three guards were just charging in from an entrance across the room. I ducked behind one of the bowling ball dispensers by the two lanes, the tang of wood polish saturating my lungs.

Another shot rang out—and then a gasp and a fleshy ripping sound reached my ears. Maybe I should question my life choices when that sound was actually familiar at this point.

I bobbed back up to see Laz twisting the neck of the third of the guards, gripping the man by the jaw so he could wrench his head off without touching the toxic metals of the man's helmet. Two other headless figures already sprawled on the floor, leaking blood all over the gleaming boards.

The troll, whose skin had deepened to a darker blue and who'd grown at least a foot in both height and width in his full shadowkind form, grinned to reveal two rows of uneven teeth and tossed the heads one by one down the lane. The first clanged into the pins helmet-first and scored him a strike.

Ruse had reappeared. "Again," he chided, "could we please be at least a tad more careful with the mortals? Spare one for me to do my work?"

Laz grunted. "Either I go straight for the throat or the gut, or they bash me with their stupid weapons before I can do much. Fucking armor makes it pretty hard to be subtle. I don't see *you* felling any of the pricks."

"Fair. Come on, let's keep moving."

We came out into a wider hall at the base of a stairwell. Thorn appeared next to us a second later. "We've searched the entire basement. Wherever the cages are, they're not down here."

I raised my chin, ignoring the increasingly frenetic beat of my heart. "Upward and onward it is, then."

Footsteps thundered toward us before we'd made it to the first landing where the staircase split in two. Thorn took one side and Laz the other, and a moment later two more gouged bodies tumbled down next to Ruse and me.

"It's raining corpses," I said with a shudder.

"As long as they're not ours." The incubus grasped my arm. "Better catch up before they tear through the entire population of this building."

We rounded the corner after Thorn, and Omen blinked into being at the top of the stairs. He'd kept his human-ish form, but traces of his hellish nature showed all over his body, from the orange blaze in his eyes to the mottled lava-gray and magma-glow twining across his skin.

"This way," he said with a jab of his hand, fangs

glinting in his mouth. He sprang back into the shadows in the direction he'd pointed to.

Racing after him, we found ourselves in a music room: a grand piano at one end, a circle of wing chairs at the other, books of music and a few other instruments propped along the wall. But we didn't arrive alone. More guards dashed after us inside.

As Thorn introduced his crystalline fists to two of their throats, I snatched up a violin by the neck. When I whirled around, the nearest guard was almost on me, brandishing one of those brilliant whips. My pulse hiccupped, I slashed out with my free hand, and he jolted backward with a flinch at the wave of heat I'd sent at him without thinking.

I couldn't care at this point whether Laz or any of the other gang members who might be watching from the shadows had noticed. Without missing a beat, I swung the violin at his helmet, knocking it to the floor and giving him a good wallop to the temple at the same time. The groaning of the violin as it cracked matched that of Thorn's current opponent, who was crumpling at the warrior's blow.

The guard I was facing off with swayed but righted himself, just in time for me to land a kick that smacked the whip from his hand. I threw myself at him with all my weight to knock him to the floor. While I yanked at the clasps on the silver-and-iron vest, Ruse danced around me, wavering in and out of view as he alternately dodged other guards and attempted to prevent our allies from obliterating this one.

The jerk managed to clock me hard enough in the head that my thoughts scrambled, but I wrenched off his last piece of armor at the same time. Ruse dropped with his knees, pinning the man's chest, and gazed intently into his startled eyes.

"Hello, friend," he said with the full force of his cubi charm. "You're going to help us free the poor wounded creatures locked up somewhere in this place."

"Hopefully quickly," Omen snapped. He'd shoved back a bookcase at the far end of the room to reveal a hidden door. His gaze snagged on me. "Let's go, Disaster. It's time for you to take the starring role."

I wished my gut hadn't lurched so much at that statement. Wished this was one of my usual capers where it was just me vs. one minor asshole collector and not a mission where the fate of all shadowkind—of Snap, of Bow and Gisele's friend, of the many other beings the Company might have captured and those they wished to destroy—hung in the balance. But here I was. I couldn't even say I hadn't signed up for it.

Resolve swelled inside me as I met Omen's eyes. "Ready when you are."

I skirted pools of blood and gore on my way across the room, the stench of ruined human flesh making my stomach churn even more than it already was from my nerves.

Just focus on the doorway. Focus on the beings in need on the other side.

In just a few more minutes, I might have Snap with me again.

Ruse's voice rose and fell in lilting tones as he and his increasingly charmed companion followed me. The doorway Omen had revealed led to a narrow flight of stairs down into a second, hidden basement.

As I descended, cool air licked over my skin, raising goosebumps on my arms. A chemical scent tickled my nose.

The room we emerged into had clearly been prepared in a rush. Crates and cardboard boxes had been shoved into stacks on one side somewhat haphazardly. The rest of the room was full of what looked like huge freestanding lockers, similar to the one the Company had brought to their hand-off with the collector. Their outsides gleamed stainless steel, but I'd be willing to stake my life and my love of curry on there being plenty of silver and pure iron embedded inside.

They were locked with keycode panels on the right side of the doors. Those gleamed less severe shades of gray, the base of the pad silver and the keys iron. No one on this mission would be able to touch them except me—or our charmed guard.

I jerked the guard over to one, my eyes watering in the glare of the overhead lights. Ruse came along too but with a grimace at the toxic vibes the metals must have been giving off around us.

"Do you know the codes?" I demanded.

"No," the guard said. "None of us—they were so strict about that—but I believe—it should all be on the computers. I don't know the password for that either—"

He'd motioned to a flashy, high-tech set-up on a desk in a corner beyond the cells. "Rex!" Omen barked.

The werewolf appeared a moment later with one of his lackeys at his side. "On it," he said, and gave the guy a shove toward the computer.

Thanks to his tech guy's expertise, we shouldn't need to run off with any equipment, only grab the data before destroying it—and hopefully the data on every computer in Bane's network as well. The lackey dropped into the chair and launched his digital assault with a clatter of the keyboard.

I turned back to Ruse and the guard. "They'll figure out that we're down here sooner rather than later, even with the doorway closed again. We should get this guy to divert the others—to say he's seen us moving to a different part of the house." Might as well make as much use of the dude as we could.

As Ruse cajoled the guard into giving frantic commands over his radio, the guy at the computer raised his hands with a brief whoop. "And we're in! Codes for the cages, where are you...?" His fingers resumed their clattering.

Omen frowned at the blank steel sides of the cells. "How will we know which code is for which cage? They don't appear to be conveniently numbered." He snapped his fingers toward Ruse. "Get that man back over here."

Ruse nudged the guard toward us. The man drew in a shaky breath. "How can I help?"

Omen's fiery eyes had simmered down now that we'd reached our goal, but they lit with a new glint that might have been partly amused at the guard's cooperative attitude. "These metal boxes have got to be labeled somehow. How do you tell which is which?"

The guard's head bobbed in eager agreement. "There are dots on the sides of the keypads. Blue first and then red."

I squinted at the edge of the panel and made out the little flecks of paint now that I knew to look for them. "This one is 3-5 then." There had to be close to twenty of the things in this space. I glanced toward the computer guy. "Do you have those codes for us yet?"

"Working on it, working on it." He tapped vigorously, sucking his lower lip under his teeth. The spines that poked from his hair at the nape of his neck quivered.

Thorn and Rex both vanished into the shadows, I assumed to fend off any guards who headed this way despite our efforts. I paced, my chest constricting.

Omen cast me a baleful look. "Too much excitement for you, mortal?"

"No," I said. "I just want us—all of us—out of here." He should know as well as I did that every passing second might mean fewer shadowkind freed—might mean our plan failed altogether. Last time we'd only managed to get him out before we'd had to run for our lives.

"There!" the computer guy said with obvious relief. "Okay, I'm going to start the virus uploading while I read out the numbers. The code for cage 3-5 is 6-9-0-2."

I braced myself as I typed in the code. Omen had already moved to the next cell, dragging the guard with him. He bent close, flinching just at being close to the toxic metals, and read off the number on the keypad there. The metals in the keys would have burned him—or any of our other shadowkind companions—too badly for him to use them, but at least we could free the captives twice as fast if the guard was punching in codes too.

As the lock thudded and the cell door in front of me swung open, Ruse stepped up to peer inside with one of his warmest smiles but wary eyes. Shadowkind didn't tend to be in a friendly state when they'd been locked away for who knew how long.

Even starker light filled the inner space from a panel up above. A streak of darkness quivered in the center of that light where the captive being had drawn its least substantial form in on itself. I couldn't make out any of its features, but somehow just looking at it, I knew we hadn't found Snap—not yet, anyway.

"Please, my friend, make your escape," Ruse said, extending his hand. "We're getting all of you out of here. And feel free to enact a little revenge on your captors as you flee."

The patch of shadow hesitated and then sprang from its confines with a shudder of knobby haunches and a clicking of scales. I didn't wait to see how it would react to its newfound freedom—I was already rushing to the next cell.

Omen and I volleyed numbers back and forth with the tech guy, and one by one the cell doors gaped open. After the first, I leapt to the next the moment the lock clicked over, not waiting to see who might be inside, as much as I might have wanted to.

A couple of the freed beings lingered in the room, watching our progress: an emaciated fae man hunched by the stack of boxes, shivering, and a shifter woman with cat-like irises prowled back and forth with darted looks toward the staircase as if she wasn't convinced it was actually any safer up there than down here. The others vanished straight into the shadows.

"Don't hang around here too long," Ruse called to them. "Take a few jabs on your way out if you like, but don't give these bastards a chance to snare you again."

We were down to the last few cells when voices crackled from the charmed guard's radio loud enough for me to hear. "The east basement! All units head there now!"

Shit. They'd realized we'd made it this far. "The rest of the numbers, fast!" I shouted, darting to another cell.

As the computer guy rattled the digits off, my fingers flew over the keypad. There were only two cells left. The guard hesitated as Omen urged him to open the cell they were at, and the hellhound shifter snarled.

"Type in the fucking code!"

Panic flashed across the guard's face. Ruse dashed over, seeing his magical influence fracturing.

I waved the computer guy on. "I can do the rest. Hurry!"

Despite the cool air, sweat trickled down my back as I jabbed in the last two codes, not even waiting to make sure they worked first. "That's it!" the computer guy shouted to me after the final one, and mashed at the keyboard a little more. "I've downloaded all the other data I can, and the virus is in the network. Should I activate it?"

"Yes, yes, get on with it!" Omen said. "We're going to burn this whole place down... in every possible way."

He shot a meaningful glance at me. At least this part I could do by regular means, no worries about uncertain powers or witnesses.

"Everyone out, now!" I hollered, just as the first figures in the new wave of guards barreled down the stairs.

Thorn, Laz, and other shadowkind I couldn't recognize from a glimpse shot in and out of the shadows between them, mashing a skull into the wall here, cracking a spine in half there. The less combat-inclined beings hurtled past them. I caught sight of smoke streaming from open wounds on Thorn's back and stiffened against the urge to run to him. I had other work to do.

I splashed the kerosene from the pouch at my hip across the crates and boxes and lit them up with a flick of my lighter.

I'd gotten too used to the struggle of using my power for the same purpose. The flames roared up faster than I was prepared for. I yanked myself backwards, slapping at a few sparks that singed my hair, and bolted for the stairs my shadowkind allies were just clearing.

My foot slipped on a smear of blood, and then Thorn was whipping me up into his arms. He barged up the stairs with me over his shoulder, smashing past another guard who'd just appeared at the top. But as he tore through the music room, a man he hadn't seen sprang from behind the piano and hurled a huge net at my warrior.

It didn't quite cover Thorn's hulking form, but it fell over enough of him that his muscles locked up with a spasm of pain. I wrenched at the silver-and-iron cords, shoving them off him as quickly as I could. More smoke poured from the fresh wounds on his back and face that would add to his collection of scars. He fell to his knees, and my feet hit the ground too.

As I hauled the net the rest of the way off the warrior, Omen leapt from the shadows to slash a claw across our attacker's throat. "Out the front!" he shouted at us, and flashed out of sight again.

Thorn staggered upright. We ran out into the hall together, his hand clutching mine as tightly as I was clutching him. With the amount of essence billowing out of him, I wasn't sure he could have carried me now if he'd wanted to.

"Did you see—" he said roughly. "Was Snap—?"

"I don't know," I said, but the hollow in my stomach didn't hold much hope. If Snap had been in one of those cells, surely he'd have stayed long enough to show himself and reunite with us properly?

If we didn't get the hell out of here, there'd be none of us left to reunite with *him*, wherever he was. Silver and iron glinted everywhere I looked—armor, nets, knives. The remaining guards were converging on us.

I wasn't finished with this place, though. We'd meant to see the whole building burn. The thick cement walls in the secret basement wouldn't let the fire seep from below into the rest of the mansion.

I grasped at my bottle of kerosene—and it slid from my hasty fingers to rattle across the rug and under a hall table behind us. Behind us, where a dozen or so guards were currently storming our way. Sayonara to that one.

We burst into a grand entrance room with woven tapestries hanging from the walls and an actual red carpet slashing down the middle of the marble floor. Ahead of us, the double doors hung open to the night, but another dozen guards stood between us and that escape.

In seconds, we'd be surrounded. I spun around, a searing heat mingling with the burst of panic in my chest.

These assholes had destroyed who knew how many beings, had tormented Omen, had nearly killed Gisele, and if they'd gotten their hands on Snap...

My jaw clenched as the heat flared into a surge of fury. They had no idea who they were dealing with. *I* could clear our way this time, and I didn't need so much as a match to do it.

I flung out my arms and hurled all the searing rage inside me at our attackers.

The carpet and the tapestries went up in a blaze. So did most of the bodies between us and the door. The guards stumbled, toppled, or flailed with shrieks of agony as the flames ate across every part of them not made of metal.

A horrified lump clogged my throat, but this was what I'd wanted. It wasn't anywhere near as horrifying as the genocide they'd planned to enact.

If I'd been thinking clearer, I might have been a little more careful. Flames raged across the entire room around us, cutting off our escape as well. I tightened my grip on Thorn's hand. He squeezed mine back with a curt nod.

"And so we dance into the fire," I muttered, and threw myself toward the doors.

The flames snagged on my sleeves and the pouch at my hip. As I soared through the doorway, I let go of Thorn so I could flip into a roll. The cool blades of the lawn's grass snuffed out the hungry tufts of fire.

I sprawled on my back, staring up at the mansion. I'd incited my blaze even higher than I'd realized. Yellow-orange light roared through broken glass on the second-floor windows. More flames leapt out to crawl across the roof.

We'd done it. We'd taken back what the Company of Light had stolen and then razed their data and their last hide-out to the ground.

And now I'd better get the hell out of here before anyone gave me the same treatment.

A few figures had charged out of the building in my wake. The guards stared at me, one of them pointing. He dashed away while the other two came at us.

Thorn swung around so swiftly you'd never have guessed he was producing nearly as much smoke as the entire mansion. His punch slammed into one guard's face, but in the warrior's weakening state, his knuckles only scraped her cheek instead of crushing it. I grabbed his elbow.

"We've got to get out of here, now!"

Laz and Rex flickered from the shadows to topple our attackers. With the mortals' shrieks and the warbling of the fire following at our heels, we ran across the lawn, leaving the remains of the Company to sink into its own ashes.

31

Sorsha

At a glance, the gathering of figures around the Everymobile looked more like a summer barbeque than a conspiracy of monsters.

Ruse had driven the RV well out of the city and parked it in a fallow field in the countryside where no buildings stood in sight. Other than him, me, and Rex's tech guy, who'd sat bent over a laptop on the sofa for the whole drive, the other shadowkind had ridden with us in the shadows. Now, coming out after a brief doze in the second bedroom, I found the entire company spread out around the vehicle.

At least, I thought it had to be the entire bunch. Omen and Thorn stood talking with Rex and a couple of his underlings near a drooping tree. A few feet from them, Ruse was shooting the breeze with Laz, Birch, and assorted other gang members, as well as the few liberated prisoners who'd decided to stick with us in our escape. To my right, Bow was sitting on the ground with Gisele lounging on his lap, her face still drawn but brighter than I'd have thought possible after the way she'd looked the last time I'd seen her. Her beaming was probably thanks to the petite, twiggy young man they were chatting with —their long-lost friend, Cori.

Everyone was smiling and laughing, their stances relaxed—except Tech Dude, who hadn't left his hunched pose on the sofa behind me. The dawn light turned the edges of the landscape golden, matching the triumphant vibe perfectly. I dragged in a deep breath of the cool early morning air, a smile of my own crossing my lips, but a twinge shot through my gut at the same time.

Snap was still missing. My instincts had been correct —he hadn't been in any of those cells in Victor Bane's mansion.

If the Company hadn't captured him, where had he gone? All the way back to the shadow realm? Was I ever going to see him again?

I'd been prepared for us to part ways when Omen's mission here was done, but the loss still gnawed at me. I hadn't gotten to say good-bye. Maybe if we'd talked, if I'd been able to talk the devourer through his doubts, I wouldn't have *needed* to say good-bye, at least not right away.

The Company of Light wasn't the only force malevolent toward the shadowkind in this world, only the largest one I'd encountered. We might have decimated them, but I wouldn't be surprised if Omen and his crew found other ways to stay busy rather than heading straight home.

And maybe I was kind of hoping they'd count me as part of that crew for as long as they stuck around. What did I have left to go back to anyway? A burned-down apartment, a handful of sort-of friends and colleagues who'd turned their backs on me...

Well, one very dedicated best friend as well. I should call Vivi and let her know it was safe to leave her watery safehouse now.

As I fished out my phone and stepped out onto the untamed grass, Pickle scuttled after me. I bent to give him a scratch between his wings before he scampered off in Laz's direction. My smile grew with the amused anticipation of the troll's nervous reaction. I brought up my contacts on the screen—

—and the tech guy burst out of the RV behind me, his laptop held up like a signal flag, gasping for breath as if he'd just run miles rather than five feet.

"Everyone! It isn't over. This isn't— That place was just *one*—"

My hand dropped to my side. As I stared at him, the others drew in closer, Omen and Rex at the front of the crowd.

The hellhound shifter's good humor had faded. "What are you saying? Spit it out—a little more coherently, if you can manage that?"

Computer Dude swiped a nervous hand across his mouth. The spines on the back of his neck jittered. "It's just—It took me a while to really dig into the files. There were a lot of layers of protection. And at first I didn't totally understand what I was seeing, with all the code names and the rest. But—there are definite references to other facilities in other cities—New York, Chicago, San Francisco, New Orleans..."

"All the best locales," Ruse murmured. Any place that attracted a decent number of artsy or otherwise quirky humans tended to appeal to the shadowkind as well—easier for *their* quirks to blend in.

My stomach had balled into a massive knot. "You're saying the Company of Light isn't alone? There are other organizations like them?"

"No, that's all the same organization." The guy swept his hand through the air. "The Company of Light has... let's call them branches in at least seven other cities in the US. It doesn't look as if all of them are currently holding higher shadowkind captive—the operation here seems to have been one of the biggest—but they're all experimenting on lesser beings and hunting around the local rifts."

The buoyant mood that had filled the gathering deflated. I exchanged a grim look with Thorn and Ruse. This hadn't been our final stand after all. The operations we'd burned down here had only been one piece in a massive puzzle of awfulness. Shit.

Omen cleared his throat, taking charge with a typical authoritarian vibe. "Have you at least determined what all this experimenting is for—specifically? How do they think they're going to conquer the shadowkind?"

Computer Dude's fingers tightened around the

laptop. "They... they've been testing all sorts of things to see what drains our essence the most, in an attempt to create a sickness that could be passed between the shadowkind and deadly enough to kill any that encountered it in the mortal world."

A deeper hush fell over the crowd. "It'll never work," one of the gang underlings said after a moment. "We don't get sick."

The guy shrugged. "They have made progress. Nothing we'd need to fend off immediately, and the virus I sent into their computer systems may have passed on to the rest of the organization over the internet and damaged their research overall, but—I won't feel comfortable while they're still working on it. They've already created bacteria potent enough to make lesser shadowkind weaken."

There was a moment of total horrified silence. It'd obviously never occurred to the assembled crowd that even that much could be possible. A shiver ran down my spine.

"Fine," Omen said. "The assholes are dangerous—we already knew that. If we didn't topple the kingpin last night, we'll just have to do that next. Did you find some indication of who *is* running the whole show?"

"It does appear that Victor Bane was in charge of operations here. The records stay pretty vague about who holds the ultimate authority, but... based on the scale of operations, my best guess is they're located in San Francisco."

"Road trip!" Ruse said, raising his fist in the air, but

even he couldn't summon much enthusiasm into his joking tone.

Murmurs spread through the crowd. As Rex took them in, he nodded. "We fought the battle we came here to fight—we kicked the bastards out of our city. The rest I'm going to have to leave to you. We've put enough on the line as it is."

The werewolf's gaze settled on me. So had that of a few of his companions, I realized. Their expressions had tensed in a way that only amplified my uneasiness.

"Especially when you've got a sorcerer working with you," Rex added, and it clicked. Of course the shadowkind who'd seen me summon fire in the entrance hall would assume I'd used sorcery, bending a shadowkind to my will. They'd seen plenty of evidence that I was mortal, and that was the only way mortals were supposed to be able to use magic.

I pulled my posture up straighter. "I'm no sorcerer. I—I'm not totally sure what I am, but I wouldn't manipulate shadowkind for power."

Rex's eyebrows shot up. "You're trying to tell me that you're a human who can conjure fire on her own steam?"

"Well, more like smoke, but..."

"It's true," Omen said brusquely. "Do you really think I'd work with a sorcerer, Rex? I'd rather eat them for dinner. If you're not sticking around, I can't see how it matters anyway."

The murmurs had heightened, more gazes turning my way. Thorn took a step closer as if he thought I might need a bodyguard, but Rex waved his people silent.

"You're right. It's your business, not ours. Come on, folks—let's leave these do-gooders to their crusade."

He wavered into the shadows. Most of the gathering followed him. I guessed they'd find a vehicle of their own to steal to shorten the trip back into town.

Let the selfish pricks have it their way. A deeper chill was sinking into my bones that had nothing to do with any shadowkind.

"Omen," I said. "At least one of the guards who saw me use my magic got away last night. I didn't worry about it because Thorn was too injured to go after him—with everything else destroyed, I didn't think it would matter. But if he tells everyone else in the Company... At the very least, they'll be ready for it next time."

"One more in a whole heap of worries. We'll deal with that along with the rest."

Someone cleared their throat. Omen turned and scowled as he noticed the Tech Dude standing nervously at the base of the RV's steps, not having left with the others. "What?"

The guy bobbed his head. "I thought you'd want to know... I think the being you were hoping to find on the Bane estate, the devourer? It looks as though they did capture him—or one of very similar description. Whichever it is, they shipped that shadowkind to Chicago yesterday afternoon. Maybe they were worried you'd be able to trace his presence if they kept him too close."

My throat closed up. "Snap." He was in one of those cells after all, pinned by the silver and iron and the searing lights—and whatever else they were already using to torment him.

"Thank you," Omen said, and the computer guy darted off after his boss. The hellhound shifter pressed his hand to his forehead. "When I get my claws into the rest of these people..."

Thorn's shoulders flexed. "It'll be a pleasure to tear them limb from limb."

"We have to get to them all first. Seven cities." Omen's mouth tightened. "Well, maybe if we shatter what they have in San Francisco, that'll be enough..."

His gaze slid past us, over the few rescued shadowkind who were standing uncertainly at the fringes of where the crowd had been, and stopped on Bow, who was just walking up to us with Gisele still cradled in his arms.

The unicorn shifter, not the centaur, was the one who spoke, her voice reedy but still silver-bright. "I think we might be able to help you out a little bit more—as a thank you for bringing Cori back to us." She shot a smile over Bow's shoulder at their friend.

"You can't try to fight when you're still recovering," I protested, but she waved me off.

"Not like that. We only... We only need the Everymobile while we're here in the mortal realm. The dryad was right—I'll heal faster shadow-side. If you can drop us off at the nearest safe rift, we're happy to lend her to you as long as you need her." She rested her hand against the vehicle's side. "Maybe I'll even bounce back fast enough to jump back into this war of yours."

Omen considered her for a long moment. Then he dipped his head, just slightly but with obvious respect. "Thank you. You've already contributed more than most would have." He swiveled back to face Thorn, Ruse, and me.

The words tumbled out before I'd thought them through, but I wouldn't have changed them anyway. "We have to get Snap back. We can't leave him in the hands of those assholes when we've got no idea how long it might take to shatter the whole Company."

I braced myself to have to argue practicalities on my lover's behalf—to point out how much *he'd* already contributed to Omen's cause and how much more he might if he got the chance, as if that mattered more than the fact that he was now facing who knew what kind of torture because of the hellhound shifter's crusade. But I didn't need to.

A tense smile curved Omen's lips. "I agree. It looks like we do have a road trip in our immediate future—and head of the Company be damned, our first stop will be Chicago. We're not leaving our devourer behind."

ABOUT THE AUTHOR

Eva Chase lives in Canada with her family. She loves stories both swoony and supernatural, and strong women and the men who appreciate them. Along with the Flirting with Monsters series, she is the author of the Cursed Studies trilogy, the Royals of Villain Academy series, the Moriarty's Men series, the Looking Glass Curse trilogy, the Their Dark Valkyrie series, the Witch's Consorts series, the Dragon Shifter's Mates series, the Demons of Fame Romance series, the Legends Reborn trilogy, and the Alpha Project Psychic Romance series.

Connect with Eva online:
www.evachase.com
eva@evachase.com

Made in the USA
Middletown, DE
03 February 2022